To Tom and Sheena

DAVID WURTZEL

THOMAS LYSTER
A Cambridge Novel

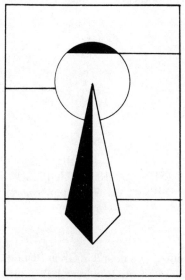

Brilliance Books

Published by Brilliance Books 1983
Copyright © David Wurtzel 1983

Brilliance Books wish to thank the labour controlled Greater
London Council for financial help.

ISBN 0 946189 30 7 hardback
ISBN 0 946189 35 8 paperback

Printed and bound in Great Britain by
Nene Litho and Woolnough Bookbinding
both of Wellingborough Northants

THOMAS LYSTER

It is a property of tear gas that it adheres to the leaves of trees. That is the only sentence in the dream. I have never identified who says it. It is spoken as I walk through the avenue of trees which stands in Sproul Plaza in Berkeley. I do not want to walk there. There is a riot going on somewhere else on campus. I can get to my lectures by another route, but I still take this one. I know that I will emerge at the other end with my eyes streaming.

But there are no tears. I am suddenly in my car, driving along the edge of campus. Just past the Hearst Gymnasium, I stop at a traffic light. In front of me are helmeted policemen. I look around. Behind me are a gang of students. The police have truncheons. The students have rocks. I. Only I separate them. I close my eyes.

When I open them, I am driving through San Francisco. The car is moving, but there are none of the normal reactions of driving. The car climbs a very steep hill. It is like the street where Susan's mother has her apartment, only steeper and longer. As I reach the crest, the car disappears.

I am now in a bedroom. Susan is lying on the bed. She must be naked. I cannot see any clothes, but neither can I see all of her body. I can smell the sweetness of her perfume and her long, fair hair. There are her slender arms and legs, and her head, but I cannot see her breasts or what is between her thighs. She smiles at me. Confidently, I move over to the bed. Without any preliminaries, I am ready to enter her. I look down, expecting to see Susan's face. Then I wake up.

I want to go back, I thought. Not to the violence of Berkeley. Nor to Susan – well, not to Susan as that symbol of innocence; of living, breathing and working without ever wondering who you are.

I don't want that again. I cannot go back at all. I am on a flight, on my way to England. Not from California this time, but from New York. New York: where I escaped with the English wardrobe I bought that year at Cambridge, and with the English books and glass and china, which were chosen for an undergraduate's set of rooms and which never looked quite right in a Manhattan apartment. I should have got rid of all that stuff. But if I had – if I were that kind of man – I wouldn't have had to make this trip. The fact

1

that I had dreamed the Berkeley dream was proof that I needed to make it, even after these two years back in America. I would have this trip to England, and then I could return, in peace.

I had gone to England in the first place for the sake of peace. From Berkeley in the last, violent days of the 1960s, Cambridge had seemed like a haven. There people would not demand the entire reconstruction of society. I had hoped that they would be less brutal in getting what they did want.

I was no warrior myself. What self-discipline I had was mental: to be reasonable, sensitive, and liberal-minded. It was a waste of time. In the great California student battles between the radical masses and the forces of order, men like me were the first to be disregarded.

I had never been to England. It would have been different if I had spent the year in London. I would have gone away with a depressing sense of a city wracked with political controversy and just learning to deal with Irish bombs. It was not a city of illusions.

Cambridge was. Other Americans came there and fell in love with the place. My affair was more personal, if no less intense. We did not envy the outside world. We knew it was there; that was about all.

ONE

'How I love you.'

I shouldn't have said that. I stood on the landing, half a flight of stairs below Susan, looked up to her, and declared my love. It was a pretty chaste announcement. It came as she stood in the half-open doorway of her mother's San Francisco apartment. She could not have had an easier escape route.

'I wish you hadn't said that, Neil.'

'Why not?' After all, I did love her.

'Because I don't know how I feel.'

'Really? Don't you really know?'

She sighed. I was making it difficult for her. 'I like you so much, Neil.'

'And?'

'And I feel so confused.'

There was a long silence. 'You won't be by the time I come back,' I said, just too late for real effect.

'I'll write,' she said eagerly.

'So will I,' bravely.

Another silence. Susan was always reluctant to be the one to say good-bye. I looked at her. She was wearing her hair down; that long, lovely, flowing blonde hair. Her dress was simple and dark blue. We had not been anywhere formal, but Susan tended to wear dark colours. They heightened her fairness. She looked so beautiful.

'I suppose I have to be going. I have a 'plane to catch in the morning.'

'Oh, of course', so worried that she had detained me. 'Give my regards to your parents.'

3

'I will.'

'Are they all right?'

'Fine.' In fact, no different – as far as I knew – than when she had asked the same question two hours ago. At least she did not ask after my brother. Susan always pandered to my temporary fantasies that I never had that tormenting brother of mine. 'Please thank your mother for the drink.' I had said that before too.

'I will. She was so glad to see you.'

Silence.

'Well.'

'Yes?'

'I guess I better be going, Susan.'

All this time we stood our ground. I had kissed her for a good ten minutes before I had walked down the half flight of steps. That had seemed to satisfy whatever desire I felt. I did not try to kiss her again.

'See you soon,' I promised.

'Good-bye, Neil.'

'Not good-bye . . .'

Slowly I ambled down the remaining stairs and out into the street. I got into the car and drove down the long, steep hill which led away from her mothers' home.

So ended the farewell scene. It was played twice: once in September, before I went to England the first time, and once the next January, at the end of my Christmas holidays. The dialogue on both occasions was roughly the same. I felt brave when I told Susan that she would know her own feelings by the time I came back. She would indeed come to know them, thought not how I predicted it.

Why did I go to England at all? I had majored in English at Berkeley; I was only going to study for a second undergraduate degree in history, at Cambridge. I wanted to escape. Cambridge had accepted me, and given me that chance. Then I met Susan. A young professor who had taught us both introduced us. He knew of my plans, and thought that I might like to meet an American girl who had travelled to Europe in the past. That was in the spring of

4

my last year.

I could have still changed my plans and stayed in California with her. I waited for her to ask me: to beg of me this fantastic sacrifice, and to offer herself as humble compensation. She never suggested any such thing. Instead, she smiled wistfully, and repeated that London was really nice. Cambridge she had not visited. I did not tell Susan that I would stay if she wanted me to. I did not tell her any of the fantasies she evoked. As I caressed her arms and kissed her lips I said that I would miss her. She said she would miss me too. I went to England, alone.

I arrived in Cambridge with expectations but no clear idea of what I would find. I had read every Oxford novel I could find, but they were obviously dated. To prepare for the England of the early 1970s by reading Waugh or Compton MacKenzie was like an European steeling himself for the riot-torn Berkeley by reading F. Scott Fitzgerald.

After World War II, the genre began to disappear. Oxford and Cambridge were no longer ends in themselves; they were just the setting for a thriller or episodes in a series of novels by which the emotionally limited amongst English male authors attempted to imitate Proust. Dons now appeared as often as undergraduates. As for the university women, they tended to write about their later life, often about finding a husband, having a child, losing the husband, losing their identity, having an unsatisfactory affair, and discovering their identify – always in that order. I learned little about Cambridge, but I found out that fictional divorced women only ever have one child. Widows, who presumably find grief less time consuming than the discovery of an identity, are allowed two children.

I had seen photographs of Cambridge, but they were misleading. It is not a city of vistas. I quickly learned that in this ancient town, things happened in confined surroundings: courtyards, colleges, staircases, sets of rooms. There was little mass feeling. If anyone suffered from *anomie*, as one did in California, they kept it to themselves.

Young men and women arrived with, and kept a sense of home and of school. However, it was also a place to lose your past. There really were men who did not quite deny that they had gone to certain public schools, and who really did suggest that their parents were permanently unavailable. They wanted me to be impressed with their new personas. If I wanted poses, we did them better in California.

Because everyone had a roommate at Berkeley, I was not disappointed to learn that I would have to share a set, consisting of two bedrooms, a tiny kitchen, and a big sitting room. I looked forward to this man teaching me about Cambridge and England, and reassuring me that I had done the right thing in coming here. I knew that I wanted to escape from Berkeley. I had, merely by coming over. Once in residence in my college, though, I felt a little lost and extremely foreign.

I had the first two days to myself. There was an Indian summer in progress. I sat in the seat by the open, mullioned windows and watched my still unknown fellows walking round the huge college lawns below. I was on the second floor, and had a splended view of the Backs.

I was not on my guard when he arrived on my second afternoon, I had come into the sitting room from my bedroom, and there was Thomas Lyster. He had had a good summer. His short, thick, fair hair was burnished and his ordinarily fresh face was ruddy. He was in shirtsleeves, rolled up twice. I introduced myself.

'Oh yes,' said my would-be mentor and friend, 'you're the Yank, aren't you?'

It was not the best way to begin. Thomas sensed it, and then went on, with the best intentions, to make it worse.

'I've just spent three weeks in Italy,' he told me, as he usurped the use of the tea things I had bought the day before, 'so when the porter told me you were American, I was afraid you'd be like them.'

'Were they ugly Americans?'

'They were all terribly good looking, but crushingly hearty. I

6

had visions of you cluttering up everywhere with sports equipment, and then complaining about the food and the lack of women – and then making such an awful racket when you did find a woman.'

'I'm pretty quiet,' I said. That was because I was a virgin, a fact I was ashamed of, especially in the face of men like Thomas who talked about sex as if it were something easy.

'Then, of course,' he went on, 'you might have a family.' As he said this he went over to the framed photograph of my parents. I had placed it on the otherwise empty mantlepiece. Thomas put it on the side table and shook his head.

'I do have a family.'

'Yes, well, who doesn't, but are they going to come over and visit us? Treat me and Cambridge as something so wonderful that they just have to take me home with them? Cloying,' he shuddered.

'They're not coming over,' I announced coldly. 'They think I'm wasting my time.'

He smiled sympathetically for the first time. 'Why?'

'Because they think I should be in law school, getting ahead of all the jerks who are doing their own thing. What can you do after you've studied history?' I flung at him, in imitation of my father.

'I don't know. Does it matter? I mean, I'm reading history too, but I can't imagine trying to get a job on the strength of it!'

'Well, what do you want to accomplish at Cambridge?'

'Nothing. It's a family tradition.'

I was wondering whether he was being serious. I know now that he was, but that he expected me to laugh. I reacted, as I did once again in a crisis, by falling back on my parents' cliches. Then, as now, I should have realised that Thomas was signalling my release from my past.

'But if you don't work hard, how are you going to get good grades?' I asked.

'You mean good exam results? What's the point of them?'

'Because otherwise you won't get a good job,' I pursued the famous line of reasoning, and felt unconvinced by my own arguments.

Thomas shrugged his shoulders. 'I don't suppose I'll ever apply for the kind of job that would turn me down because I didn't get a First.'

Now I had caught him. 'But what if you changed your mind? Wouldn't you want to have that choice, rather than have an employer choose for you?' I could almost see a gleam of approval in the eyes of my parents, as they suffered the pangs of banishment on the side table.

'I suppose it doesn't matter. I got a First last year. Perhaps I can scrape another one this year.'

'Why didn't you say so to begin with?'

'Why ever should I?'

So Thomas and I did not really hit it off. We became polite strangers. We rarely saw each other anyway. He was playing wing three quarter for the college First XV that term, and, like many undergraduates, he took every opportunity to go down to London. I had little sporting side to me, and I wanted to stay in Cambridge and savour the place.

It was rare to find Thomas alone. He was the star attraction of a large group of friends who crowded our sitting room. For no real reason, I shied away from them. He was also a sexual magnet. He talked about sex as if it were something easy because it was easy for him. There were women in his bedroom as often as three or four nights a week. I scarcely even met them. The seductions took place either before I arrived or somewhere else: I was never expected to leave; when I came in, the girl either followed Thomas into the bedroom or was taken home.

I never referred to these episodes. I was brought up with the idea that the sexual athlete is contemptuous of the virgin. I did not call attention to my undoubtedly contemptible state by asking Thomas about his activities. He treated them as matters of course, unworthy of comment.

I was alone a lot of the time. I did not mind. Cambridge seemed incredibly beautiful that autumn, and I enjoyed playing the tourist. I visited every church and chapel, and took day trips to Ely and Norwich. Academically, I was required to write an essay each

8

fortnight, and to read it to my tutor. My essays were, if anything, over-researched. My thoroughness baffled my tutor, who ended our sessions by giving me a glass of sherry and by expressing his hopes that I would enjoy my time at Cambridge.

I remained devoted to Susan. I wrote to her three times a week. She replied with sincerity, if less frequently. I think I held back from getting involved because of her. I wanted to be able to say, I have loved no one and nothing aside from you.

Of course I made acquaintances. They were men in college. We talked about our lectures. They asked me about America. They were fascinated by Thomas Lyster, who had the pre-eminent reputation in college for drinking, womanising, and arrogance.

I remember one night, about the middle of November, when I invited two or three of these college men to coffee after Hall. One of them said that he was supposed to meet up with a school friend, so could he bring him along too?

He brought me Matthew Jenkins. His friend, and whoever else was there, have faded from memory. I can only recall being in the room with Matthew. This was not due to any physical pre-possessiveness on his part. He was of medium height, pale, and thin, with straight black hair. He wore the sort of maroon jumper that some undergraduates wear daily for three successive years. He was uncomfortable when he came in. He paced around, and then looked at the row of invitations on the mantlepiece.

'You go to a lot of parties,' he admired.

'My roommate does.'

'Oh. Who's that?'

'A guy called Thomas Lyster.'

'You share this set with Tom Lyster?' He asked the question differently from everyone else. They either tried to be roguish themselves or expressed sympathy at having to put up with the reputed excesses of Thomas's behaviour. Matthew Jenkins seemed to believe everything he had ever heard about Thomas Lyster, and it put him in awe. He looked at the two bedroom doors, and wondered which was his.

'Do you know him?' I asked.

'Not really. Well, we're in CUCA – the Conservative Association – together.'

Thomas never discussed his political activities with me. I did not think he had many. I expected him to be a Conservative. But Jenkins? What in the world did the Tories have to offer a man like him? He looked a born radical; a walking indictment of the class system that had kept Jenkinses away from Cambridge until now.

I wondered what I should tell him about Thomas. I saw him daily. I saw him hung over. I caught glimpses at the pretty girls who were willing to pleasure him. I unfortunately also had to listen to all those maddening questions that began 'why ever . . .?' as if I had never properly thought out anything until Thomas came round to point out the absurdity of my ways. Obviously he was a handsome athlete. But I didn't think he was that heroic.

I did not pursue the point. Anyway, Jenkins looked a little embarrassed at having mentioned Thomas at all. But as everyone got up to leave, I could not resist opening Thomas's bedroom door, and announcing, 'this is where the great man sleeps. Pretty messy, isn't he?'

His room was indeed a mess. There were piles of clothes on the floor, plus his rugby kit, and a jumble of books and papers. It was a miracle that he managed to look so well groomed. Jenkins alone took the opportunity to look in. He gazed at the narrow room, with the much-used single bed, the wardrobe, and the chest of drawers. The gaze became a stare. I have never seen such a look of hunger on anyone. Jenkins wouldn't have dared to touch as much as a door handle, but he would have given anything to swallow the room whole.

I did not tell Thomas about the incident, but I began to think that I was wasting the opportunity of sharing with him. He was the sort of Englishman upon whom I could dine out in California. I also thought it was time that he learned something about America. Thanksgiving was coming up. I invited him to a celebratory lunch. Aside from breakfast, it was the first meal we would have eaten alone. I looked forward to dropping my priggish role, and hoped that we would both get drunk together. It was, in the event, the turning point.

I chose the restaurant of the Blue Boar for lunch because they had turkey on the menu. Otherwise it was an unatmospheric choice. Unbeknownst to me, while I was in revolutionary Berkeley and dreaming of a solid, rooted England, some British – architects, builders, local councillors – had been busy smashing up the place. *People want something different*, was their excuse. I did not blame them for wanting to appear modern. I did not blame the great property speculators of the time for wanting to make money. I was just appalled at the ghastly mess they left behind.

'It's very good of you to invite me,' Thomas began conventionally when we sat down. He looked at the menu. 'Why ever do you think restaurants serve fruit juice as a first course?'

'Beats me. Go ahead and eat something substantial.'

'Thanks. I'm starving.' He put the menu down and looked around. 'Isn't this place awful?'

I had genuinely not noticed it before. Now I looked at the trim, dark blue chairs and the multi-coloured carpet and the lighting. I nodded. It did look a little tacky.

'The international anonymous style,' Thomas sneered.

'It's all I've ever known,' I said.

'I hope not. I'd like to think that if I walked into a Californian restaurant, I'd immediately say, this is California. But here! You could be anywhere with an owner who doesn't know what he wants.' I shrugged my shoulders. 'Are you interested in design and architecture?'

'Kind of. I've noticed that college is old, and this is new.'

He laughed. 'But, seriously, aren't there some places you can't stand being in? I mean, how do you bear doing all that work in the faculty library?' The history library was designed to resemble a greenhouse. There was nothing admirable about it. It was uncomfortable inside, and looked out of place in Cambridge. I had ignored that fact. At Berkeley, smoked glass and concrete stood shoulder to shoulder with the Greek revival.

'The books are there,' I said.

'Pity. Books deserve some place better than that.'

The waitress arrived and took our orders for avocados with crab and for the turkey. Thomas took the wine list, and spent a lot of time choosing a bottle.

'Terrible choice,' he complained after he ordered. 'Does the American Thanksgiving mean a lot to you?'

'I like the idea behind it. As a matter of fact, though, it's the first time I've ever spent a holiday away from home.'

'Gosh. I've never wanted to. But I usually get stuck.'

'Don't you get along with your folks?'

'Get along with Father? Whatever for?' He swallowed a piece of avocado. 'Still, things were rather better this summer.'

'What happened?'

'I drove him mad. You see, he hates the fact that I'm so healthy, so I played cricket constantly, and when I couldn't find a match, I took runs and lifted weights. Then I started discussing Proust at dinner. Especially when they had guests.'

'Had your father read him?'

'Father? Read books?'

I was fascinated by this account. It would never have occurred to me to imitate such behaviour. I was drowned with love at home. When away from my parents I alternated between guilt, because I did not love them enough in return, and guilt because they financed whatever I wanted to do, whether they approved of my activity or not.

'I haven't mentioned literature to my parents in years,' I said. 'It would upset them.'

'Gosh. How loyal you are.' He didn't understand what I was talking about, but he was careful not to mock.

'I'm very grateful to them. But I like showing up my brother.'

'Oh, do you have a ghastly brother too? You've never mentioned him. Mine's awful.'

'I'd rather not think he's alive.' That was the strongest I had ever put it. Thomas was delighted.

'Wonderful. It gives us something in common.'

'Us and about five million other people with brothers.'

'Five million people have nothing in common with me. Anyway, I bet they just put up with the little bastard. But you and I don't. We've made ourselves better, haven't we? Because we are better.'

I marvelled at his confidence. 'I never thought about it like that.'

'Why ever not?'

'Because . . . well, because my brother's the all-American boy. Great athlete. Great businessman. Great bully. Great sexual performer . . .'

'How do you know that?'

'He tells me about it.'

'He boasts about it?' Thomas asked contemptuously. As I say although he had had more women in two months than most undergraduates had in three years, Thomas never referred to it. The women were shadowy figures. Sex for him was just another bodily function. It was this attitude that we all envied. It impressed me that such a man poured scorn on my brother. I had been told that 'he who talks about it, doesn't do it', but that was the sour grapes of the virgin: my brother talked about it, and I was sure he was telling the truth. I never talked about it because I had nothing to talk about. My brother was vulgar, but I never denied him the right to boast. I supposed that that was the prerogative of the male sexual athlete. Thomas was the first man I respected who said that that wasn't so.

'He tells me every anatomical detail,' I explained. 'He's very thorough. He's that way about everything. He's a real workaholic. No nonsense.'

'What's his definition of nonsense?'

'Books. Plays. Music. He reads *Time* and *Fortune*. Oh, and I think he likes musicals.'

'And you never thought yourself superior to that?'

'Not superior. Just better at different things, like getting good grades. He's the man, though: I've always had to concede that.'

'Christ. I hope he isn't coming over to England.'

'Hardly. He says you're all decadent and washed up. A flop. No killer instinct.'

'I'd love him to tell me that to my face.'

'He's a big guy.'

'And I was rather good at boxing at school.' He grinned. 'You must be so glad to be here.'

'Yes. Of course.'

He took out a pack of cigarettes. 'Do you mind if I smoke before the cheese?'

'Go ahead.' I disliked his smoking, but I got used to it.

'Neil . . .'

'Yes?' I could sense that this was preliminary to something.

'Are you really enjoying Cambridge?'

'Sure. Why?'

'I wondered. You obviously don't dislike it, but you don't seem very enthusiastic either. Do you know what it means to be here?'

'I feel very privileged.'

'Damn that. It means that no one's looking over your shoulder.' I nodded, uneasily. 'Tell me, why don't you read books?'

'I do.'

'Not an assigned text; a book just for pleasure.'

'I don't have the time.'

'Make time.'

'Just like that?'

'Why not? The problem, though, is that we don't have any interesting books in our room. We need something on art, or architecture. Something you can pick up and get lost in for an hour or two. And some novels. I've got stuck into reading the Powell and Raven series, but I hate waiting until the library has them, or they come out in paperback.'

It was the first time Thomas had talked of our room in the first person plural. It was also the first time he had expressed an opinion on what it ought to be like. We had occupied it for so long without ever living there. I had hung on the walls one thing: my Berkeley diploma, with Ronald Reagan's signature on it. Thomas had a few old prints from home, plus a decent stereo and a dozen records of Mozart, Tchaikovsky and Brahms symphonies. That was it.

This now seemed like a waste. Thomas was obviously trying to

14

streamroll me into buying things. Why not, if he were correct? Why occupy a room that gave the impression that I lived somewhere else? It was no wonder I seemed unenthusiastic about Cambridge. For all that I had taken advantage of it, I might have been at any university anywhere. I felt as if I were cheating myself.

'Funny,' I said, 'we've never really talked about the room before.'

'We never talk to each other.'

'Frankly, I thought you'd dismissed me the moment we met.'

'Really?' he looked concerned. 'How?'

'Do you have any idea how scared I was when I arrived here?'

'No.'

'Well, I was. I didn't know whether I'd done the right thing or not. It all seemed so foreign and different. And there you were, saying '*so you're the Yank*' and complaining about the Americans you had met in Italy.'

'And that upset you?'

'Weren't you trying to put me in my place?'

'Not particularly. Is that what you thought?'

'I wouldn't exactly call you friendly the last few months.'

He put his cutlery down and looked at me. 'Then why ever did you invite me to lunch?'

'For your own good.'

'You mean, you thought that I had behaved badly towards you, and yet you react with this absurd generosity? For my own good?'

'That's right.'

That attitude towards life had obviously never occurred to him before. He was silent for a while. He must have been wondering whether or not I was a fool. At last he made his decision . . . 'I believe you,' he said. 'I really do believe you.'

'Then I'm glad I invited you.'

'Chirst, you must think I'm a shit.'

'Forget it. Let's talk about what we're going to do about the room.'

'We need books. And a decent bookcase to put them in.'

'What about the shelves we've got?'

15

'Better for china. A bowl of pot-pourri and some vases, so we can have fresh flowers at last. And a few photographs. I think I've got one of my grandparents at the black Ascot in 1910.'

'Anything else?'

'Some decent prints. I rather like political portraits, but the odd painting would be nice. We really ought to go to the London auction rooms. They've got all kinds of marvellous things that no one ever bids on. And we could get a rug there too.'

'Hey, how much is this going to cost?'

'Hundreds. Or thousands. It's easy to spend money; it's damn difficult buying something worthwhile. Goodness it's fun browsing, though. The best things just fall into your lap.'

'Then why haven't you done any of this yourself?'

'Because Father gives me a miserly allowance, and he's too rich for me to get a grant. I worked a bit during the summer, but that all went on travel.'

'All right,' I said. 'Let's get started this afternoon.'

So our room began to be transformed. It was done by a division of labour: my money, and Thomas's taste. Spending my money was just another way in which Thomas both gave and took pleasure. He would not have done it unless he knew that I enjoyed it too.

I loved it. I was learning for the first time what it meant to impress one's personality on a room. I was also learning to tell reproductions from originals. It would have been wonderful to have spent more time in the auction rooms, but we did far too well out of our first sale. There was even some money left, though not after Thomas had marched me up and down Jermyn Street.

'You see,' Thomas said just before I left for Christmas in America, 'something of you is left behind here. Something to come back and recognise.'

I returned in January the day after Thomas did. In that time he had put the room back in order. I took it as a favour to me. It was like coming back home.

TWO

I dreamed the Berkeley dream several times at Cambridge without warning. I remember it happening late in January. It was the morning of the lunch party. Thomas and I had entertained together before, but this was the largest occasion, and for a lot of reasons it sticks in my mind.

The dream was so strong that it awakened me as soon as it ended. I lay in bed, trying to figure out where I was, and then I switched on the lamp.

This was always the worst moment. If Susan had walked in right then, I was sure I would have taken her, and purged the dream forever. I could bear living without her while my memory of her touch failed. But just after the dream I could still smell her sweetness. Her restrained letters were no substitute.

Thomas's behaviour seemed as incomprehensible as ever. What did he feel like with those girls? What did he feel to begin with, to drive him on? I couldn't guess. Thomas was younger than I was, and in comparison I felt very old, very pale, very dry.

Sterile. That was the word. And boring. Boring was one of the words I picked up at Cambridge. Both could have described my bedroom. In it was stored the suits and tweed jackets I'd had made up, and the stacks of Turnbull and Asser shirts and ties, Beale and Inman trousers and jumpers that Thomas talked me into buying. They filled the wardrobe and chest of drawers. And they were all immaculately put away. The only decoration was the photograph of my parents, which had now migrated to the top of the chest of drawers, and the Berkeley diploma, now that everyone had seen and commented on Ronald Reagan's signature.

Yet the mere fact that I was dissatisfied with the room was a sign

17

of how far I had come. Two months before I would have considered tidiness to be an end in itself. Now I knew better – and I also had some idea of how to put things right.That comforted me.It was Thomas's genius that he could challenge everything I believed in, overwhelm me with his own notions of good taste and right behaviour, and yet never undermine my self esteem. I liked myself when I was with him. It just so happened that I also wanted to improve myself for both our sakes. It was the first time I had admired someone without, feeling myself inferior to him.

It was different from life with my brother. He boasted because he wanted to subjugate me. He succeeded. Thomas never acted like that. I felt safe with him. I also felt warned: I must not take everything he said seriously.

It was eight o'clock now. I got up, washed and shaved at the basin in my room, and dressed. Only then did I leave the bedroom. I was always the first up. I lit the gas fire in the sitting room – the only source of heat – and opened the curtains. The sun had only just risen on what turned out to be a glorious, if cold day. I never got tired of our view of the Backs. I used to think that whenever I returned to Cambridge I would come back to this window and this view, and then everything else would come flooding back.

I went into our little kitchen. The college provided us with a kettle and an electric ring. I had bought a percolator and a toaster. I put on some coffee and a saucepan for boiling eggs. Then I went out to the landing to collect the post and the newspapers.

Thomas emerged at just about the time that breakfast was ready. He wore the huge, heavy dressing gown which belonged to his grandfather. It was too big on him. I once asked why he did not get a new one that fitted. He replied that he couldn't find silk like this any more, and that it was the finest dressing gown in Cambridge. When I understood that, he explained, I would understand England.

'Oh well done,' he said when he saw the food. He sat down, and propped the sporting section of the *Daily Telegraph* against the vase of carnations which I had bought in the market place the day before. I opened *The Times* to the overseas news page.

I was a little ignorant of British news. Thomas's political friends relished it, although their discussions seemed no more relevant to the real world than their discussions of historical events or points of nineteenth century case law. It was just something else to talk about, like who was expected to run for office in the Union or the Conservative Association. The prime example of this breed was Peter Harding, one of Thomas's biggest admirers – Thomas tended to have admirers rather than friends; Peter spoke of him as if he were someone he had read about in a book. Peter had a reputation for niceness, although no one could ever cite an instance where he had done something kind for another person. His passions were sport and politics, and he rattled off the names and voting of Members of Parliament as easily as he expounded cricket statistics.

It bewildered me. I began by watching the news on television, but one night saw one of the new breed of exuberant, Camden Town, stripped pine lady reporters asking a Durham miner what he served at his dinner parties. I gave up after that. I justified my ignorance on the grounds that I was going to spend an apolitical year.

Of course I was aware of the great issues. I knew that Conservative politicians came and told us that British industry was straining at the leash, ready to explode with prosperity the moment the markets of the European Community were open to them. I also knew that the trades unions had a sense of outrage against the government, matched only by the outrage of American students against whatever they happened to be against at that moment. I learned that the British intelligentsia was staunchly Labour. It would be some years before they suddenly discovered that the unions did not appreciate them, whereupon they went off in a huff to form a social democratic party all their own. It all seemed far away from Cambridge.

'Where were you last night?' Thomas asked. Conversation was usually limited during breakfast, and almost non-existent if Thomas had a hangover.

'Visiting a friend.'

19

'Oh?'

'You don't like her.'

'Not Nancy, I hope,' he grunted as he broke open his egg. Nancy Wright was a tall, buxom American PhD student who had thrown her arms around me one day in the library and said, 'I'm just so glad to find another American here.' She had been having a difficult time in Cambridge.

'She's all right,' I defended her.

'She has a social manner the like of which I have never seen.'

'She says the problem is that Englishmen can't cope with intelligent women, and British women lack consciousness.'

'What in the world is consciousness?'

'It means being aware of yourself.'

Thomas looked around the room and then at his hands. 'I am sitting in a chair, eating my breakfast. Does that make me aware of myself?'

'In a way. But you're not aware of yourself in . . . in a cosmic sense.'

'Tell me: does Nancy include herself among the class of intelligent women with whom Englishmen can't cope?'

'She's very bright.' That was true. It was also true that I was never quite sure what to do with Nancy. She had come to Cambridge with preconceptions, but they were fairly accurate, namely, that there were a lot of virile English youths here who needed a woman of experience to tear away the layers of inhibition.

Thomas did not need such a woman. He also had an irrational prejudice against American ladies. He claimed that it was grounded in history, and produced for me the Lyster Theory of the Pernicious Effect of American Women on British History, starring Lady Astor, Mrs Simpson, and the wives of most of the current Labour front bench. I did not argue with him. I had learned that there was a point at which Thomas went beyond argument – like refusing to use the aesthetically horrific history library. With anybody else I would have suspected him of being afraid of Nancy, but he was the only man I knew who never was.

'And she's coming to lunch today,' I added.

'Neil. You didn't invite her, did you?'

'Why not? You invite who you want to invite.'

'Yes, my friends.'

'Nancy's my friend.'

'But she won't get along with mine.'

'Are you sure about that, Thomas?'

'That woman's a walking lion's den . . . Christ! You haven't invited her to seduce someone, have you?'

'And if I did? Isn't this our day for the sheets to be changed?'

He laughed and lit a cigarette. 'Perhaps it will be amusing. I wonder who'll she'll devour.'

'What about Peter Harding.'

'Don't you dare try that.'

I shrugged my shoulders. It was precisely Peter Harding that I had had in mind.

'So what is a soiree at Nancy's like?' he asked, calming down.

'A couple of men; a couple of women from her college. Bourbon and Henry James.'

'Bourbon?'

'She had a duty free bottle. I suppose it really was a bourbon party. Henry James doesn't go with bourbon. If I remember correctly, we dropped him and started reading scenes from Tennessee Williams's plays instead.'

'Nancy Wright as Blanche DuBois?'

'Well, it was her party.'

'Who was Stanley Kowalski?'

'Not me, I'm afraid.'

'You looked pretty tired by the time you got in.'

'I was. I was pretty tired beforehand. I left early. Leaving Stanley with Blanche.'

'Spare me the details.'

'You seemed to be having a jolly party when I got back.'

'A few friends.' Thomas always described his drinking sessions as 'a few friends'. 'Pity you wouldn't join us.'

'I said hello.'

'Didn't you want to talk to Peter?'

'I said hello to him too.'

'He likes you so much. He must've thought you were angry with him.'

'Don't be ridiculous.'

'Your light was on for ages.'

'I was reading.'

'I thought you were exhausted.'

'Thomas, I like to read before I go to bed.'

'But how could you be too tired for my friends but not too tired to read?' I looked at him. 'Very odd,' he concluded.

I slammed my newspaper down. Thomas looked surprised. He leaned across the table and put his hand on my arm.

''My dear fellow; is something wrong?'

'I wish you wouldn't be so bloody sometimes. I. . . I didn't get enough sleep last night. I woke up too early.'

'Too much bourbon?'

'It was not too much bourbon, I. . . I dreamed about California.'

'I'm so sorry.'

'Why? You don't know what I dreamed.'

'It's pretty obvious that you didn't dream that you won the sixty-four million dollar question.'

I was tempted to tell him the truth, but it would open up too many issues. Anyway, I was not at all sure that Thomas would be sympathetic. Everyone else was interested or at least tolerant about Susan. Nancy was positively ecstatic about her. Thomas, without actually saying anything, gave the impression that he thought I was wasting my time.

'It doesn't matter,' I said.

'Well, try to make your – what was it? – your consciousness, try to make it think of Cambridge. California doesn't matter any more.'

'Swell; lop off twenty-two years and forget about it.'

'I didn't say that. It just doesn't matter over here.'

'But I've got to go back.'

'I suppose so – eventually. Meanwhile, if you mull over

22

California it'll be – oh, what was that word with all the syllables that means useless?'

'Counter-productive.'

'That's it. Don't be counter-productive.'

I got up. 'I've got to get ready to go. Have you arranged everything for the lunch?'

'I think so. Oh. . . I've forgotten the port. Can you go to Peter Dominic's in the Market Square? They should have Dow's 1960. Or 1950, if you can.' He lit another cigarette.

'Aren't you going to any lectures today?'

Thomas sighed. 'I made a New year's resolution that I wouldn't miss any more. I have been pretty regular, haven't I?'

'More or less.'

'But your notes are so good. And your handwriting! I've never seen anything so neat.'

I leaned against my doorway and stared at him. 'What are you going to do this morning?'

'I have to run an errand. Politics,' he added. This surprised me. Although his friends were deeply involved, and talked to Thomas as if he were an insider, he never seemed to do anything himself.

'Isn't it a little early in the day for cabals?'

'It's not a cabal. I have to go and see someone. If I don't run him to ground in his room, I'll get stuck with him in public. I'd rather keep this short, and private.'

'Do I know him?'

'I certainly hope not.'

'He wasn't here last night?'

'God forbid.'

'Hey, what's wrong with him?'

'He's the greyest man in England.' 'Grey' was the worst word that anyone could use to describe a fellow undergraduate.

'So why see him?'

'It's a long story. There's no reason for both of us to be bored by it. People take politics so seriously here.'

'Not as seriously as at Berkeley.'

'That was violence, not seriousness. You were concerned about issues, and ideologies. People kill each other over that. There are no issues at all at Cambridge; just personalities. No one's going to get killed here, but they'll get far more impassioned.'

'Which is worse?' I asked, as I put on my bicycle clips.

'That's a good question. Killing people doesn't bother me, as long as there's a good reason for doing it. The fact that they disagree with you is a bit strong, I admit. But it's honest, and it does settle the argument. To be stabbed in the back metaphorically is rather like a long, lingering illness.'

'Which are you going to inflict?'

'I'm just going to tell someone the facts of life. What he makes of them is entirely his own business. I couldn't care less.'

Thomas was not likeable in such a mood, but I had to admit that there was something disturbingly exciting about his indifference. It is a cliche that power is an aphrodisiac: ugly but highly influential men are as attractive to women as any Adonis. I suppose there is a strength, akin to power, in genuinely not caring what other people think.

I left Thomas to his cigarette and walked downstairs. On the way I ran across our bedder, Mrs Dipper, a short, ageless lady who looked after the occupants of the staircase whom she insisted on referring to as her gentlemen.

Mrs Dipper made beds, changed the bottom sheet once a week, and emptied wastepaper baskets. She did no cleaning. Whether she had a religious objection to the removal of dirt, or whether she was unable to relate to a dust cloth, I never learned. She was brilliant at making beds. She adored Thomas, he made such a mess of his that to reassemble the sheets and blankets gave her a deep sense of worth. She respected me for my tidiness.

'Good morning, Mrs Dipper,' I shouted as we passed on the concrete stairs. 'I mustn't be late for my lectures.' Thomas, no matter what his real hurry, would have stopped and passed the time of day with her. Well, he wasn't doing anything upstairs at the moment.

'Oh, Mr Fielding . . . no, you mustn't be late,' she agreed.

THREE

To leave college was to leave the incubus. As incubi go, mine was pretty large. Quite apart from the Regency Gothic wedding cake of a building which I inhabited, there were three, big redbrick court-yards, the newest of which was 300 years old, and which followed one another from the porter's lodge to the river. They contained the chapel and the hall, both built on an equally grand scale.

It was said that the town was the colleges and the colleges were the town. If so, it was a world perpetually looking in on itself. Thomas was quite right when he said that the battles were only over personalities. Labour and Conservatives fought fiercely amongst themselves, and clashed only at Union debates on Monday nights. The clearest distillation of current student Tory philosophy was the cry of Peter Harding's mob, 'lefties out'. They were ignorant of political philosophy, but it was the sort of thing which well-born undergraduates earlier in the century might have shouted. The current Conservatives were bourgeois to a man. Matthew Jenkins was not the least grand of them. I could never understand why they all aped and adulated a class to which they did not belong, and which offered very little either to them or to the country at large.

I knew several of my fellow historians by now, and generally sat with the same group. Occasionally we had coffee afterwards. No one suggested a fuller social life together. We just hung around together on the Sidgwick Site, that ghastly attempt to create a campus for the arts students.

I liked the fact that my lectures were smaller than at Berkeley, but the opportunities arising out of that were wasted. No one asked questions, and the lecturers seemed slightly at odds with their audience. They obviously would have far preferred going back to their research or their colleagues. No one performed, as only a California professor with star quality could.

My second lecture was over at eleven. I declined the invitation to coffee offered by the others. I fetched my bicycle – old, with a huge basket tied to the handlebars – and pedalled into town. I chained the machine to the railings of the Senate house. A lecture had obviously just finished in the Old Schools – the law faculty – and groups of men were drifting in my direction. There were a few women, but I noticed only one, Sally Lloyd. She was tall, and wore her black hair pulled severely back, which emphasised her sloping nose and those incredible, high cheekbones.

She had another importance as well. Thomas was known for the brevity of his affairs. Few lasted longer than a night or two, and never more than four or five. Sally had been having an affair with Thomas for two weeks. Even more significantly, I had actually been asked to keep away from the set on the first evenings when she was brought back. I had never wished to inhibit Thomas's activities, but he treated sex so casually that he had never before been bothered whether I was around or not. He had cared whether Sally succumbed. When she did, I was allowed back. We quickly became friends.

Her relationship with Thomas was perhaps the oddest aspect of her being a woman at Cambridge. It was not easy then. The ratio of men to women of seven to one did not ensure a fantastic social life for all the female undergraduates. On the contrary, they had to be that much brighter to get in at all, and once there, they had to contend with men who were frightened or contemptuous of intelligent women. An absurd number of women just wound up as one of the boys.

Sally was not cut out for that. She sat with glazed eyes while the men discussed law. She smiled with barely suppressed boredom as they unloaded their soul-searchings on her. Sally had an imagination, and ambition. She wanted to be a great woman, and she wanted a great man who owed a lot to her.

I did not know how far she wanted her and her man to go. I was brought up on the ethos of the alcoholic, madly self-indulgent, tortured genius writer. At school we were taught to marvel at wonderful Scott Fitzgerald and Hemingway and, in particular, wonderful Thomas Wolfe, with his egoism and utter lack of discipline. None had a reputation for treating women particularly well, but that never seemed to matter. Women begged for the role of The One Who Understands, and those kind of men settled for nothing less than a completely adoring woman. It all got mixed up in my mind with my brother's dictum about women liking being treated as dirt. I found the whole thing unattractive. I trusted Thomas and Sally to have a lot more good taste.

When she saw me, Sally broke away from a group of men and came up. She was a popular girl, and I basked in the reflected glory of her attention.

'Neil; what're you doing around here? Aren't you making something marvellous for us for lunch?'

'Thomas has talked the college into doing the cooking. I'm here to buy the port.'

'What's Thomas doing?'

'Being charming?' I grinned. 'Actually, he said he had to go run a political errand.'

'Thomas?' she was as surprised as I was. 'I wonder . . . oh, no; I can't imagine it.'

'What's that?'

'About an hour ago, I got trapped into going to have coffee now with the most mournful-looking man in Cambridge.'

'Who's that?'

'Matthew Jenkins.'

'Matthew . . .'

'Do you know him?'

I thought of that look of hunger as he stood at the doorway of Thomas Lyster's bedroom. I had not seen him since. 'I met him once. I guess you could call him intense.'

'To say the least. Now he's involved in politics, but I can't believe Thomas would go off and see him. Can you?'

I thought of how Jenkins would love nothing more than for

Thomas to speak to him. I remembered Thomas saying that he was a grey man, whom he would not want to see in public. Nevertheless I shook my head.

'Anyway,' Sally went on, 'I heard something so odd this morning.'

'What's that?'

'I dashed into the library – to look up a law report – and I overheard two blokes in the next bay. One of them was saying "what do you mean, why is Sally hanging around with Tom Lyster? she's his girlfriend".'

'Aren't you?'

'Am I? What does Thomas say?'

'Nothing, of course. Does that bother you, Sally?'

'How can I put it . . . when I'm alone with Thomas, the rest of the world doesn't matter. When I leave your room, I feel as if he and I have a joke on the rest of the world. We've been terribly happy and they don't know. But it doesn't matter that they don't know. There's something about Thomas which makes me feel self-sufficient. With other men, you just want to run and tell a friend how marvellous it all was. I don't feel that with Thomas. He's a world in himself. Does that make any sense?'

'I think so.' I hadn't a clue; life with Susan had never quite been like that. 'So is it intrusive, that everyone else has found out?'

'Oh, I hope it's not everyone else. And yes, I don't like being labelled. After all, how long does Thomas have affairs with women?'

'Not as long as with you,' I said truthfully.

'Exactly. Perhaps we're in overtime already, and I didn't even realise it.'

'I don't see any signs that he's about to dump you.'

'Oh? What are the signs?'

'Uh . . . the girl doesn't reappear.'

Sally laughed. 'Is she found floating in the Cam?'

'Wait and find out.'

Sally took my arm, and we walked across King's Parade to the railings of Great St. Mary's.

28

'It's just so impossible being sure of Thomas,' she told me. 'Everyone always says, that you can't walk into one of his parties without thinking that he's been to bed with everyone there.'

I nodded. Everyone had not told me that. I got stuck on the second 'everyone'. Thomas had once said that he was sexually initiated in the boiler room at school. I had only just learned that there were no girls at Radley. The vista of his sexual experience now became even broader. I was unaware of him having any sex with men while I had known him. Whenever would he have had the time or the energy?

The jibe, if true, confused me. To my knowledge I had never met someone homosexual. I was brought up in the liberal school of condescension, that is, that homosexuality was abhorrent, but that one should not hold that against a man who practised it. I could not imagine myself condescending to Thomas about anything.

There was something else. In the past week or so, I had been conscious of Sally and Thomas being together, in a way that had not happened with any of his other girls. I was acutely aware of the comparison between their activities, and my own: masturbating as an act of desperation; for the sake of relief, not pleasure. I thought of my own body – tall, pale, with my auburn hair and freckled forearms; perfectly respectable in tennis shorts or swimming trunks. I began to fantasise that I was the man in Thomas's body. The Freudian explanation of that suddenly became obvious. I immediately resolved never to think about it again.

Sally looked up at the clock on the west front of the church. 'Heavens, I'm late already. I hope that doesn't make Matthew positively suicidal.'

'Just think of what a wonderful time you'll have with us afterwards.'

Sally looked directly into my eyes and smiled. 'I always do.'

I blushed. 'Well . . . I suppose I must get the port.'

'Just make sure that you've got the biggest glass of wine waiting for me.'

FOUR

Thomas had decided that the theme of the lunch party would be red. We ate borscht, smoked salmon, red caviar, roast beef, and red stilton; we drank hock with a drop of Cassis, burgundy and port. It was all very much a throw-back to earlier days. Since the world-wide student revolution, and the rise of class guilt and reverse snobbery, undergraduates had toned down their entertainments. I knew that our guests would gorge themselves with an easy conscience. Even if they weren't the descendants of people who had once carried on this way, Thomas was. He simply thought that this was the proper manner of entertaining.

We were ready for the guests a quarter of an hour before they were due to arrive. While waiting, I asked Thomas,

'Why do you always invite Jenny Seymour?' Jenny was a painfully shy and plain Girtonian. Her parents had known the Lysters for years.

'What's wrong with Jenny?'

'Nothing. She's just so different from your other friends. I don't think I've ever heard her say a word to anyone.'

'She certainly talks less than the others.'

'She doesn't talk at all.'

'Chatty people need an audience.'

'But does she like being an audience?'

'I don't know; ask her.'

'Hardly.'

'All right; why don't we just get her to play the piano? She plays beautifully, and – you know, it's fascinating: when she is playing, she suddenly is beautiful.'

'Thomas . . .'

'Yes?'

'We don't have a piano. Do we?'

'No. Pity that.' He shook his head and looked wistful. I knew that look. This party was expensive enough.

'I'm not going to buy a piano, just so Jenny can come and play for us once a term.'

'Certainly not. That would be an awful waste.'

'Thank you.'

'But I'm sure you could hire one.'

'Not just for Jenny?'

'Neil, don't you play?'

I hesitated. 'No. My parents told me that boys don't play musical instruments.'

Thomas looked delighted. 'Really? What fun. Father said the same thing.'

'Then if neither of us . . .'

'But there was such a nice music master at Radley. By the time the fees for lessons showed up on the bill it was too late. Mummy made him give in.'

'Tell me about your political errand,' I asked bluntly.

He strained to remember what I was talking about. 'Oh . . . grim.' He went into the kitchen and checked again on the platters and the bottles of wine. 'Any bets on Peter Harding being the first to arrive?' he called to me. 'He's turning into such a glutton.'

'He certainly likes his drink,' I agreed.

'And his food. Peter Harding,' Thomas suddenly said, as if making a general pronouncement, 'knew the pleasure of good food before he knew the pleasure of good sex. That, Neil, is the definition of a moral member of the upper middle class.'

'I thought he didn't have a girlfriend.'

'Why ever should you think that he has?'

'Well, if he knows about good sex now . . .'

'Yes?' Thomas asked.

I felt a fool without understanding why. 'I suppose he just picks girls up then.'

'No.' Thomas dipped a spoon in the borscht and tasted it with

31

seriousness. He was satisfied. 'Why does it have to be a woman?'

'For God's sake,' I began, acting on instinct, and then stopped, remembering what Sally had said. 'Is he queer?' I asked, trying to sound worldly.

Thomas shrugged. 'Why don't you ask him?'

I was about to speak when I saw Thomas looking over my shoulder. I turned round. There was Peter Harding. He stood by the sitting room door, grinning.

'Hello, you two,' We joined him. 'Ask me what?'

'I don't know,' Thomas said. 'Neil, what were you going to ask Peter?'

I picked up a bottle of wine, filled a glass, and handed it to the guest. 'Here. Have something to drink,'

Inevitably, most of the guests arrived at the same time. I was kept busy, circulating the drink. I greeted the silent Jenny Seymour and handed her over to the man most likely to need an audience, an aspiring politico who talked constantly and made notes in his diary as to who the other guests were. Jenny smiled and said nothing.

Just before we were about to ladle out the borscht, Nancy Wright came in. She wore a white suit, and looked like an illustration for a nineteenth century novel. She walked up and hugged me.

'How's my little darling?' she asked. I was taller than she was.

'Good to see you, Nancy.'

'I'm so sorry to be the last person to arrive. I . . .'

'You're not,' I told her truthfully if tactlessly.

'Oh. Then I'm just so happy I haven't held anything up.'

'Only your introduction to Peter Harding,' I whispered. 'Come on.' I took her over to Peter – Thomas was safely on the other side of the room. Peter was already a little drunk. I hovered slightly in the background as he asked,

'What are you reading?'

'English.'

'Where do you come from?'

'Nebraska.'

'How do you know our hosts?'

'The moment I heard Neil, I threw my arms around him.'

'Oh.'

'I was so starved for another American.'

'I suppose this party is . . . well, rather English.'

'Yes. Isn't that great?'

'Of course. I . . .'

'I think this conversation is very limited, Peter. Have you ever talked to a girl differently?'

'No one's ever complained before.'

'But you haven't heard anything I've said.'

'Yes, I have. You come from . . . Nebraska.'

'True. But it's not my fault.'

'And you go round throwing your arms around men.'

'My friends say that I'm too physical. What do you think?'

'Well . . . you haven't thrown your arms around . . . Thomas,' have you?'

'No, but wouldn't you love to?'

Peter nearly choked. 'Thomas is a great friend of mine,' he managed to say.

'I'm not passing judgement on him. Of course I know he doesn't really approve of me . . .'

'I'm sure . . .'

'Please. Thomas and I are completely honest with each other. At least we would be, if we'd ever spoken to each other. Still, it is a shame, as Thomas is the second most gorgeous man in Cambridge.' She smiled straight at Peter.

I have rarely seen a young man look as terrified. Peter was a tall, hulking youth, who was suddenly powerless. I remembered Thomas's dictum that his guests should know how to look after themselves, so I did not intervene. Anyway, the best part of Nancy was that she knew when not to be subtle. Peter desperately needed someone to clear away the sexual cobwebs. It must have emanated from him like an odour. At the time, of course, I could not reconcile his terror with his apparent knowledge of the pleasure of good sex.

Of all things, Peter opted for a literary allusion. As a law student he was not required to have any intellectual tastes, and he had none. He owned perhaps a dozen works of fiction, mainly by P. G. Wodehouse. Nevertheless, he waded in with 'You're like a minor character in Henry James.'

'Minor! Minor! Peter, I am Isabelle Archer.'

This was quite untrue, but Peter didn't know that. He had no idea who Isabelle whatsit was. Wasn't this girl called Nancy? After some time, and by utilising his legal powers of so-called analysis, it finally seemed to dawn on him that Isabelle Archer was a major Jamesian character.

At this point I asked, 'Wouldn't you like something to eat? There's mounds.'

Nancy slipped her hand through Peter's arm and went towards the sideboard. As they moved off I noticed silent Jenny Seymour had been left stranded.

'Hello,' I said to her.

'Hello, Neil.' She smiled. She paused. 'This is a super party.'

'Thanks.' We looked at each other. Our standards were obviously very different. 'Don't you want something to eat?' I asked.

'It looks super,' she said, without moving.

'What about a drink?'

'Oh . . . I'm being brought one.' I wondered how long ago the man with the diary had promised to bring back a glass of wine for her. Still, she believed him.

'Thomas and I must get you to play sometime,' I said.

'But you don't have a piano.'

'If we had one, though . . . would you play?'

'Oh, yes.' She smiled, and this time I saw what Thomas meant about music transforming her.

'I thought of arranging to have one delivered. Tomorrow, if I can.'

'Oh. But . . . getting a piano . . . isn't like ordering lunch.'

'I don't know anything about it. Will you come and help? We could go to Miller's tomorrow afternoon.'

'Oh . . . I . . .' She stepped away. 'All right.'

34

'Good. That's settled. Now I can't let you starve . . .'

She walked obediently to the side table where the other guests had descended like the proverbial locusts. By chance, I looked towards the door. There was Sally.

She just stood there, her hands resting in the pockets of the duffle coat that so mercilessly camouflaged her figure. I went up to her.

'Neil. I'm glad to see you.' She took the glass which I had brought with me. 'Thanks.'

'You're welcome.'

'How are things going?'

'Fine. Would you like some lunch?'

'No.' She drained her glass.

'More wine?'

'Please.' There was a bottle nearby on the floor. I retrieved it and filled her glass.

I was a little alarmed. Quite apart from her manner, it was Thomas who could down a bottle in the time it took Sally to sip a glass.

'Can I take your coat?'

'All right.' I held on to her glass while she took off the coat.

'I'll put it in my bedroom,' I volunteered.

'Not yet.'

She restrained me by placing her hand on my arm. I thought I could feel it as firmly as if she had been holding on to my bare flesh. She looked around the room. So did I. I felt proud of myself as a host. People would remember the party. I would remember them as they were that January afternoon, during that brief period of our lives when we had something in common.

'How do you remain a decent person in these surroundings?' Sally suddenly asked.

I laughed. 'I don't know. Cowardice?'

'Be serious.'

'Well . . . I guess, that when a crisis comes up, I know what the right thing is.'

'How?'

'Sally, are you all right? Can I get you something?'

'Yes; answer my question.'

'Instinct.'

'What kind of answer is that?'

'The truth. Whenever I've had a crisis in my life, I've looked at myself in the mirror in the morning and said, do that. I don't know what I'd do if I had a moral crisis late at night.'

'There are no moral crises late at night.' That came from Thomas, who had joined us. 'Hello, my love.' He leaned over to kiss Sally, and just got away with it.

'Bastard,' she said.

'Don't tell Father that. He'd be so upset.'

I felt that whatever crisis was going on, was between Thomas and Sally, I would just get in the way – and display my general ignorance in such matters. I took the duffle coat to my bedroom, and then started circulating with the wine bottle again. I found Peter and Nancy still together.

'Have you been to a CUCA meeting?' he was asking. Peter was chairman. This, short of cricket, was his home ground.

'I'm afraid I don't know anything about British politics.'

'Neither do half the MPs who come down to talk to us,' he joked.

'Then I wouldn't learn anything if I came.'

'But it would please me if you did. You see, I'm chairman this term.' He smiled boyishly.

'Then I will attend, Peter. But what should I wear? Are your meetings date affairs?'

Peter laughed. At last he was able to feel superior to this endearingly ignorant colonial.

'Of course,' Nancy went on, 'I think you ought to know that I don't approve of Cambridge men sublimating what they should really be expressing.'

'I beg your pardon?'

'Politics is sex.'

'Is it?'

'And I'm afraid that I've always assumed that English undergraduates are homosexual. Unless I've tested them myself.'

Never had anyone so effectively killed every other conversation in the room.

Peter grinned at Nancy. He took his diary from his top jacket pocket and opened it to January. 'You really must come round for tea.'

'What about your meeting?' she asked. He waved the question aside. 'Of course, I don't really relate in group situations anyway.'

'What're you doing tomorrow?'

Nancy looked through her handbag and found her own diary. Conversation slowly picked up again. Thomas gave me a quick glance that would have been enough to kill an army, stone dead.

'I'm afraid I'm very busy for tea tomorrow.'

'Then come round for a drink afterwards.'

'Now would that be wise I ask myself. Tea at Cambridge so often turns into drinks. I might not want to leave that early.' Peter closed his diary. 'But I'm not doing anything tonight.'

He opened the diary again. He must have seen an entry referring to his promised dinner with Matthew Jenkins, an event of which I learned more later. Nevertheless, he said, 'How odd. I'm free too. Why don't you come round my rooms . . . oh, say at six-thirty?' He told her where he lived.

'I'm sure that'll be just lovely.'

The party was now at its prime. The red caviar and smoked salmon had long disappeared. There was still plenty of wine and port, though not from lack of trying by the guests. Most of the people were more or less drunk. They chatted happily in groups by the window seat or lounged against the mantlepiece, where they stole glances at the row of invitation cards. Overall there was a distinct odour of good drink, rich food, and of young, taut, washed bodies.

Only Sally was miserable. Thomas had steered her over to other people and then ignored her. Only after some time did he go up to her. She was sitting in the large, soft chair next to the fireplace. He sat at her feet, draping his long arms over his knees.

'I'm leaving for a supervision in five minutes,' she told him.

'You couldn't possibly discuss law after a lunch party.'

'I'll manage.'

'What you mean, is that you won't talk to me.'

'I thought you were avoiding me. It's too late now.' She started to get up. Thomas grabbed her wrist. 'I could embarrass you,' she said.

'Tell me what's wrong. Then go whenever you damn well please.'

She sat down, slowly.

'I spent some time listening to Matthew Jenkins this morning,' she said.

'Poor you.'

'Thomas!'

'All right: lucky you; fancy listening to Matthew Jenkins; gosh, golly, wow.' She folded her arms and glared at him. 'Christ, Sally, what is it about Jenkins?'

'You could start with what you said to him.'

'Really? What did he say I said?'

'Don't you remember?'

'Of course I do. But what did *he* say I said?'

Sally hesitated. She had not expected to be thrown onto the defensive. 'Well, to start with, you woke him up.'

'It was 9.15. We country people are up much earlier.'

'He'd been up until past three, working.'

'Swot'

'And you just walked in, sat down, and ordered him to make you some coffee.'

'I walked in and said, "terribly sorry, Jenkins you should've been up hours ago." He didn't tell me not to sit down, so I did. Then I said "it looks as if you could do with a cup of coffee". I might've volunteered to do it, but of course I had no idea where he kept his stuff.'

'He was terribly embarrassed. He had nothing on.'

'True. I saw that when his arms came from under the covers. I could tell that I was about to see something quite revolting. So I got up, very casually, and looked out the window. That gave him plenty of opportunity to put on some clothes. In fact he put on what I'm sure he wore yesterday. And I suspect that yesterday wasn't the first day he'd worn them. It amazed me that he could walk into a shop full of clothes and actually choose to buy those.'

'You're impossible.'

'No, I'm not. The size of a wardrobe is immaterial; what matters is whether you've chosen it with taste.'

'It's easy for you, Thomas. You'd look good in anything.'

'Thank you, my love,' he smiled. He got up and offered her his hand. 'Now you've got to go to your supervision.'

'No.' She did not move. 'I'm not being fobbed off.'

'I'm sorry. I thought it was I who had to force this out of you. What would you like to say?'

'That you behaved abominably today. Going and telling Matthew that he didn't belong.'

'I don't think I used the word belong.'

'That if he stood for office he'd get a lot of votes . . .'

'True. Pity there are so many grey voters, but there it is.'

'Votes which should go to your friends.'

'Not necessarily my friends.'

'All right, to the people who think God's asked them to rule the world. That there was a group that was supposed to run things and that Matthew wasn't one of it, so he should stick to his books and get out.'

'I believe I also suggested that he take up rowing. You don't have to be good at games to row.'

'Thomas!'

'Sally, do calm down. I wish one or both of us was sober. Look, I did nothing more than tell Jenkins what my opinion was. I was deputised to do so. Peter would've done it himself, only he's going to Jenkins's for dinner tonight, and he thought it'd be a little rude to do it. Jenkins may make of my opinion what he wishes. He can stand for office or not. I have absolutely no interest in the man.'

'Thomas, that's it.'

'What?'

'The fact that you're so utterly indifferent to him. That you were quite happy to play the hatchet man.'

'Why shouldn't I be indifferent?'

39

'Thomas. Matthew Jenkins happens to worship the ground you walk on.'

Thomas looked at her and then burst out laughing. He rocked back and forth, shaking his head in disbelief. 'I don't believe you.'

'You'll have to,' she said wearily. 'He told me all about it. "Effortless grace, Sally, I wish I had it". He's got it into his head that if he became a political star here it would prove to you that he also was interesting and able. And then he'd have to become one of your glittering friends.'

Thomas gaped at her. 'The man's mad.'

'He thinks you're genuine aristocracy.'

Thomas did not reply. He sat quietly on the floor by her side for some time.

'When he told me,' Sally went on, 'I thought, "I must tell Thomas; he'll think it so funny". And then I realised you really were a brute about it. I was right.' Again Thomas did not reply. 'Don't you have anything to say?'

'Yes. You shouldn't have come to this party. You were upset and confused, and this is no place to get over it. You should've waited until we could be alone.'

'And have you nothing else to say?'

He shook his head. 'If I say anything, you'll only think it was the drink talking. I'll get your coat.' He went into my room to fetch it, and helped her on with it.

Reluctantly, Sally let herself be propelled towards the door. She managed to step backwards just as Thomas was leaning down to kiss her.

'Thank Neil for me, for lunch,' she said.

'I helped a bit too.'

'You're a shit, Thomas.'

He grinned at her. 'What makes you think you'll ever love any other kind of man?'

Thomas stood out of the landing while Sally ran downstairs. When she was gone, he came back into the room. He paused at the doorway, and then came up to me and Peter. He took Peter's arm.

'Dear boy, you must listen to this. It's the best Matthew Jenkins story ever.'

He then proceeded to tell us what Sally had said. I knew just how accurate she was. I was tempted now to tell Thomas about the incident weeks before, just to give him some sense of moral responsibility. I did.

'Then the man really is mad,' Thomas said. 'But imagine, Peter, effortless grace!'

Peter laughed too. Effortless grace had just become the new joke phrase.

FIVE

About half an hour after Sally left, Thomas came up to me.

'I hope you don't mind,' he said, 'but I've just borrowed five pounds from your wallet.'

'What for?'

'I have to take a taxi.'

'Where? Edinburgh?'

'No, Girton.' This was Sally's college. 'But please don't say anything.'

'What about your guests?'

'They can look after themselves.'

'But why . . .?'

He put his hand on my arm and let it linger there. 'You didn't have anything smaller than a fiver.' Then he disappeared. Along with being extremely lithe, Thomas had a great talent for getting through a crowd.

Most of the guests started to leave soon afterwards. By five o'clock there was a hard core of half a dozen or so – the tweed jacketed, flannel-trousered politicians – sitting on the Chesterfield and the arm chairs, passing round the port bottles. I grew restless for them to go. They finally went at half past six, showering invitations on for me for dinner that evening, all of which I declined.

When I was rid of them, I stacked the remaining glasses and plates on the sideboard, and put the furniture back. I opened a window, to air out the port and smoke fumes. It was much colder now, and had begun to drizzle. I pulled an arm chair very close to the gas fire, collapsed in it, and proceeded to feel depressed.

I guess it was an ordinary reaction after a long day. I brooded on it, though. I thought of Thomas and Sally, having a romp of a reconciliation or at least of Thomas getting drunk somewhere. I thought of the lunch guests: all very obliging and appreciative, but in the end going off in relief to the sort of people they understood. That did not include unsure Americans; even Americans wearing thick corduroy trousers, heavy brogues and a blazer. I was having one of my bouts of foreignness.

Thomas had introduced me to his friends. We got along very well. I remained untouched. It bothered me rarely, but then I suddenly realised that I did not have a single, real emotional tie in Cambridge. Other visitors, as I said, fall in love with the university and the town as a whole – I guess in the same way that people fall in love with movie and pop stars whom they will never meet. That was not enough for me.

I tried to think of any time when I had known the intimacy I was craving at the moment. At home? I was simply the object of love, received not because of the kind of man I was, but because I happened to a son/grandson, nephew/cousin. I had had lots of friends, but no one to whom I could tell everything. Only with Susan had I come close.

Susan, who believed implicitly in my manliness; who was impervious to the values of people like my brother. On this freezing English night I tried to recall the warm Berkeley days, when I put my bare forearms around Susan's shoulders, our skins separated only by her thin cotton blouse. If only I had been more aggressive then. I accepted that any fault there was mine; I was the man. What was I waiting for? I blamed my hesitancy on my sexual shyness, and that, in turn, on my brother, whose achievement had been to instil in me an ineradicable sense of my own weakness.

Sitting there, I felt that I had to rouse myself. I would go mad otherwise. The chief lesson of twenty-two years of chastity was self control. Whenever I felt overcome by sexual frustration or shame, I forced myself to do some ordinary chore: to quell the inner turmoil by outward ordinariness. I would . . . I would write to Susan.

First I put a record on. I decided to have a joke with myself. I chose the Letter Scene from *Eugen Onegin*. Then I closed the window, and drew the curtains. Finally I sat down at the davenport which I had bought in London. I took out the box of college writing paper and the fountain pen which Thomas had finally persuaded me to buy and which I never used at mere history lectures.

I wrote the date. 'My dear Susan,' I began. Once I daydreamed that as a matter of course, I could start with 'Darling Susan' or even 'Darling S'. I had never dared go beyond 'My dear Susan'.

I have not heard from you since I returned.

Of course it is the fault of the post office.

Anyway, I am sure you will understand if I write to see how you are feeling . . .

I tore up the sheet and began again. I re-phrased it, 'write to ask what your feelings are'. From the stereo speakers I could hear what Tatiana's were.

That was enough of that subject. I tried to stay casual for the rest of the letter. I told her about the lunch party. I made a few remarks about my progress in squash, which Thomas had started to teach me.

Susan had no interest in athletics, but I wanted her to know that in England I was a man amongst men. I had won two of our nine games the day before, and had played so much better that Thomas had gone to the college bar and bought a bottle of champagne, which he could ill afford.

I filled up four sides and stopped. I could not think of anything else to say. At the same time the letter was much shorter than any other I had sent. I scrawled 'Love, Neil' and put the pen down. I put the letter inside an envelope but did not seal it. As I got up I remembered a phrase which Susan had written last October: 'the need to love is deep within you'. I could not bear to think of it now.

I went to the Chesterfield and picked up the third volume of Proust. It failed to hold my attention, which wandered to thoughts of what Thomas and Peter were doing.

Weeks later, when the three of us were on holiday in Italy together, Nancy admitted that all through that evening an old song had been playing through her mind's ear, 'I'm gonna make you love me'. But even she turned coy when it came to the details of how she had initiated Peter without wounding his male vanity.

She did say that she found Peter's room as she had expected: an untidy collection of papers, law books, fixtures cards and sporting kit. Sitting down on a chair which had been hastily cleared, she had given the impression of sniffing.

'Is anything wrong?' Peter asked.

'No. But there is . . . an odour about this room.'

'Really, I . . .'

'Is it damp?' she asked aloud.

'It is raining outside.'

'No, not damp. I think I've decided that there is a distinctive odour amongst upper middle class Englishmen, especially those with fair hair and who only bathe every other day.'

'Considering the fact that I have black hair and . . .'

'This is a very masculine room.'

'And a jolly good thing too.'

'I can feel it. You see, Peter, I'm testing the vibrations.'

'Vibrations? What are you going to do? Organise a seance?'

'Not a seance.'

The phrase 'but a seduction' came to their lips simultaneously. They saw it in each other's face and were so pleased with their respective cleverness and with having found someone who was obviously equally clever, that they burst out laughing.

'That made things easier' Nancy told me in Italy.

'Good. Then what happened?'

'What do you mean, Neil?'

'Well, what happened after you laughed?'

'Honey, you don't want to know about *that*.'

I laughed, knowingly, and pointed out that we were in a famous piazza and that the ruin on the right was of the temple of the vestal virgins.

Meanwhile there was a dismal affair going on elsewhere in Cambridge. I was to learn about Matthew Jenkins's dinner party – the one that Peter cut in order to be seduced by Nancy – a few days later. I happened to be at another party where the conversation turned to an exchange of reminiscences of embarrassing incidents. One of Jenkins's guests told me, in almost venomous detail, about the dinner.

Jenkins had planned it as a means of launching his political career. No one knew why he chose to have a dinner in his room. He not only had never cooked before; he only had at his disposal the electric ring and the tiny oven provided by the college in the gyp room. He served tinned soup, frozen steak and kidney pie, cheese and fruit. For the six people he had bought two bottles of the cheapest college wine.

It is true that very few undergraduates knew much about food or wine. They were usually happy so long as they were given enough alcohol to dull their senses. Jenkins however gave them obviously bad food and not nearly enough to drink. Sober throughout, the guests were all too aware of what they were eating, and of who was in attendance.

Those who came at all, came late, a serious matter since Jenkins had prepared the meal on the basis that his guests, like him, always arrived a little early. About twenty minutes after the appointed hour the first three young men wandered in. They said that they did not mind about the food being burned. They expressed a great deal of interest in who was yet to arrive.

'It seemed,' my narrator said, 'as if Jenkins had pulled off the coup of the term. I mean, the President of the Union and Peter Harding.'

'Had they really accepted?'

'Jenkins never lies. I have no doubt that they said yes. Of course that doesn't mean that they hadn't said no on any number of previous occasions.'

'But they didn't come?'

'No. We waited for at least half an hour. The food was ruined by then as well, so we tried to make the best of it.'

'What did you do?'

'Pretend as if nothing were wrong. The three of us knew each other well enough, so we talked between ourselves. Jenkins just sat there, looking like stone.'

'Didn't he give away any of his feelings?'

'Not really. At one point he said that he'd been reading Nietzsche. He asked if we believed that the weak really could develop a morality that would make the strong their slaves.'

'What did you say to that?'

'Looked even more embarrassed. One chap did ask if Jenkins had read E. M. Forster. Then I changed the subject. Asked why none of us had been invited to your lunch party.'

'Did you ever find out what had happened to the other two?'

'Yes. The President of the Union simply chucked it. Typical. Peter rang the college porter's lodge at six and left a message to say that he was ill and terribly sorry that he could not come.'

I thought of Peter's reputation for niceness and wondered if he had had any qualms of conscience while he sated himself with Nancy. 'What happened to the message?'

'The porter left it in Jenkins' pigeonhole. He found it there, the next morning.'

'Poor Jenkins,' I said.

'Yes, he's an odd fellow. Welsh name, but very Hendon.

'What does that mean?'

'Well, you know his father owns a kettle shop on the North Circular Road.'

When I was told this story I was still very naïve: I thought that the narrator was unique in his insensitivity towards his fellow man.

Thomas returned to the room about ten. His tie was off, but otherwise he looked no different.

'Oh, hello,' he said. 'Wonderful lunch, wasn't it?'

'I think so. Did you get to Girton?'

'Yes. Thanks.' He scooped the change from the taxi from his jacket pocket and put it on the edge of the side table.

'You know I didn't care about the money.'

He grinned. 'You mean the *après-dejeuner*?'

'Is everything all right between you?'

'I think so.' He leaned against the doorway to his bedroom and

47

hugged himself. 'Sally was in the most absurd state at the party.'

'I saw.'

'It was ridiculous for her to get drunk, especially when she had a supervision afterwards. She looked like hell by the time she got back to Girton.

'Was she glad when you called on her?'

'I didn't call on her.'

'How do you mean?'

'I was already there when she got back.'

'Yes, but . . .'

'In her room. Sally always leaves her door key in her coat pocket. I removed it.' He smiled again. 'Not bad, considering how drunk I was at the time.'

'How did she react?'

'Not very favourably at first. But she was shocked. That was good tactics. I'd also had time to strew books and my jacket and tie over the chairs. There was nowhere left to sit except the bed. By the time she walked in, the fire was on, tea was made, and I was happily stretched out on the bed, reading a novel.'

'A picture of domestic bliss.'

'That's rather what I was trying to convey, though of course I don't believe in domesticity. Cloying.'

'Did you choose an appropriate novel?'

'Now that was remarkable. I expected Sally's bookshelves to be full of law and feminism.'

'What were they full of?'

'Jean Plaidy and Colette. Fascinating.'

'So in the end you got your way?'

At first Thomas did not answer. He remained where he was, slowly taking off his jacket, then his cufflinks and the blue-and-white striped New and Lingwood shirt which he folded over his crossed arms.

In the brief silence I noticed how impressive Thomas's physique was. He had done a good deal of sport at school, quite apart from his holiday training, and he had the body of a more than usually muscular athlete. The veins were prominent on his forearms and hands. The October brownness had long ago faded to a light gold. The skin was taut across his cheekbones and broad forehead and he had a smooth chest.

'I don't know,' he said, shattering my reverie, 'if I'm convinced by reconciliations that simply end in sex.'

'If they didn't, I bet a lot of reconciliations wouldn't take place at all.'

'Perhaps. But Sally wasn't annoyed with me because I'm a poor lover. She was annoyed because she thinks I behaved like a shit this morning. We had an ecstatic time in Girton, but she must know that I'm not going to be any nicer to Matthew Jenkins.'

'Maybe she invited the quarrel? To provoke you into a reconciliation?'

'She's a bloody good actress if she did. Still, I am feeling rather pleased with myself at the moment.'

'What more do you want?'

'Have you turned cynic?'

'I don't think so.'

'So you've turned sarcastic. It doesn't suit you.'

'I'm not!'

'Then what do you mean by asking what more I want?'

I was completely puzzled by his anger. 'I'm just using your standards . . . and thinking . . .'

'What?'

'Well, have you ever asked for more from a girl than sex?'

'For Christ's sake . . . I'm not worried about whether she has capacity for feeling. Most people I know can turn love on like a tap.'

'Some taps . . . need sinks.'

Thomas sniggered. 'That's rather funny.'

'It wasn't meant to be. It was just a lousy simile.'

'I know what you're saying; I haven't had any experience in it myself, though. I suppose you'd say that I had too many sinks and no taps at all.'

I shook my head. 'I don't know . . .'

'I can remember what a funny old colonel said to my brother

years ago. We were out shooting together and he must've decided to take William under his wing. Anyway, I can see him killing a pheasant, putting down his gun, turning to William and saying "sex is like shitting".'

I smiled politely. 'Is it?'

Thomas went over the the side table and, finding a cigarette, lit it. 'Sex is, yes.'

'Maybe you should introduce the colonel to Nancy Wright.'

'That girl.'

'Peter doesn't mind her.'

'Have you been match-making?'

'Didn't you see them at the party?'

'I heard her once. I pretended not to notice. Bitch.'

'Come on . . .'

'Sorry, I just feel rather . . . proprietorial about Peter. Of course he's going to attract women, but he doesn't have to fall into the clutches of some latter-day Wallis Simpson.'

'Peter can look after himself.'

'How do you know?'

'Well, he's a nice guy and . . .'

'How would you know when and where Peter can look after himself?' I was too taken aback to answer. 'Sorry. Again. It just goes back to that little affair in the autumn.'

'What's that?'

'That little affair I had with Peter.' He said it so matter-of-factly.

'Oh. I didn't notice.'

'I must tell him that. I didn't care whether or not you knew, but he did.'

'Then why did he . . .?'

'Because he really is absolutely insatiable. He can't bear talking about sex and if you ask him about anything sexual he sounds like a puritan, but once you've torn away that ridiculous exterior . . . I hope Nancy's going to be pleased,' Thomas said nastily. 'I wonder if he's going to be paranoid about her too.'

'It's a bit more acceptable, isn't it?'

He looked at me with his cynical stare which always gave me a sinking feeling. 'What the hell did you people do in Berkeley?'

'You mean sex-wise?'

'Yes.'

'I guess about everything. The whole campus reeked with the ethos of the right of one man and one woman to have sex in as many different positions as they liked. It was a very liberal place,' I added.

'No it wasn't.'

'The rest of the country thought we were positively radical.'

'Did it? With undergraduates with notions of acceptability drilled into their heads?'

'That's me. I guess I'm just conventional.'

'But what if someone had stood up in your Sproul Plaza and shouted, "let's strike for the right of privileged young Englishmen to go to bed with each other". What would they have called that kind of behaviour?'

'Decadent.'

'Exactly.'

'Okay, Thomas. But I'm liberal.'

'That's the funny thing. You really are tolerant of things you're completely ignorant about.'

'Isn't that what real tolerance is all about?'

Thomas smiled and shook his head. 'Sometimes you're so good that by rights you ought to be incredibly boring as well. But you're not.'

'Thanks.' I was willing to accept that as a second best compliment to being worldly.

'Christ, let's not talk about sex seriously.'

'We never talk about sex at all, Thomas.'

'Do you want to?'

'No.' I preferred being 'safe'.

'Good. It's quite useless. I mean, I enjoy talking about a book or a painting or a symphony or even a history essay – it's quite likely that the other person could point something out that you'd never noticed otherwise. But no one can teach you anything about sex, except the person lying next to you.'

51

'Sure.'

'You ought to know that being attracted to Peter took me by surprise. Of course I'd known him for a year, and then suddenly he said something – I can't even remember what, except that it was incredibly awkward and embarrassed – which showed that he could be available. And all of a sudden I couldn't do without him. But of course it only lasted a week, so that's all right.'

'Sally's lasted all of a fortnight.'

'Yes. My great achievement. Two weeks with the same girl. We might make it all the way through this term at the present rate. Bloody, bloody good.'

'Thomas, what's the matter?'

'Look, do you mind if we talk about something else?'

'All right.' I sat down.

'What have you been doing since the guests left?'

'I wrote a letter to Susan.'

'Her.' I got up and started to walk towards my room. 'Neil . . . look, I'm sorry. Come back, please. Oh, come on, and don't sulk. Tell me what you wrote to her.'

I went over to the davenport, and handed Thomas the unsealed envelope. He read it to himself.

'It's good,' he said, as he handed it back to me. 'Just the right tone.'

'Thank you very much.'

'I shouldn't have mocked. But don't you ever wonder, what you're doing here while she's there? I mean, if you are in love with each other?'

'I've explained it all to you. By the time we met, she'd been accepted to law school, and I'd been accepted here. I couldn't ask her to give that up, and she obviously didn't feel as if she could ask me to give up England. I'm sorry if that much delicacy of feeling confuses you.'

'As I said, I shouldn't have mocked. I just don't know what it feels like to care that much for someone.'

It was an admission of what most people guessed about Thomas. Unlike every other pronouncement by him of his attitude towards life and the people who inhabited it, he was not boasting. He may have realised it for the first time. I was anxious to ask him why he had gone to all that fuss to make it up with Sally, but I felt warned off.

'I hope you care for the piano I'm going to hire.'

'What?' he beamed.

'Jenny Seymour said she'd help me choose one tomorrow. You seemed to want it so badly, and it would be nice to . . .'

'Oh, don't talk about it. Let me think how wonderful it's going to be.' He paused. 'Oh, Neil . . .' He stood there quivering with delight like a little boy. 'I know. Let's go play squash. Right now.'

'Now?'

'I'm much too excited to go to bed. I might as well work it off with exercise. There won't be anyone on the college courts.'

'Well . . . if you don't mind winning all the games . . .' Not that there was any fear of his minding that. Although it felt as if it had been a very long day already, I had caught my second wind and ten o'clock did seem too early for bed. I agreed to play.

The college courts were one of the least attractive aspects of the place. They were cold and draughty, especially now in winter, and had none of the claims to 'charm' with which I had to dismiss most of the inconveniences visited upon me in Cambridge. There was a booking system, but we correctly guessed that no one would be playing now.

I had typically spent too much money on buying clothes to play in. At least I looked very smart in my immaculately laundered white shirt and shorts. Thomas, correspondingly, was a little grubby. To keep warm he wore the long socks he had used when playing rugby at Radley and, over his shirt, an old school cricket jumper.

We ran across the cobbled courtyard to the squash courts, not so much for the exercise as to combat the cold. I was proud of the fact that I did not feel stiff after yesterday's game. It was the first sense of athleticism I had ever experienced, despite my love of swimming.

I did not have a great deal of native talent for squash, but I tried to make up for it by strenuous effort and by expending the last of my resources of stamina. Thomas played with less effort and almost perfect form. He had grace because that was the only way he knew how to play, squash was not 'his game'.

Thomas won the first game with ease, and the second with a little more effort. That seemed to satisfy him, but he could not suggest ending there before I had the chance to even things. Nevertheless his enjoyment obviously lessened, and he lost concentration. He started losing the serve as quickly as he gained it.

At the same time I became uncharacteristically wily. Thomas consistently stood well back, able and willing to meet any powerful hits. I'd confounded him by being able to tap the ball just above the bottom red foul line. When he did occupy the central point in the court I managed to direct the ball into a far corner. Once or twice I became too clever by half and slammed the ball into the metal barrier and thus lost a point or a serve, but in general I kept Thomas off balance sufficiently to win the third game.

'Tired?' Thomas asked. He was much too polite to say that he was.

'No; I'm just waking up,' I replied in my selfish flush of victory and handed him the ball to serve.

It was the most see-saw game we had ever played and took twice as long as any other. Both of us played as if there would not be a fifth game and expended all our effort. The court was no longer cold. Thomas had long ago taken off his jumper. His shirt, like mine, was clinging to his chest, and he kept pushing his hair out of his face. My own hair, was wavier and less of a problem.

Both of us found it difficult to gain a commanding lead. We would win the serve and then a point whereupon the other would take the serve back. Towards the end I felt almost too exhausted to go on and Thomas pulled ahead, just failing to win 9–7. This escape cheered me and in a last burst of energy I pulled ahead, 10–9.

At this point I stood in the server's box and paused. My legs felt like lead and I had difficulty holding on to the racket. I rocked back and forth a little and squeezed the ball in my sweaty hand, while trying to forget how crucial this serve was and how tired I felt. It was a wonderful fatigue; that legendary exhaustion which was reserved for athletes and which I had read about without any sense that I might one day know it. It was another experience Thomas had introduced me to. It may have been trivial, but it seemed as if he, albeit unconsciously, had gone to a lot of effort to put me in a place of equality. No one else ever had, and it was the more remarkable because of his own *laissez-faire* attitude towards other people.

I threw the ball up and hit it as hard as I could. It was a poor serve and Thomas smashed it back easily. It rebounded from the front wall and came like a bullet towards where I was still foolishly rooted in the server's box. More through self-defence than any conscious manoeuvre I swung my racket into a backhand position and returned it with equal force in a straight line only inches from the wall.

Unable to think of anything else, I threw myself against the wall. It was the only way Thomas could get to the ball. I closed my eyes, heard his movements and his breathing, then the swishing noise of his racket and . . . and then the second bounce of the ball. The game was mine.

'Well done' Thomas grinned.

I couldn't think of what to say. 'Want to play again?' I offered.

'Haven't we played enough? I'm dead.'

'So am I.'

'And . . . and I'd rather leave it, like this; a tie.'

We did leave it there. It was my one moment of athletic glory, fairly earned and not forgotten. In later weeks, when someone would ask, in our room, if I wanted a game of squash, Thomas would always intervene with 'didn't you know? Neil and I play together. We tie.' Somehow that deflected the challenge, and I never did play with anyone else. I just had the reputation that I was as good as Thomas Lyster.

SIX

I was born a swot, and I was a swot for much of my life. I grew up in a prosperous neighbourhood, where it was safe to send the children to the local schools. My father, like many others, spent all day exhorting his employees to work harder, so that he could make bigger profits and pay them larger salaries. He came home and exhorted his sons to study harder, so that they would get into university. They needed a degree in order to have a good job. He himself was uneducated, and my mother used to say that she did not need a diploma to know how to change a diaper. But their sons would succeed.

I was obsessed with the need to fulfil their ambitions. All through school and Berkeley I had a nightmare that I was approaching exams but had somehow failed to open a book on the subject. Time was running out, and I was doomed to failure.

At Cambridge, Thomas kicked me off the treadmill.

'You can do your work during the vacation,' he told me.

'How do I know that'll give me enough time?'

'It will. What goes on during term at Cambridge is far too wonderful to miss out on. Bury yourself in books when term is over.'

'Well . . .'

'All right, I'll prove it to you. Come and stay with us over Easter.'

'With your family?'

'I'm afraid that that is a liability.'

'I didn't mean that. But . . . it's very generous of you'.

'Nonsense. We're the sort of household where the guests and the animals are treated much better than the children.'

56

'I'd love to come.'

'Excellent. You go to Italy with a clear conscience,' – I had just arranged to spend a fortnight there with the budding romantics, Peter and Nancy – 'Now put down that history of the revolution of 1848. You've got to get well into Proust by the time you arrive. I want to discuss it over dinner.'

'Thomas, I'm not coming if I'm going to be made a tool in your arguments with your father.'

'All right. I'll try to be good. If you force me to.'

Easter seemed a long way away on the evening in February when Thomas issued the invitation. My mind in any case was only on one thing: Susan, and the four page letter I had just got, saying that she loved me; hoping that I would forgive her the months of not knowing her own mind; and promising to come to England in June, as soon as her finals were over.

I am in love, I told myself. I am in love and I am loved in return. It was all so innocent and simple. It made me very happy. It also gave me increased confidence in enjoying Cambridge. I was sure that I could even go out with flocks of English girls now. Nothing would shake my loyalty.

I didn't realise how far I was into Cambridge until, in late February, I received my first and last American visitor. Rob Berman, a Berkeley acquaintance, had written that he was giving up graduate school, in order to bum around the world. 'You can't understand what's going on inside yourself,' he wrote, 'unless you get physically outside your environment.' On a fine winter morning, just before the first crocuses appeared along the river, Rob arrived at Cambridge station.

He tried not to react to seeing me in a light brown tweed jacket, Viyella shirt, and yellow silk tie. I looked at his faded work shirt and jeans as at an alien costume. Nevertheless, I dutifully took him on a tour of as many colleges as we could fit in in a day. I had learned a lot about Cambridge during my lonely time in the autumn and kept up a running commentary. He seemed to like the town. Over lunch he called Cambridge 'a far out place'.

In the afternoon we went to King's College. I thought I was

saving the best for last. Even in my most ignorant days, I was bowled over by the chapel, and had spent a long time, trying to find the best position from which to marvel at the fan vaulting and the majesty of the nave.

'Don't you feel the dead hand of the past?' Rob asked me as we stood in the choir. 'And all this money spent on religion.'

With a sinking heart, I took Rob to the set for tea. Thomas was there – lying in wait, I thought.

'Neil belongs here, I guess,' Rob conceded. He took the proffered tea cup and saucer and then looked confused, having no idea where to put it.

'I think he likes it,' Thomas said.

'But you really have to be into old things to appreciate it. London seems so old.'

'Rome,' Thomas warned him, 'will probably seem even older.'

Rob shook his head. 'I don't know if I can hack that part of Europe. It's okay, if you don't have any choice. But I always thought that the past is really only there to fuck you up. That's why I left the States.'

'Why ever did you come to Europe then?' Thomas asked.

'Well, maybe I was thinking of my own past. I like the future. Maybe England was just the wrong country to come to. I mean, you don't really think it has a future, do you? With all the class system and everything?' I felt acutely embarrassed. Thomas smiled in a sinister manner. Fortunately Rob was uninterested in anyone else's point of view. 'How are things with you and Susan?' he asked.

'Fine. Wonderful.'

'It must be difficult to relate when you're so far apart and having different experiences.'

'Relate?' Thomas said. 'I didn't know you were cousins.'

I ignored the sarcasm. 'There's not much we can do about it.'

'Yah, it's the shits all right. Say, where do you pick up girls? There don't seem to be many around.'

'One manages,' Thomas said.

'What about you, Neil? Don't tell me you're playing Mr Faithful to Susan all this time. You know, chastity is its own punishment and all that.'

'My dear fellow,' Thomas smiled, 'whatever did you get up to at Berkeley?'

I shrugged. Rob said. 'Oh, Neil kept pretty quiet. You never knew what he was doing, but there were girls creaming themselves for him.' I was sure that Rob was putting on an act. And I wished someone would bring down the curtain. 'I bet it's the same here,' he proclaimed, 'if there are any girls.'

'I'm sorry,' Thomas apologised, 'but I'm afraid that Neil and I don't have any to spare at the moment. Otherwise, we would've been delighted to look after you.'

Rob laughed. 'God, that English sense of humour. That's all right, though. There was a girl on my flight over, and we shacked up in London. I need a rest. I've got to start thinking of my mind, anyway.'

'What's wrong with your mind?' Thomas asked.

'That's what I've got to find out. I've decided that I've got to think about myself.'

'Neil told me that Berkeley students are out to re-make the world.'

'Not any more. It's look out for number one now. That's what the '70's are going to be all about. Sure, I've gone on demonstrations and tried to stop the war and all that. But that's over.'

Thomas got up. 'I'm afraid that I must be meeting some friends for dinner. It was so nice to meet you.'

Rob stood up to shake hands. 'I guess I better be going too.' He looked at me, obviously expecting an invitation to stay for dinner if not the night.

'It was great of you to come up,' I said. 'I'll walk you to the bus stop – you can get to the station from there.'

'That's all right. I'm hitching from here.' He had arrived with a small nylon bag, which I guessed contained all the bodily necessities he needed for his journey of the mind.

I escorted Rob to the Huntingdon Road. He produced from his bag a small sign that said 'Somewhere – Anywhere' and prepared to hold it up.

'Thanks for everything,' he said as he held out his hand. 'I guess people change. That's the first lesson I've learned so far. I guess I'll learn a lot more before I'm finished.'

'Yes,' I agreed. 'Keep in touch.'

Coincidentally, on the following Monday the Union held a debate on the special relationship between the United States and Great Britain. I went out of curiosity, inspired in part by the fact that Matthew Jenkins was due to speak. I asked Peter Harding how Jenkins had achieved this honour of a paper speech.

'Guilt,' he told me.

'How's that?'

'He invited the President of the Union to dinner a few weeks back, and the President jacked. Jenkins came round his office the next day, and just to shut him up he told him he could have a paper speech.'

Peter had, of course, snubbed the dinner as well, but his feelings towards Jenkins had hardened.

'It was an idiotic thing to do,' he went on. 'It makes Jenkins look respectable. Christ, I'd like to kick that man downstairs sometimes. The next thing is that he'll come to my meetings and behave as if we should take him seriously, just because the Union does.'

As always, the whys and wherefores of Cambridge politics confused me. Peter's enthusiasm was even a little irritating. How could he get so excited about trivia? I could imagine him in later life, embroiled in the details of the golf club and deeply involved in the intricacies of the law: the kind of man who everyone likes even though he can only talk shop. Peter succeeded in Cambridge because there was a myth woven round him. No one, I learned, had ever stood against him for office, because it was assumed that no one would ever beat him. He was completely untested.

We went together to the Union debate. Peter sat there glowering because Jenkins was speaking at all. I paid attention to what Jenkins said. He talked about America's great liberal institutions. I, who knew how little that liberalism existed below the surface, thought it was nonsense. But his manner struck me. He was desperately intense and gawky. I tried to put that to one side. What mattered was that he hungered for what he wanted. I remembered the quoted remark from his dinner party, about the weak developing a philosophy that would help them to vanquish the strong. Matthew Jenkins should not have been talking about liberalism; with a bit of polish he would have been a superb rabble rouser. I wondered how long it would take him to realise that himself. And once he did, all the handsome, muscular, vacuous Peter Hardings of this world wouldn't stand a chance.

I could find no one to agree with me about Jenkins. Everyone I knew either loathed him or felt sorry for him. My reactions were considered to be naive. I shrugged my shoulders and lapsed into apoliticism.

As the term wore on, my life became completely involved with that of Thomas and Sally. I kept up with Peter and Nancy, partly because of the already made plans for Italy, and partly because Nancy had decided to 'adopt' me as her little friend, an appropriation which was extremely difficult to avoid.

I remained officially a part of Thomas's circle, but I did not have a great deal in common with them. The politicians pursued their trivia, and the gentry were like beings from another planet. The gentry was the name I gave to that majority of Thomas's friends who were people of his own kind, that is, their families were like the Lysters. They went shooting in the autumn and winter; they went to hunt balls; they did no work in term time; they ostetnatiously avoided intelligent women. One took me into hall at his college, Magdalene. I looked down the long table and saw rows of wine bottles – far, far more than in any other college in Cambridge. These men took drinking seriously. My host then entertained me by telling me where every man within earshot had gone to school. Only he and I had not been to Eton or Harrow. After that, Peter Harding's discourse on the upcoming Conservative Association elections was a relief.

Of course it made Thomas that much more intriguing. The

politicians spent a great deal of time with him, even though they gained no political advantage from it. The gentry happily drank through evening after evening with us, although Thomas found them as absurd as I did.

It would have been against Thomas's nature to ask for any depth of feeling from his friends. I often wondered what he wanted from Sally. In the short term, he kept things at a very high pitch. When they quarrelled – as they often did – and if Thomas won – as usually happened – he would send her a dozen roses and never refer to the matter again. If she won, he would sulk for a few days, go up to Girton, play the little boy until she took him back, and then re-assert his dominance. Sally never quite knew where she stood, except that Thomas insisted on always being in control.

I hated being around when they argued, but as the fights flared up unexpectedly, I had to choose between taking that risk and not seeing them together at all. The latter would have been intolerable, and anyway, they both claimed that my presence was essential.

'Thomas is nicer when you're around,' Sally said.

'That's because I look up to him; he doesn't want to be a bad influence on me,' I joked.

'Do you? Do you look up to me?' Thomas asked. 'That makes you the only creative thing I've ever done.'

Our favourite activity was to go down to London together, which we did four times that term. It was a very happy experience. In the winter London was relatively free of tourists. The city seemed to belong to us. It saw that we three were young and healthy, and gave a blessing to our exploits.

On one Saturday we spent the early afternoon at Kensington Palace, which then housed the London Museum, and then went to a five o'clock matinee. It was one of the most successful plays that season, and the theatre was packed when we arrived. I escorted Sally to our seats in the stalls, while Thomas ordered drinks in the bar for the interval. As we sat down, I noticed that there was an empty seat on my left; next to that was a woman who appeared to be alone.

I could not imagine that she would be alone for long. I only saw her profile, but it was beautiful: creamy white skin, rich black hair and large, dark eyes. I thought she was in her late twentys. From her poise – legs crossed, eyes straight ahead at the curtained stage, back straight – I imagined she was a worldly woman. I immediately began to fantasise that the only men she had ever known were full-blooded characters, who had moved with ease from the playing fields to the bar to the bedroom.

When I first noticed her I gaped appallingly. She took no notice.

Recovering myself, I turned to Sally and looked at the programme which she held. Out of the corner of my eye I stole a glimpse at the woman. It was then that I saw the impossible: she was actually looking at me. Quickly I looked back at the programme. I stole another glimpse. This time it was unmistakable. Even by scarcely moving her head, she had trained her eyes on me.

My first conclusion was that she was looking at someone else. I glanced around. There were no other likely candidates. I turned to my right, expecting to see Thomas, but he was still in the bar.

'Something wrong?' Sally asked.

'No. I mean, Thomas is going to be late.'

'The management wouldn't dare start without him,' she observed drily.

She was right. The moment Thomas sat down the lights went out and the curtain went up. The stage lights faintly illumined the row where we were sitting. I summoned up my courage, turned to the woman on my left, and grinned in my most charming way. She, who had come to see the play, did not notice.

That was enough to defeat my efforts. At the end of the first act I followed Thomas as he led the way to the aisle, over the feet of the two couples who sat nearest to it and who resolutely remained seated while the other patrons climbed over them. Thomas waited in the gangway for Sally and I. I saw him look over my shoulder and then say,

'Caroline Camden!'

I turned round to see the lady in question smiling at my roommate. 'Hello, Thomas.' With measured steps she slipped past the seated couples and joined us. I could see now that she wore a very simple, dark green wool dress.

Thomas leaned over and kissed her cheek. He grinned at her. I knew that grin. It was given to his favourite women. Then, to make the current position plain, he put his arm around Sally's shoulders.

'You don't know Sally Lloyd, do you? Caroline Camden,' he repeated, nodding towards her. The two women exchanged short greetings, the sort of greetings which are swapped between the woman who is no longer a threat and the woman who has nothing to fear. Still, neither liked the look of the other. '. . . and Neil Fielding.'

She gave me her hand which I shook with care. 'I'm very glad I got to meet you,' she said.

'Who are you with?' Thomas asked, as he indicated that we should start to move towards the bar.

'I'm alone.'

'I don't believe it!'

'It's true.'

'Who did you ditch?'

Caroline laughed. It was the laugh of someone who always enjoyed herself. 'You're the only man in England charming enough to phrase it like that.'

'Well?'

'Someone worth ditching. Thank goodness I had the tickets.'

I may have an inadequate sense of money, but the idea of going alone to the theatre with two tickets struck my middle class conscience as being too extravagent. Still, I was becoming partial to extravagance.

'Then you'll join us?' Thomas said.

'I'd love to.' As she said this she smiled at the three of us but in particular caught my eye. I melted.

'What do you do, Caroline?' I asked, as if that might explain her own sense of money.

'Nothing.' She giggled.

'Caroline's the most beautiful woman in London,' Thomas said. 'That's a full-time job.'

'What a little edge we have to our charm.'

Thomas enjoyed that remark. We were now in the bar. It was crowded and there was virtually nowhere to sit aside from one table with chairs. It was here that Thomas had managed to have our drinks placed. The ladies sat down.

'Can I get you something, Caroline?' I asked.

'Why . . .'

'I will,' Thomas said firmly, and propelled me towards the table. 'I know what she drinks.' Then he disappeared into the mob near the bar.

'We're all at Cambridge together,' I said, as no one else seemed eager to talk.

'I thought so.'

'Thomas and I share a set of rooms.'

'I'd like to see that.'

'Were you – are you – at Cambridge? I mean, is that how you two know each other?'

'I'm one of those stupid people who didn't go to a university.'

'What a pity,' Sally said without a grain of sympathy. 'What did you do instead?'

'Nothing.'

'Of course. I forgot.'

Thomas returned at this point, proving again that he could extract drinks faster than any man in England. 'One large gin, twist of lemon, half a bottle of tonic water, no ice.'

'Thanks.'

'I'll never get used to warm cocktails,' I said.

'I've never like ice cubed. I love cold drinks, but not ice cubes.'

It took me a moment to figure this out. 'That leaves you with . . . white wine and champagne.'

'Yes, please,' she smiled.

The bell rang, signalling the end of the interval. After the performance we invited Caroline to dinner with us, but she declined.

'I've got to go to a dreary dinner party.'

'Why don't you ditch them as well?' I suggested. I had spent most of the second act staring at her – without a reply – and fantasising a bit more. I had forgotten that I was now actually speaking to her.

'I'm very tempted', and I was glad that I had made the suggestion. 'But I've really got to go.' Turning to Thomas she added, 'It's your sister's party.'

'Then it won't be dreary.'

'I know. I didn't want you to think that I was looking forward to leaving you.' Then she said good-bye and left.

The three of us had dinner in Soho. During it I asked Sally what she would have done if she had gone to the matinee with a man while knowing that she had to go off immediately afterwards to dinner.

'Don't ask me. I'm one of those intelligent people who went to a university.'

Thomas looked quizzical so I told him that his return to the drinks table had prevented what looked like a row.

'What do you have against Caroline?' he asked.

'I hate women like that.'

'How many others do you know?'

'I know the type.'

'What type's that?'

'The ageing deb of the year . . .'

'Sally . . .'

'She's twenty-seven if she's a day.'

'And a jolly good day it is.'

I tried to make peace. 'I suppose it's pretty bad, her not having a job.'

'She's had lots of jobs, but she spends longer between them than in them. That's why she calls them 'nothing'.'

'The only job she was brought up to have was to get a husband. And she's failing,' Sally added.

'I'd imagine,' Thomas mused, 'that that's a blessing all round.'

'Well I liked her,' I said. 'I think she's . . .' I was at a loss for adjectives. 'She was nice to me.'

Sally groaned. 'As if no one else is.'

'All right; I think she's very sweet.'

'That's probably just what her young man thought. Before she ditched him.'

Thomas rubbed the back of her hand. 'Why are we so prickly tonight?'

'I'm sorry. I didn't mean to ruin your evening. It's just . . . I don't like being patronised. Caroline patronised me like anything.'

'I don't see why she should. She doesn't have half your brains and she'll never find life half as interesting as you will.'

'Exactly.'

'She has to make up for that somehow. So she was born with beauty and she has more chic than any woman I've ever met, and she's probably jealous as hell because you're beautiful *and* intelligent. It's an insult to women like that to find that brillant girls aren't ugly and revolting.'

'All right, I'll be compassionate. What about her?'

'That's not her style at all.'

'You seem to know her pretty well.'

'We were well acquainted at one stage.'

'I bet.'

'That's my business.'

'Male prerogative,' she mocked. 'One girl's much the same as another.'

Thomas picked up her hand, pressed his palm against hers, and looked Sally in the eye. 'So why do you go out with me?'

She did not hesitate. 'Because you're the only man I know who can take me out of the foul mood that you've put me in yourself.'

When we got back to Cambridge Sally went to Girton, while Thomas and I returned to college. Once back in our room, Thomas asked,

'Did you really like Caroline?'

'Yes.'

'Then invite her up for a weekend. She loves Cambridge.'

'Invite her . . .? Where would she stay?'

'Here.'

'That's asking a lot of her.' What I meant was that the prospect

67

scared me to death.

Thomas shrugged. 'Then invite her for the day. Take her punting. Or go to London. She has less to do than you.'

'Maybe I could invite her for the day.'

Thomas leaned against the mantlepiece and slowly took out his cufflinks. 'Christ, Sally is a chore sometimes,' he said.

'I guess she was upset.'

'She has no cause to be.'

'Did you . . . was Caroline your girlfriend?'

'Dear boy, there's a Caroline in every man's life, and there have been numerous men in hers.'

'I thought so.'

'Doesn't that please you? Isn't it what you wanted?'

'Kind of.'

'Susan will think you're Byron by the time Caroline gets through with you.'

'But what if I fall in love with her?'

'Do you fall in love with every girl you have sex with?'

'No.' That was strictly quite true. 'But I don't know if I'm going to like this.'

'Why shouldn't you?'

'I guess I'm not very sure of myself.'

'Don't let Caroline find that out. She'll have you for breakfast.'

'Oh, I think she likes me.'

'Yes?'

'Before you got to your seat – before the first act tonight – she was undoubtedly staring at me.'

'She's not a fool, you know,' he said and walked into his room.

Caroline replied to my jaunty note from a yet unfashionable part of London. She said she would love to come to Cambridge for the day. We fixed up the last Sunday of full term. A day which also saw the Conservative Association elections. I was oblivious to them at the time.

I met her at Cambridge station wearing my blazer and a newly-bought boater. It was a balmy March morning, one of those days

68

which give false hope to the end of winter and a tantalising hint of the summer yet to come. Caroline stepped off the train wearing a Liberty print skirt and a dark blue blouse which showed off the whiteness of her skin. Twenty seven years old, but the complexion was perfect, as I carefully if surreptitiously noticed.

'Welcome to Cambridge,' I said, taking off my boater.

'I was hoping you'd ask me,' she said. 'But you will keep the hat off, won't you?' She smiled like a little girl who knows that she is being a little naughty.

'I thought . . .'

'I came to see Neil, not any old twee undergraduate.'

'All right.' I tucked the boater under my left arm. As we passed the ticket barrier she slipped her hand through my right arm. There were two men I knew who were in the railway lobby, and they saw us.

The taxi ride to the town centre was a short one, but it gave me a good deal of vexation. I had just read a passage in an Evelyn Waugh novel where the heroine felt surprise tinged with contempt when a man did not take the opportunity of a taxi journey to make a pass at her. Did Caroline expect me to? In broad daylight? In Cambridge? Hesitantly I leaned my elbow on the back of the seat but then let my hand hang loose. It looked absurd in that pose so I used it to gesture while I spoke in a manner which was completely contrary to habit.

We got out at Magdalene Bridge. The restaurant was next to a punt station. I wanted one event to appear to follow upon another.

'I'm sorry about the boater,' I said when we sat down.

'I'm sorry I said anything. It's a lovely hat. I'm just feeling naughty'

'Do you want to be punished?' It was I who was punished for that clumsy remark, with silence. 'Do you really do nothing? Thomas said that you've had lots of jobs.'

'That's cheating.'

'What is?'

'Asking Thomas about me. Aren't you interested in finding out on your own?'

69

'Didn't I just ask the question?'

'True. Sorry.'

'That's the second time you've apologised.'

'I know. It makes me feel guilty.'

'Don't tell me you like feeling quilty.'

'It's a habit I can't break.'

The waitress came over to our table. I ordered paté since I like it and roast beef since I thought this is what an Englishwoman would expect to eat on Sunday.

'It sounds funny to hear people talking about guilt,' I said. 'That's so Berkeley'.

'Perhaps I'm just saying the first thing that comes into my mind. Does that confuse you?'

'A little.'

'It'll help if I tell you that my favourite writer is Trollope.'

'Why?'

'Because you know after the first hundred pages or so what's going to happen. Then you've got the pleasure of seeing it all unfold before you.'

'Then you like certainty.'

'I've had certainty all my life. I always come back to it, whenever I get tired of being irresponsible.'

'How often is that?'

'Ask Thomas.'

'I thought I'm not supposed to.'

'But you will, as soon as I'm back on the train.'

'I can keep my own counsel.'

'I'm sure you can. But Thomas is a special case.'

'How's that?'

'You're besotted with him.' I gaped at her. 'I don't mean you're having an affair, though you wouldn't be the first man to abandon his sexual principles for him. I mean that you take your cue from him in everything you do.'

'He . . . he's been a great influence on me.'

'Of course. He influences everyone. Extraordinary, when you think how flippantly he behaves.'

'Thomas isn't as superficial as everyone thinks.'

'So I'd like to think. When he finds out that he's got a soul and a conscience . . . it'll be amusing to see how he handles it. Of course you influence him too.'

'I do?' I was astonished.

'Well, you must've made some impression. Thomas expects other people to do things for him. If he leaves you with the ladies while he fights the sweaty mob to get a drink for a woman he abandoned a year before . . . that means something.'

It had never occurred to me before. At the same time I was rather disappointed that the conversation had turned this way. Caroline was here in order to fall into my clutches, not to become a source of Wise Advice on Thomas Lyster.

'I didn't invite you here to discuss Thomas,' I said.

'Oh?'

'And I was having such a good time, listening to you talk about yourself.'

Caroline smiled, and I got lost again in those lovely huge eyes.

After lunch we duly went out on the punt. I had done a little practice on this, and although I was fairly slow I was reasonably proficient. I took off my blazer and rolled up my shirt sleeves just twice, as Thomas did, although I wished there were more veins in my white, auburn freckled forearms.

'Does Cambridge seem very different to you?' I asked. 'You have been here before.'

'I first had lunch with an undergraduate longer ago than I ought to admit to. I remember being terrified.'

'Why?'

'Because I was only eighteen and he was all of twenty one. I'd scarcely ever been out with a man before. I was convinced that I'd be raped. We always used to discuss rape at school and wonder what it would be like.'

'That's a bit gruesome.'

'Children's fantasies usually are. But I didn't have to worry. He was very nice about it.'

'Did you . . .?'

71

'I didn't want to spend my young womanhood waiting and wondering and not knowing what to do once I met a man I really liked. The most sensible thing seemed to be to find a gentle, pleasant, reasonably experienced, good-looking chap, and let him have his own way.'

'Namely that fellow?'

'He was just what the doctor ordered.'

Caroline's attitude flustered me. She was obviously used only to experienced men. At the same time her attitude towards sex was far more indifferent than I was used to. I was not Mr Right. I was just another highly eligible young man. I hoped that would make things easier.

'People say that Cambridge is much more puritanical now.' I volunteered.

'In those days – when I first came up – everyone slept with everyone else. Don't they any more?'

'No. And they smirk at those who do.'

'How silly.'

I nodded my agreement. I wanted to be as worldly as she. I also wanted to feel part of a tradition, albeit a sexual one. It was funny to think that Thomas, by his behaviour, was part of Cambridge, whereas men like, say, Matthew Jenkins, were some modern aberration.

'You said you'd like to see our room,' I mentioned casually when the punt ride was over.

'I'd love to.'

We got there at about five. I had fussed a good deal in the sitting room, buying two vases full of flowers. The weather was warm enough to keep the windows open, and for almost the first time that academic year the actual scent of Cambridge came in.

I knew that this was the crucial part of the day. Caroline casually chose the easy chair. That was bad. It would have been easier to make The Move if she were on the chesterfield, where Thomas's girls sensibly sat.

In my nervousness I let the conversation lapse. During one silence Caroline began to sing, softly. She had a lovely voice.

'What're you singing?'

'The Brahms alto rhapsody, very badly. I love it.'

'I wish I had the record.'

'So do I. My great-grandmother was Austrian. She knew Brahms. She didn't like him.'

'My great-grandmother was Austrian too. I don't think she ever heard of Brahms.' Stupid! The remark made me feel clumsy and Caroline guilty.

'I suppose I shouldn't stay late. You must have a lot to do at the end of term.'

This was It. The moment when I should say, of course you should stay. There are lots of trains in the morning, hint, hint. I nearly did say it. I had all the usual symptoms I felt before a momentous event: heart racing, hands fidgeting, and a horrible sense that I would never succeed.

'Do you have another dinner party to go to?' I asked instead,

'No.' The moment passed. I was fed up with myself and this depressed both my spirits and what was left of the conversation.

'I've had a lovely day, Neil.'

'I'm glad you came.'

'I'm glad you invited me.'

'Will you come again?'

'Of course.'

'Now that we know each other . . .' I could not think of any way to finish the sentence.

'Look,' she said kindly, 'I don't mind if you don't.'

This was Absolutely It. The Second Opportunity. The Last Chance. The invitation to go over to the chair, lean down and kiss her; to tell her that if I could not have her body as well as her friendship then I would mind very much indeed. Instead I sat rooted to the spot. My heart raced again. I ached to touch that lovely white skin. I remembered something my brother had told me years before, when he was trying to be kind. He said 'don't worry about being shy with girls. You'll get so horny that you'll have to make the move.' Was this not such a moment? And if so, where was that irresistible wave of brutal male lust which would

73

sweep Caroline into my arms?

'I like you,' I said. Lucky Caroline. I hated myself. By God, she knew that too.

'So do I. But you can't love someone who doesn't love themself first.'

'No wonder Thomas is such a success.'

She smiled. At that moment there was a knock at the door. I had not sported the oak, which was the usual sign that one was not at home. The new guest therefore had no qualms about barging in. It was Peter Harding.

'Neil . . .' He saw Caroline and blushed. 'Sorry I . . .'

'Come in.' I introduced them. 'Peter's the most important Conservative in Cambridge.'

'Not any more. We had the elections this afternoon. There's a new chairman.'

'Thomas will tell me all about it.'

'Thomas didn't come to the meeting. He said he would.'

'He probably forgot.'

'Forgot? But he didn't vote. And because he didn't vote, Matthew Jenkins was elected to the committee.'

'Does that matter?'

Peter looked at me as if I were mad. I looked at Caroline who was smiling politely. Compared to her, Peter and I must seem twelve years old.

'I must go,' she said.

'I'll take you to the market place. That's the best place to get a taxi.'

'Lovely.'

We said good-bye to Peter and set off. As we walked through the old redbrick courtyards Caroline began to hum the alto rhapsody again.

'You realise, Caroline, that I'll never be able to hear that without thinking of you.'

'What a lovely idea.'

There was a taxi waiting in the market place, and he would be able to get her to the station with only a few minutes to spare before the next train. I gave the driver fifty pence, far more than was needed for the fare.

'Thanks again.' she said.

'My pleasure.'

'Do you ever come to London?'

'Only *en passant*. I'm going to Italy for ten days with that man who burst into the room, and then a week with the Lysters. I'll call you'. I kissed her cheek, as Thomas had done in the theatre.

'Good-bye, Neil.'

'So long Caroline.'

She disappeared with the taxi. I walked very slowly back to college, while my feelings of self reproach warred with a curious sense of relief.

SEVEN

The Nonagon dinner was the night after Caroline's visit. The Nonagons were the college dining society. The name was chosen because the membership was limited to nine homogeneous members. Noting the destruction of glass which usually followed the event, someone had once suggested that the body should expand slightly and call itself the decimators.

Thomas had been elected to membership in his first term. In January he got me elected as well. We had invited Peter Harding to be our guest.

Bathed and dressed in our dinner jackets, we awaited Peter in our sitting room. We were also expecting Sally and Nancy for drinks. Nancy had decided that the two of them should have a dinner party of their own.

The weather was balmy, and we had the windows open. The clocks had been turned forward the previous weekend, and so at six-thirty it was still light.

I had every reason to feel happy that night except for one extraordinary event which had been revealed in a letter from home that morning. It had come not from my parents, but from my brother. It was, I think, the second letter I had ever received from him. He broke his silence to announce what he said our parents could not bring themselves to say. The letter was full of rationalisations and the usual bullying. It took some time to sift through it and to realise what he was saying. Stan Fielding, God's gift to women, had turned queer.

'I'm writing to you, little runt, because Mom and Dad, can't say it themselves. I'm not saying that I've given up women for good. I'm just saying that for the time being I can't live without men. It

76

all has to do with sex, so you wouldn't understand.'

I had memorised the letter by the evening which was my first real opportunity to discuss it with Thomas. I was not pleased at the prospect.

'My brother,' I began hesitantly, 'has changed the whole direction of his life.'

'That seems to be an occupational disease in California.'

'This is serious.'

'What's happened?'

'Well . . . apparently . . . he's given up women.'

'In favour of . . .?'

'Men.'

'Gosh.' Thomas tugged at his shirt cuff without interest.

'This is serious.'

'I'm sure it is. Are you shocked?'

'Of course.'

'Outraged? Your moral sense revolted?' Thomas was in full attack.

'No.' I might not have said that six months ago.

'It isn't very acceptable, is it?'

'I don't care about that. It's just . . . rather a lot to take in at once.'

Thomas stroked his clean chin. 'I'm just trying to think of the same thing happening in my family. I can't. Fancy my brother turning queer in his old age.'

'I bet it would kill your parents.'

'They're tougher than that.'

'Well, maybe they wouldn't find out.'

'I think they're cleverer than that – but I won't go into it. It would certainly be very sad for poor William.'

'I bet.'

'For one thing, homosexuality for him would be a single ticket to chastity.'

'Oh, Thomas . . .'

'It's true. The most objective thing that can be said about William is that he's ugly. At least now he has a fiancee. That's one guarantee of a sex life for both of them.'

'I'm sure . . .'

'You've never met them, so you can't be sure. Believe me, no man could look at William and no other man would look at Sarah. I wonder if that's what they have in common.' He paused. 'Men are so superficial about beauty.'

'Are they?'

'At least about male beauty. Think of all those Simon Raven novels. One beautiful cricketer falls in love with another. The only crisis is Will The Others Find Out. And Brideshead. Charles Ryder falls in love with a fabulously rich and charming and handsome aristocrat. So who wouldn't?'

'I don't think that's the point.'

'But it is the reality. The beautiful cricketer never falls in love with the boy with the Ugly Body and the Beautiful Soul. Those poor sods are left to the women.'

'Women complain about it too.'

'Really? Which ones?'

'Women's Lib. It's one of their gripes.'

'What's Women's Lib?'

'It was a movement at Berkeley last year. They don't like the popular notion that a woman's delighted to have any man at all, so long as she's got a man.'

'I agree. I wouldn't want to be left with the dregs either.'

'Have you ever?'

He paused, modestly. 'No.'

'So you think people do abandon their sexual principles because of one particular person?'

'There are no such things as sexual principles. There are lots and lots of principles about the way you should treat other people. Sex is a matter of habit or choice, and there's no reason why you shouldn't abandon women for men or the other way round or have both at the same time though not very many people can handle *that*.'

'But men and women are different.'

'Beauty isn't. It's a world we use to describe a landscape and a

78

person. Sally's body and Peter's torso are both beautiful. Why shouldn't they both excite me?'

'It sounds as if you'd like to fuck the landscape.'

'I do. I'd appreciate it all the more.' He walked from the mantlepiece to the side table, where he had set out the bottles of sherry and of gin.

'What's going to happen to my brother?' I asked.

'Isn't he the all-American boy with the all-American physique in one of your family photos?'

'Yes.'

Thomas nodded. 'With that body, he'll be all right.'

'I don't care whether or not my brother's going to be a success with men.'

'So what's bothering you?' He gulped another drink.

'You don't understand. I've spent my whole life trying to be – wanting to be – fantasising myself – as more of a man than he is. And now . . .'

'And now he's a fairy.'

I was about to say yes. Then I looked up and saw Thomas staring at me, half-drunkenly. I wished he wasn't trying to get drunk so early. I realised that I had been on the verge of insulting him. I had always thought, automatically, that homosexuals are queers and fairies are men who are more female than male. But my brother wasn't. Neither was Peter Harding, for that matter. It sounds incredibly naïve, but once Thomas smashed the stereotype, I had no idea what to think. That, of course, was the idea.

'Don't use that word,' I said lamely.

'Why ever not? You would've, wouldn't you?; Anyway,' grinning, 'you don't know what sort of tastes your brother might appeal to. I bet he'd look splendid in uniforms.'

'Don't be disgusting.'

The grin vanished. 'I haven't heard sex described as disgusting since I was at school. Sometimes you talk as if you were still a schoolboy yourself.'

I looked down at my hands. 'If I do . . . If I do, it's because that's about all I know.'

'You're not sixteen years old.'

I paused. 'In one sense, I am.'

Neither of us spoke for a moment. Thomas lit a cigarette. 'I've been pretty bloody insensitive,' he said.

'It's my fault. Twenty-two year old virgins aren't what everyone expects to meet.'

'Not even Susan?'

'Especially not Susan. God, it makes me feel guilty.'

'Why?'

'Because when the time comes, she has the right to expect me to be experienced, and I won't be.'

'I thought perhaps Caroline might . . .'

'Nothing doing.'

'She really was keen on you.'

'Maybe. She must've left thinking I was an idiot.'

Thomas poured himself another gin. I wished he would stop. 'Has this always bothered you as much as it seems to do now?'

'It's been bliss here at Cambridge.' I felt as if the pressure were off. It was hell at Berkeley. Every term I'd come home and my brother would ask whether I'd scored yet.'

'Did you tell him the truth?'

'Why bother lying? But I hated it. Every quarter I'd go back to the campus and think, this is it. It's this quarter or never. And somehow . . .'

'Yes?'

'Somehow, I didn't feel anything inside me. Like yesterday. Caroline looked so lovely, but I just couldn't feel anything to push me on.'

'Did you ever think of paying for it?'

'Pay for it?' I was astonished at the suggestion. 'At Berkeley? In the sixties? I couldn't ask someone where a house was.'

'Oh, Neil, Neil, Neil. You're so sensible about everything else. This is absurd. Why can't you . . .'

'I tried,' I interrupted him. 'Last year, my brother actually came to the rescue. He fixed me up with a girl who was supposed to be easy. Rang her up and said it was me. Of course, he was so smooth and cool, she couldn't wait to meet this Neil Fielding.'

'And?'

'I got scared. I was sure she'd guess, and then how would she feel? I think I would've preferred a prostitute then. At least it would've been honest. But the prospect of an evening with a woman I had nothing to say to . . . pretending to be the kind of man I'm not. He even said I had to take her to a stupid movie just because she was stupid too.'

'What did you do?'

'I rang her up and said I was sick. My brother died laughing.'

'Your brother's such a shit. Are you sure he isn't coming over here?'

'No, we're safe. He ended his letter asking if I were still wandering around the ruins, looking for the phoenix to rise from the embers of a dying civilisation.'

'Where'd he pick that up from?'

'Probably *Time* magazine. He's too busy to read books.'

Thomas slowly shook his head. He finished his cigarette and came and stood over me.

'All that doesn't matter any more,' he said quietly.

'How can I forget it?'

'Try. You're free. I promise you.'

'Sure. Sure I am.'

'You are. You can't be hurt any more.'

'I . . . I guess that's right.'

'Of course it is.'

I smiled at him. 'It'll be funny, living without expectations. I won't even know what everyone wants me to do.'

'Thank God for that.'

'Yes.'

'Now. What are you going to do with your freedom?'

I thought for a moment. I wasn't free, just like that. I couldn't just throw overboard all those years of expectations. Even sitting there, my future seemed to loom ahead on exactly those fixed tram lines it had always run on.

I had wondered before how I would consummate a marriage

when I had no sexual experience. I had worried before why I did not feel this famous male lust. I had always rationalised it in the same way. I did once more.

'I think I'm going to ask Susan to marry me,' I said. Marriage, I always thought, would solve everything.

Thomas's reaction was violent. He spun round so quickly that he nearly knocked the glass out of my hand. He looked as if he would storm out of the room and slam the door behind him. Instead he strode over to the windows, jammed his fists into his pockets, and stared out. I was too surprised to say anything. After a while, and just as suddenly – he calmly turned round again. He went over to the piano, which had been in the room for weeks. He sat down at the stool and leafed through some of the music. He began to play a Chopin prelude. I was hurt by his disapproval, but I did not say so. We were becoming aware of each other's sensibilities – like my not offering to pay for him to come to Italy with us. After a while Thomas stopped playing.

'Have you seen Peter since yesterday?' I asked.

'No.'

'I wonder if he's recovered from Jenkins being elected to the committee.'

'He'll get used ot it.'

'He really was annoyed.' Thomas sniggered. 'Of course it's Sally he ought to blame.'

'Sally?' Thomas turned round on the piano stool.

'She organised all her friends to vote for Jenkins. That's how he scraped in.'

'She never told me about it.'

'She didn't want you to stop her.'

He thought about the implications of that and then said, 'She couldn't have many friends if he only scraped in.'

'Why didn't you run for the committee yourself? Jenkins would never had made it then.'

'Peter got me to talk to that man. It's not my fault if he didn't take my advice. And I've been on the committee of CUCA. It's as boring as hell.'

'When was that?'

'Last year. I was told that no freshman had ever been elected at the end of his first term, so I stood and won. It was a bit pointless after that.'

'Haven't you thought of running for office again?'

'At Cambridge?'

'I know it's sandbox politics, but . . . I don't know; sometimes when I look at all these politicians sitting around here, I think that they're just waiting for you to give them a lead. And you make them all look so second rate.' He smiled and shook his head. 'Okay, I know you don't give a damn what anybody thinks of you . . .'

'I don't know.' He paused. 'The point . . . the point is . . .' I looked at him intently. He was actually finding it difficult to say something. 'You see, I believe in myself. That's something so strong, that it frightens even me. It makes Cambridge politics irrelevant. It also means that unless it has some outlet. I'll go mad.' I recalled my own use of madness when thinking about my sexual frustration. Well, Nancy had said that politics is sex.

'What do you want to do?' I asked.

'Damn it, if I knew that . . . but whatever it is, it's something that's only open to men like me.' We looked at each other for a long time. I felt that Thomas was waiting for me. When I said nothing, he laughed, and said, 'Christ, let's have a drink.' He staggered over to the sidetable and looked at the bottles. 'I say, why not champagne?'

'I give up; why not?'

'There must be some in the college bar.'

'I'll go down,' I offered.

'No. I will.' He opened the door, just as Peter Harding and Sally Lloyd were coming onto the landing. He explained what he was doing. Peter insisted on accompanying him, and Thomas later gleefully told me the contents of their conversation . . .

'Three cheers for democracy,' Thomas said as he closed the door on Sally and me.

'Damn Jenkins. Why didn't you stand?'

Thomas replied, 'You know I wouldn't do that. My job was to tell Jenkins the facts of life. I did. I said that he could stand if he wished, and that some people might vote for him. Both quite correct.'

'You did a bloody good job with him, didn't you?'

'My dear Peter; you will remember that I never wanted to go near that man. It was you who wanted it done – but you were too much of a coward. Said you couldn't stab a man in the back in the morning, and sit at his dinner table that night. If memory serves me right, you wound up doing neither.'

Thomas began to walk downstairs. Peter followed. They were a strong contrast to each other. Thomas's shirt, with its wing collar; and his waistcoated dinner jacket, looked as if they had never seen a crease. Peter was beginning to fill out early, and the dinner jacket which he had bought as a freshman made him look like a night club bouncer.

'Why did you go if you didn't want to?' Peter asked.

'You know why.'

'So?'

'It was because you pleaded with me. You had that certain look in your eye. I hadn't seen it in months. And you know that I can't resist you when you look like that.'

'Look, can I talk to you about that?'

Thomas stopped at the bottom of the staircase and smiled up at Peter. 'Please do.'

'I wish you wouldn't refer to . . . to that.'

'To what?'

'You know.'

'No. I don't.'

'Damn you . . . you know I find it embarrassing.' Thomas shrugged his shoulders. 'Thomas . . .' As he began, Thomas put his hand on Peter's arm. He slowly caressed it until his fingers reached Peter's hand, which was resting on the iron bannister. Peter folded his arms in front of his chest. 'People change,' he announced. 'And as far as I'm concerned, I've never touched anyone before Nancy.'

84

'Really?'

'Well, don't you feel the same about Sally?'

'Sally . . .' He said the name as if he weren't sure who she was. 'Oh, Sally. Neil tells me that she's responsible for Jenkins winning. Wasn't that thoughtful of her?'

'Thomas, please. You have changed too, haven't you?. Everyone does.'

'Then why worry about it?' Thomas smiled. 'I bet that American woman is letting you get fat. What do you say, I can get to the bar faster than you can.'

With that he turned round and began to sprint across the bridge. Peter followed him over and into the courtyards. Thomas got to the bar first without difficulty.

'Told you,' he gasped, as Peter finally caught up. 'Fatty.'

Peter grinned. Thomas put his arm around his shoulder and led him into the bar. Peter chose to take it as an innocent gesture which said that everything was all right now.

As soon as we were left alone, Sally sat down in the large easy chair by the fireplace. She had a shawl on, and she wore her dark hair up. It made her resemble a heroine in Jane Austen.

'Looking forward to the Nonagons?' she asked.

'Oh yes. But you sound as if I shouldn't.'

'I have no idea what goes on at these all male dinners. I'm sure they're very amusing.'

'You sound like Nancy, telling us not to sublimate ourselves.'

'As an Englishwoman, I suppose I'll have to get used to men needing these civilised brawls. Do they have them in America?'

'I guess so.' The only equivalent I could think of was a fraternity affair. I had never been to one of those. Instead, when my Berkeley friends wanted to escape they got stoned, not drunk. Suddenly it seemed odd to be asked what went on in America. It felt as if I had been away from it for ages. Indeed, there I stood in a dinner jacket and a tunic shirt with wing collar, in an old room, in an ancient college.

'I envy you going to Italy,' Sally said.

'Have you been there yourself?'

'I spent the most wonderful seven months of my life in Florence. Before I came up to Cambridge. It was the first time I had ever been away from everyone and everything at home.'

'God, don't tell me you wanted to run away from home too.'

'Of course. The world of a Cardiff solicitor's daughter is not exactly a glamorous one.'

'And I always thought that British people had all these roots.'

'We do. But roots tie you down.'

I sat on the hearthrug in front of Sally. 'Then where did you get your sense of decency from, if it wasn't from the accumulation of generations of Cardiff solicitors?'

'A sense of decency? You know, I haven't thought about that since the day of your big lunch party.'

'Oh, yeah? Then why did you go out and get Matthew Jenkins elected yesterday?'

'I can't explain it. In a way I felt manipulated. I felt guilty about him.'

'Why should you feel guilty about Jenkins?'

'That's the point. There is no reason – except that he's Matthew and ugly and intense and resentful, and he makes me think that the world should somehow compensate him.'

'God, that sounds sinister.'

She laughed. 'You see, I've spent two months with Thomas Lyster, and I'm completely corrupted. 'No values any more.'

'That's silly.'

'It sounds silly, but . . . look, I promise you, to fall in love with Thomas is to abandon yourself completely. You live on his terms and with his values. Unfortunately, it's also the most exciting and frightening thing that's ever happened to me.'

'I didn't think he was as bad as that.'

'Oh, he's terribly considerate. He makes sure you don't miss what you've left behind. I think he's aware of every need I have. He may not cater for it, but he knows that it's there.'

'Golly . . . it makes the rest of life sound pretty dull.'

'That's why no one ever walks out on him.'

'My own life's going to be a lot duller.'

'At least a girl can trust you.'

'I hope so.' I paused. 'I'm going to ask Susan to marry me.'

'Oh, Neil. How wonderful! Why didn't you say so the second I walked in?'

'Well, I haven't asked her and she hasn't said yes.'

'Of course she'll say yes; unless she's a fool.'

'I hope so. I hope so.'

'Is there anything wrong?'

I got up and leaned against the mantelpiece. 'Sally, I feel so . . . well, as if I've let Susan down.'

'Why? Because you're a virgin?'

'How . . .?'

'Dear Neil, I realised that long ago.'

'I wonder if Susan does.'

'If she's the girl you should marry, it won't matter.'

I shook my head. 'I wish it were that easy. You see, I look at Thomas, and he's so good looking, and he finds sex so damn easy, and I can't see how I can ever . . .'

Sally stood up and came next to me. 'Listen to me, Neil. Forget Thomas. People talk about the Chemistry between men and women, but that's rubbish. chemistry is rational. I want you to know, that if I had any sense, I'd be in love with you, not him.'

I was staggered by this. 'Oh, Sally . . .'

'It's true. But there's no point trying to tie Thomas to rationalism.' She leaned up, and kissed me lightly on the lips. 'There. If I loved you, it wouldn't matter how many girls you'd kissed before.' She paused and then sat down.

The moment she stepped away I felt a stab of desire – the same stab I felt when Caroline sat in that chair. I wished I could have gone over to her and taken her in my arms and . . . well, whatever one did after that.

'I'll be scared to death if she says yes.'

There was the sound of Thomas's and Peter's footsteps on the stairs.

'Neil, has it ever occurred to you that you're also a very hand-

some man?'
  'No.'

Veterans claimed that it was the best Nonagon dinner ever. The small, panelled room, just sufficiently lit by the Georgian silver candlesticks, enclosed the fourteen of us in a magically small world where age and poverty and stupidity and ugliness did not exist. Anything could have been going on in the outside world; it didn't matter. I never felt so insulated. I indulged nothing but my own palate until I was too drunk to judge the quality of the port. It was like the big lunch party, with the smell of expensive wine and cigars and of rich bodies.

Most of us adjourned to our set of rooms, where we got through two more bottles of port, three of whisky, and smashed half a dozen more glasses. Thomas sat down at the piano and started to play the Appassionata.

'Too drunk to appreciate it,' someone shouted.

In response, Thomas played his own medley of show tunes. He wound up with 'Salad Days'. Peter Harding happened to have been brought up with the record of the show. For our benefit he boomed forth, over and over again, 'I'll remind you to remind me; we said we'd never look back'. Never look back.

Two days later I left for Italy with Peter and Nancy. That morning I went to the Trinity Street post office and sent a cable to Susan: Would you consider marrying me? Love Neil. As I left I realised that the only address she had for me was college. I went back to my room and asked Thomas to arrange for all my post to be forwarded to his parents' address.

EIGHT

'God, you look well,' Thomas said as I stepped out of the carriage at Ipswich station. 'Do you mean to say that the sun is actually shining somewhere in the world?'

'It is in Italy.' The sun had indeed followed us along from Rome, deepening the tan which I tried to set off with a light blue shirt. I turned to get my suitcase but Thomas insisted on carrying it over the bridge and to the front of the station.

'Christ, how much did you pack in here? No, no, I'll take it Neil. You've no idea how fit I've become the last fortnight.'

'How's the work going?'

'Splendidly. I lead a spartan existence: I run two miles before breakfast and another before tea; lift weights; and otherwise work non-stop between meals. No potatoes, nothing to drink, only half a dozen cigarettes a day, and bed by ten. I feel so well, it's almost enough to put me off debauchery forever!'

'I think I understand your postcard now.' Awaiting me at Thomas Cook in Florence there had been an old picture postcard of a rural Suffolk scene. On the other side Thomas had written, 'There is absolutely nothing of interest for you to miss save one who without his natural audience does not count. Thomas'.

'Oh, you got it then? That says something for the Italians. Your letter took ten days. It arrived this morning before breakfast.'

'Sorry.'

'I'd rather have the gen–u–ine article,' he said, stretching out the phrase in what he supposed was an American accent. 'I gather you liked Italy.'

'Oh, Thomas, it was wonderful. Imagine what it was like, getting up in the morning in that flat in Rome: The Piazza Farnese before you – the Fountains – the Michaelangelo Frieze – the Act II rooms from "Tosca" – and then in Florence . . .'

'Not very Ipswich.' We had reached the front of the station. The station hotel was uninspiring, and the view of new architecture in the distance was almost depressing.

'But I was so glad to get back to England,' I said with surviving conviction. 'When the train went through East anglia I felt . . . well, kind of as if I belonged . . . as if I were coming home to some place I had the right to love.'

Thomas grinned at me. 'It's an ugly part of the country. If you can fall in love with England here, you must be a fanatic.'

'Aren't you just as fanatical?'

'Of course,' he said without further comment. He threw my suitcase into the back of the estate car, narrowly missing the screen which was placed there to keep in dogs.

I hesitated, 'Did any other letters arrive?' I asked.

'Afraid not,' he said, and got in. When I joined him he added, 'but I went into Cambridge a few days ago and stopped by the porter's lodge. They had a letter from your parents. I saved them the trouble of forwarding it.'

It seemed to be neither the time nor the place to tell Thomas the depth of my disappointment at not hearing from Susan. I said nothing but looked miserable. He, in turn, pretended there was nothing to be said on the subject. Instead he took me on a brief motor tour of the city, through the old town centre and past the non-descript town hall where Mrs Simpson got her divorce. I expressed some interest.

'Speaking of American women,' Thomas said, as we headed into open country, 'tell me about Peter and Nancy. Has love survived abroad?'

'Yes. You were quite right about him. Behaves as if sex doesn't exist until – I presume – the bedroom door is closed.'

'Was it very boring being the third person?'

'Sometimes. It's not like you and Sally – being three friends. Nancy's hands are never off Peter the whole day.'

'How that must have amused the Italians.'

'I don't know. I never knew what to do. There we were in the Forum, which was about the only place Peter got interested in, and just under the arch of Septimus Severus, Nancy says, "now that you've seen Italy, don't you think that Peter's just the most gorgeous thing in the whole world?"'

'What did you say?'

'I was caught off guard. I said that Peter's looks were Greek, not Roman, so I couldn't comment. Later I thought of something better.'

'She didn't say it again, did she?'

'Oh, yes. In the Uffizzi.'

'And?'

'I said that Sally seemed to think that you were probably the handsomest man in England, and since Peter's English too he can't come second here and first in the world. The jury was obviously hung, and so I could only declare that there was no verdict.'

'Not bad.'

'She didn't ask me after that. Now I'm afraid she thinks I don't take her seriously.'

'Join the club. But you and Peter got along well?'

'It's impossible not to. He's completely uneducated, but he's just so nice. I basked in it. And he was glad to have me there so he could talk politics.'

'I know. I got a letter from him with four pages of gossip. And the end there was one sentence saying that he couldn't praise you enough and that the three of you were having a "nice time". Apparently his feelings towards Nancy don't translate easily into the written word either.'

'Peter told me he doesn't want to leave Cambridge before he sees you well on your way to being Chairman, like he was.'

'Did he?' A look of annoyance came over Thomas, although, to be fair, he was at the same time negotiating the car around a tractor which had caused him to change down gears for the first time since leaving town. He looked at the rear-view mirror. 'Did I cut him off?' he asked.

'I don't think so.'

'Good. He probably recognised the car, though. Father disapproves of my driving, especially when I drive arrogantly at people he has to do business with. The truth of course is that I just like driving fast, which is well-nigh impossible in the sort of cars he runs. Anyway, I've heard him say "what's that bloody vehicle doing on the road?" more often that I've had hot meals.'

Since I had never before seen Thomas at the wheel of a car, I felt unable to comment.

'Oh, as someone who's interested in English behaviour, I'm sorry you missed the discussion at dinner last night.'

'What was that?'

'My parents were giving me a small lecture about how I'm more privileged than most people and therefore had to watch out.'

'Watch out for what?'

'Hangers-on. Spongers.' Since it was I who paid for the wine which filled the 'sponges', I thought that the Lysters' concern could have waited one more evening before being expressed. Thomas laughed. 'And of course women.'

'Goodness, Thomas, are they expecting you to get married?'

'I certainly hope not. But they have this notion that marriage should come at about the time when one is ready for . . . let us say, the pleasures of marriage. Well, Mummy thinks that, being a woman. Father thinks that young men should go through about a dozen women a year until they're thirty or so, and then marry the richest virgin on the market. Only it's all gone wrong in his family.'

'Oh?'

'My own theory is that William – my brother – is marrying the only girl he's ever been to bed with, and that she extracted his proposal as the price of her virtue. If virtue she still had. While I, on the other hand, despite bringing home at least six girlfriends to Sunday lunch, have been a source of concern since Radley.'

'They know what went on?'

'Not officially. But there was a little bitch of a master who wrote off reports about me. Mummy never noticed a thing, but father's the sort of man who's more intelligent reading between the lines than he is reading what's actually on them. Let's say he has a hunch'

'Doesn't he discuss it with your mother?'

'No. Why should he?'

'In my family, "the children" are about the most important topic of conversation.'

'How odd. Don't your parents have lives of their own? I think my parents think about us, but they can't discuss me. They disagree about me completely.'

'Don't they want to sort it out?'

'Not at the price of an argument. I'm almost twenty one as it is. It's easier to leave me to sort myself out. It keeps order in the house.'

'But what abour your father's "hunch"?'

'What about it? To him, all those girlfriends could be a front.'

'But marriage isn't a front?'

'No. I told you he hasn't read Proust.' He sighed mockingly. 'The family is getting so bourgeois.'

'Do they at least agree on the sort of girl you should marry?'

'More or less. They both told me not to marry a girl without money. Father in particular seems to have no faith in my ability to make any of my own.'

'Why not?'

'Ask him. I've never had the opportunity. I think I've got that killer instinct your brother talks about. I must: even Father thinks I'd make a good officer.'

'Do you want to join the Army? You've never mentioned it before.'

'No – because it's one of Father's suggestions. It might be something to do for a few years. Some of it sounds fun. A lot of it sounds deathly.'

I thought for a moment of the nervous, youthful National Guardsmen at Berkeley, with their bayonets fixed against an unarmed mob screaming for martyrdom. 'Do you think you could kill someone?' I asked.

He thought about it. 'Depends on the circumstances. Generally speaking, I'm sure I could.' He grinned at me. 'I'd certainly kill anyone who tried to lay a finger on you.'

'But that's a kind of self-defence.'

'Perhaps, but there are other things, aside from friends, that I'd fight to defend. What does it matter, though? It's all second best to the only thing I'd really like to.' Before I had the opportunity to ask him what that was, he stopped the car slightly off the road. 'Would you mind getting out for a moment? There's something I want to show you.'

I obeyed. The countryside about us was much the same to what we had been seeing since we left Ipswich: flat, with a few early signs of the greenness of spring. Thomas started to climb what seemed to be the only hill in the area. In his battered Barbour coat and Wellingtons he strode on quickly and then waited patiently for me at the crest as I picked my muddy way in my best city clothes.

'This is Netherbridge Lyster,' he said, when I joined him. 'Flat; not very pretty. That's the house where my parents live; roomy, not very beautiful. But there are lots and lots of acres. I'll tell you all about them later on. We've only recently lived in that house, but we've always had the same number of acres.'

'It's . . . lovely.'

'Beauty is not its significance. I wish that we could stand here like Sebastian and Charles and I were showing you a great valley and a great house. I'm afraid I can't even show you something which is or will ever be mine.' He stood there for a moment and then lit a cigarette. He smoked it slowly, I said nothing, waiting for him to go on.

For a long time Thomas simply looked out at his father's farm. After a while a strange look of indescribable sadness passed over his face – a look I later learned that I was only the second person to witness. I tried to think of something to match the depth of my friend's mood but as I could not, I said nothing. Gradually the look passed away. Thomas finished his cigarette and stamped out the end. Then he began to walk down the hill towards the car.

'Come on,' he called, 'let me introduce you to my parents.'

NINE

We drove in silence for the small part of the journey which remained. As we did so, I became increasingly apprehensive about this visit. I had never been to a British home before, let alone stayed with a family for a week.

I had grown up in what I assumed was a normal family: love gushed endlessly and the children were gods. The apparent estrangement between my brother and myself was a source of agony to our parents. They believed that brothers existed to love each other, just as parents and children existed to love each other. 'Love' was, indeed, the key. I often wondered whether my parents were capable of making a reliable judgement on any of my attributes or abilities. Or even if they were aware of what they were, aside from the fact that 'Neil's brilliant'. But I never doubted for a moment that they absolutely adored me. Things were obviously very different at the Lysters'.

They lived, as Peter Harding had already coached me, in a house in the country, not a country house. The unimpressive entrance was a long porch capped with Victorian trellis work: 'like a scrunched-up railway platform', Thomas said.

The drive we entered from the road opened into a large circle by this porch. Thomas parked the car and went round to the back to get my suitcase. As he did so I noticed the carefully tended lawns which lay on either side of the house below bow windows.

Thomas led me inside. The front door was not locked. It led merely to another hallway and a cloakroom where he hung up our coats amongst the existing collection of jackets and boots. There seemed to be far more of them than there could be inhabitants of the house.

Thomas stopped in the hallway and then shook his head. 'I told Mummy that you liked music, but she's obviously forgotten to put something on. I don't think we have much anyway, aside from Elgar and Christmas carols from King's College chapel.'

At last we went into the sitting room.

'Hello, Mummy; hello, Father. This is Neil Fielding.'

I was immediately struck by his tone. I wasn't just that one word was affectionate and even childlike while the other simply covered the biological relationship. He made a clear distinction in the way he talked to each. The two parents were also a physical contrast to each other. Mrs Lyster was extremely fair and almost slight. Mr Lyster was a big man, taller than his son and broad, with thinning black hair and a red face which did not come from exposure to the sun. I shook hands with both, and then Mrs Lyster took over.

'We're so glad you could come,' she said, sitting down and indicating that I should as well. She leaned over to the tea trolley, which seemed to have arrived just before I did. I noticed that she wore a dark blue, high-necked jumper, which set off her fairness, a drab tweed skirt and sensible brown shoes.The only jewellery was a brooch and her wedding ring. 'Would you like some tea? You must be so tired after all your travelling.'

'I'd love some, thanks. I . . . I think I was in Milan when I woke up this morning. It's extremely kind of you to invite me.'

'Not at all; we're delighted to meet you. Tea, Tommy darling?' She had already served her husband.

'Oh yes, please.'

'Did you have any difficulties with the trains, Neil? They can be so troublesome.'

'Oh, no. Thomas gave me perfect directions. And it arrived in Ipswich exactly on time.'

'Really?' Mr Lyster said. 'Tom must've driven rather quickly to get home by now.'

'There wasn't much traffic.'

Both men were correct.

It occurred to me that my friend insisted that the world call him by a name no one used at home. Everyone who knew Thomas at

Cambridge soon learned that he liked to be called 'Thomas'. To say 'Tom' was a give-away. He frequently winced when someone used it. Until now I had assumed that he was protesting at an acquaintance purporting to be a friend.

'I must apologise for the absence of the rest of the family,' Mrs Lyster said. 'William, our elder son, is staying with his fiancee's people, and of course Lucy's married and in London now. They both said how sorry they were to miss you.' I had never met these people, and never expected to. I was surprised that I was the cause of disappointment amongst the other children, since we were only failing to accomplish what no one had thought would take place.

'I . . . I'll look forward to another time then.'

'Did you enjoy Italy?' she asked me. 'You certainly got very brown.'

'It was marvellous. It's like a treasure house, isn't it?'

'We were in Venice once.'

'We went there too. And Florence and Rome. Isn't it great just sitting out in the Piazza San Marco? And the cathedral – of course it's so different from the Duomo . . .' I had been made to feel so much at home' that I comfortably launched into a very long story about what we had seen and done. Mr Lyster fiddled with his pipe as I spoke. Mrs Lyster smiled politely but seemed to have difficulty finding something to do with her hands. Thomas's eyes never left me.

'Yes,' she said at the end. 'How interesting for you. We're not great travellers ourselves. In fact, I was thinking the other day that I wouldn't care if I never left Netherbridge again.'

'With increased age comes increased responsibility,' Thomas chided her good-naturedly.

'Dearest, I don't seem that old yet, do I?'

'Not a bit. It's Father who's such an old man.'

'My age,' said Mr Lyster, 'is a contrast only with your continuing juvenalia. William doesn't think me old.'

'That's because William's already the oldest middle-aged man under thirty. Still, I suppose that makes him a good man to marry. Since he has the imagination of a forty-year old when he's only twenty five, Sarah will have lots of time to learn how to cope with him by the time he really is forty. But by then, it's going to feel as if she's been married to him for a very, very long time.'

'Some day, Tom, when you decide to add human gifts to your other achievements, you'll learn that there is rarely enough time to be with someone you love.'

'Is that why time seems to hang on your hands when you're with me, Father?'

'Tell me about your family, Neil,' Mrs Lyster said, as if this were the next logical remark to make. 'Do you have brothers and sisters?'

'I have an elder brother. He's in business in California.' This elicited no response, so I added, 'he's done the right thing – staying at home.'

'Is it a family business, then?' Mrs Lyster asked.

'We are,' Thomas interrupted. 'But in our kind, only one son is allowed to stay at home.'

'Isn't it time for your afternoon run, Tom? Or perhaps Neil would like a rest.'

'Neil hasn't finished his tea yet.'

I picked up the cup and saucer with the flower pattern from where I had left it on the carpet, next to the chintz-covered chair. 'I don't want any more, thanks.'

'Nonsense,' Thomas insisted, 'you haven't had any of Mummy's cake yet.'

'Well, I'm finished,' Mr Lyster said, and got up. I started to follow suit but he waved me down. 'No need; stay as long as you like Neil. I'll see you at dinner.' Then he left the room.

His departure changed the atmosphere from the formal one of family tea-taking. It was a room which was designed for formal occasions, with the carefully arranged chairs and the decanters placed on the highly-polished mahogany table. There was a fire in the grate and above the mantlepiece hung a rather bad eighteenth century painting, the figures in the foreground being out of proportion to the large Jacobean house behind them.

'Really, Tommy darling,' Mrs Lyster began, 'you promised that you'd have a closed season on baiting your father. At least until the flat racing starts.'

'That's the racing at Newmarket,' Thomas explained. 'It begins in April – the day after you leave. That's why I promised. All right, Mummy, I'll be good.' He got up and kissed his mother. 'Come on, Neil, I'll show you the Suffolk version of a view from a Roman piazza.'

'Thanks a lot for tea, Mrs Lyster.'

'Not at all, Neil. I hope you'll enjoy your visit.' She smiled at me but did not move from her chair.

The moment we left her alone I reminded Thomas, 'I never did get a piece of your mother's tea cake.'

'Really? I thought you said you were finished.'

We collected my case. The staircase was in a corner between the kitchen and the dining room, so we had to walk the length of the house to get there. I noticed, in the hallway, another painting of the Jacobean mansion, done in the nineteenth century.

Upstairs there was a very wide corridor. We went to a room at the end of it, and at the front of the house.

'I've missed you the last fortnight,' I said. 'I kept thinking how it was wasted on Peter, and how you would've enjoyed it.'

'I couldn't stop thinking the same thing. I've tried blotting it out by sweating over jogging and sweating over books. But I couldn't wait for that train of yours to get to Ipswich. Now I have you to myself.'

'Thomas, I didn't realise things were that bad with your father.'

'Oh . . . I couldn't have you think that Father liked having me about. But don't worry, he just feels outnumbered at the moment. Expect reinforcements to be brought to the dinner table very soon.'

Thomas opened the door and let me into a spacious bedroom, with more chintz covered chairs, a plain writing desk, and a basin in the corner. There was a double bed. On the table was a bottle of Malvern water and half a dozen books, mostly memoirs by minor Royalties.

'It's my sister's bedroom,' he told me. 'She's so nice. In fact, I don't think I've ever heard her say a bad word about anyone. I don't see how she does it. She's the only Lyster who loves everyone in the family.'

'Doesn't your mother?'

'That's a good question. Anyway, although she and Father are some sort of distant cousins, she wasn't actually born a Lyster.'

'It's a nice room.'

Thomas put his hand on my shoulder. 'The important thing is that it's Lucy's. I wouldn't let you sleep in William's bed. And we're virtually in a separate wing here.'

'Oh? Where's your room?'

'Come and see.' We walked directly across the hall. Thomas showed me a room as big as mine but impossibly cluttered – like the bedroom in Cambridge. Piles of notes and newspapers lay everywhere, sometimes held down by items of still damp running gear. There were three barbells, a set of dumbbells, and an exercise bench. 'You see, I've copied out all your notes and read almost all the required books. I could start revision tomorrow.'

'I'm impressed.'

'I wanted you to be.' He grinned at me. 'But you look absolutely exhausted. Don't you want to rest?'

'I wouldn't mind.'

'Then go and lie down. I'm going for another run. We don't congregate for drinks until half past six.'

I slept for nearly an hour. The central heating had come on, and I woke up to a warm room. I decided to have a bath before dinner. The bathroom, I found, was almost as large as the bedrooms. I could stretch right out in the tub, and fully admire the effect of the Italian sun on my body.

Lying there was also one of my rare chances to have time to myself at Netherbridge. I felt adrift here. At the same time, Netherbridge seemed to be even more of a world in itself than Cambridge. My prime feeling about this house was that it was isolated: not surprising, since one could not even see where the next human dwelling was.

It meant, of course, that I was entirely dependent on Thomas. I could relax only with him. It was a little like being on holiday together.

Any incipient good mood, though, was destroyed by thoughts of Susan. Why was there no letter? Not even a note, saying that she was thinking about it? She owed me at least that much.

I felt angry by the time I got downstairs for drinks. The Lysters were all waiting for me.

'Oh, Neil, how nice to see you,' Mrs Lyster said, as if I were an honoured guest.

'What do you drink?' Mr Lyster asked. 'You musn't be shy about that here. After dinner I'll show you where the whisky is, and then you can get some for yourself whenever you want it.'

Thomas, if possible, looked even healthier than before. He poured me a strong gin and bitter lemon. As he handed it to me he touched my arm, and told me again how well I seemed.

The men were in various stages of drunkenness by the time we sat down to dinner. Mrs Lyster brought out various bowls and platters from the kitchen and put them on the hot plate which was on the side table behind me. She served her husband; then I helped myself, followed by her and then Thomas. It was a very English menu: game soup, roast pork, roast potatoes, sprouts, carrots, gooseberry fool and Stilton.

Thomas poured the wine. I saw that it was a 1962 vintage from Berry Bros.

'And where does your family live?' Mrs Lyster asked me.

'California.'

'Neil was at Berkeley,' Thomas added, to give everyone their cue. As he said this he dropped a little wine on the white tablecloth by his mother.

'Tom, don't be so clumsy,' Mr Lyster snapped.

Mrs Lyster put a little salt on it and asked, 'Berkeley university?' She prounounced it in the English manner. Her voice mingled interest with reassurance: interest at knowing someone who had experienced terrible events which she had only read about; reassurance that her instincts were, after all, superior to the prejudices of the popular newspapers. Most young people were like

Thomas and me, and resistant to the allure of transient, urban, intellectual radicals. 'Were you there during the troubles?'

'Which ones?' I laughed.

'The ones we read about in the newspapers here,.'

It was hardly a helpful indication of what she knew or didn't know. I guessed that she would be unable to remember a single incident she had read about, so I just told them,

'What stands out in my mind is that the first theatre I ever saw in California was a performance on a Berkeley sidewalk. Street theatre.'

'What in the world is that?' Mr Lyster asked.

'Revolutionary drama. People spontaneously acting out their political views.' Everyone looked baffled. The whole thing was so ludicrously remote from their existence here in Suffolk.

Mr Lyster, however, had heard his cue. 'Revolution, you say. If you stay in England, you'll probably see it here. And if they want revolutionary theatre, the trades unions will provide a cast of thousands.'

'I don't think so, Father,' Thomas said. It was the opening shot of the evening. Was it being barked at over the wine, I wondered, or just the same old battle. Probably the latter. 'For one thing, those east end boys aren't nearly as tough as countrymen.'

'I wasn't talking about a punch-up.'

'Oh. Then do tell us what you were talking about.'

'I'm talking about the unions taking over this country.'

'They can't. We have a Conservative government.'

'Huh! Not until they tame the unions.'

'They can't do that.'

'And why not?'

'Because a democratic government can't "tame" anyone. It's got to jog along until people come round. Anyway, what would you say if someone came up to you and said, "listen, mate, I know better than you do, so go away and obey me. I'm just the cleverest thing going". Hmm?'

'You know perfectly well what I'd say.'

'Exactly. So why should a trade unionist have less self-esteem

102

than you do?'

'That,' said Mr Lyster, turning towards me, 'is supposed to be the authentic voice of young England.'

'No, it's not, Father. It's the authentic voice of old England; Harold MacMillian and Rab Butler and Walter Monckton. Your boys. My chums haven't been given the chance yet to sort out what you've left us.'

'And what will you do with that chance, Tom?' Mr Lyster's voice was like ice.

'I shall remember that most men are guided by what their fathers taught them.' He smiled benignly.

'That, Tom, is something you will obviously never understand,' he fired back.

Thomas shrugged his shoulders, got up, and uncorked the third bottle of wine. 'I think we ought to discuss something that Neil can contribute to,' he said.

TEN

On my first two mornings in Netherbridge I woke early, with a start, as if I had been dreaming, though I could not remember what. I stumbled out of bed, still half-expecting to see the Italian sun. Instead, there were torrents of English rain – and a drenched Thomas Lyster, returning from his morning run, with his shirt stuck to his torso and his blond hair matted against his forehead. A moment later, I could hear Thomas's footsteps along the corridor, the bathroom door open and the taps being turned on. I would go back to sleep.

I was awakened by a knock, and by Thomas coming in with a pot of tea and two cups. He was fully dressed, though his hair was still wet. He sat on the edge of my bed, discussing his proposals for the day while drinking most of the tea himself.

Thomas was reluctant to honour his promise that I would work at Netherbridge. In the mornings he took me on tours of Suffolk churches. After lunch we sat before the fire in the sitting room, reading and commenting on *Country Life* house adverts and on catalogues from Harrods and wine merchants.

Because we ate breakfast and lunch at odd times, we rarely saw his parents before tea. Mr Lyster ran the farm, though I never learned exactly what he did. Mrs Lyster ran the house, with the help of a woman 'from the village', who did the cleaning and helped with the cooking if there was a large dinner. I found Thomas's mother to be friendly but remote. She made no dramatic outbursts about the joys of having her son home, as happened in my house. Neither did she lecture us about the need to be self-conscious about one's body, or about the basis of a successful marriage being founded in sexual compatibility and money, as my mother did. I did not figure out what kept the Lysters together, but both seemed satisfied with their arrangement. I could see how the children had been left alone: William, the eldest, to lapse into being boring, and Thomas, to develop his imagination and ambitions.

Reinforcements were brought into dinner on my third night. At least we had guests, the most notable being Geoffrey Stephenson: retired Major, Member of Parliament, and the head of the oldest family in the neighbourhood aside from the Lysters. He was also the family's closest friend.

'Of course, he's been terribly lonely since his wife died.' Mrs Lyster warned me. 'Even though he has two lovely daughters.'

'Each of whom live about 200 miles away,' Thomas pointed out.

'Married to countrymen and very nice fellows,' Mr Lyster said.

'Geoffrey wanted a son,' Thomas told me, 'and a real one; the sort of son who'd keep him up to the mark. Instead of which, he had two daughters who took after their mother: found men they could manage, and married them.'

'Have I heard of him?' I asked. 'Has he spoken at Cambridge?'

'He was there last year. Whenever there's a chairman who wants someone to rouse the troops, he invites Geoffrey. Peter's under the delusion that Geoffrey's out of date, just because the Prime Minister won't give him a job.'

'He has the shrewdest judgement in the House.'

'Father, I couldn't agree more. And about the safest seat.'

I found everything about Geoffrey Stephenson to be large, including his bitterness. He was in his mid-sixties. As a young man he may have been an Adonis. If so, he had been cashing in on it for forty years. He was now bloated and paunchy. His vigour had gone, but not his presence. It was still easy to see in him the ghost of a splendid man.

He was the last to arrive that evening. When he walked in there was an appreciable change of tone in the room. He kissed Mrs Lyster hello. He then turned to the other guests – a couple of about his age and their unmarried daughter in her late twenties. They had known each other all their lives, and the women kissed him with the air of indulging a naughty boy. For all I knew they had good reason to think him that. He was introduced to me and I shook his fleshy, still-strong hand. Finally he turned to Thomas.

'There's Tommy,' he grinned. I imagined his striding into this same room fifteen or so years ago, when he was still a vibrant man, and crying 'There's Tommy', to a delighted little boy who would run to his arms. Even now, when Thomas said, 'hello, Geoffrey', he looked at him as I had never seen him look at anyone. Especially his own father.

I did not talk to Stephenson during dinner, where I was placed between the neighbour's daughter and Mrs Lyster. For tonight I had been demoted, and sat on her left. I might not have spoken to Stephenson at all, had the ladies not decided to retire. It was not that I did not believe that anyone followed this custom any more, I had not realised that it existed. When Mrs Lyster stood up and said, 'would you like some coffee?' I said, 'Yes, please'. Thomas had to tell me to sit down.

As Geoffrey Stephenson had been on Mrs Lyster's right, we were left alone at that end of the table. He did not move up to join the others. I did not know any better and stayed where I was.

'I understand you've been to Rome,' he said.

'That's right, sir.'

'Did you know anyone there?'

'Kind of. My friend's brother-in-law was sent there by the Foreign Office. We stayed in his flat. It was beautiful.'

'Figures. Taxpayer's money.'

'Oh no, Major Stephenson; he has much more money than the government does. Seriously, they have a painting – it's supposed to be School of Titian but it might be Giorgione.'

'School of Titian? I suppose those fellows couldn't make much money out of art, so they opened a school to teach other chaps how to do what they couldn't make a go of themselves.'

My instincts to attack rose up, but they were dulled by a good deal of wine and port. Instead I replied,

'There's more to life than being a success.'

'Such as?'

'Well . . . fifty years after you're dead, people may think you were a genius.'

'That counts as the same thing, Neil. They're still judging you on what you did. What's the good of failure? Of being weak? Cowardly?' He leaned over the table as he pressed his point. I could see his face getting redder, in reverse proportion to the colour of his political views.

'I didn't say it was "good".'

'Excellent!' he boomed. I had more to say, but he had been in politics a long time. That meant that he listened to nothing more than a cue line from which he could again pick up the thread of his monologue. 'Too many people think it is good. Too few people believe what I have to say.'

'Oh, no.'

He smiled. 'I may have my prejudices, but I'm not a fool. Do you know what the expression "passed over major" means?'

'No.'

'It's an officer who will never make colonel. He'll never be promoted again and everyone knows it. He'll walk into the mess and feel that the other fellows don't have to worry if they snub him a little. He has no pull at all. Unless, of course, they think that he's a nice chap.'

'That's something.'

'Neil, when I was your age, if someone tried to get me to escort his cousin to a dance I'd ask, "is she pretty?" If he replied, "she's charming" – do you see what I mean?'

'Yes.' I nodded.

He shrugged. 'I was a passed-over major, and I quit. Now I'm a backbench M.P. It's the same thing. Perhaps I'm a nice chap – I don't know – but I'll never get an office. And Parliament isn't like America – you can't go over the Cabinet's head to appeal to the people. Sometimes it takes freshmen MPs months to figure out who I am.'

By then I was reeling. I was unused to English people saying anything about themselves and their ambitions. I was also surprised by the rapid pace at which he trotted out his confession. He

107

went on to say, as if we were discussing the weather:

'The problem is that I like power. And once you know that, it's no good just being a nice chap. You can be a nice chap whether you're Prime Minister or a dustman.'

I already suspected that he was not particularly interested in my views on that remark either. I was a treat to him; simply because I was a presentable stranger who had never heard him before. He could bring out all his opinions and because they were fresh to me, for that evening they would appear to sparkle. Stephenson was civil enough, and I was courteous enough to egg him on. Anyway, I could not believe that Thomas could adore a failure. I kept searching for the ghost of greatness which the Lysters still called the reality.

'Surely your life hasn't been without compensations,' I urged.

'Here and there. On the way.' He paused for effect. 'Perhaps too many.' He punctuated this little self-deprecation with a boyish grin. It was the sort of smile I had seen on the faces of fit young men as they stumbled out of drunken Cambridge dinner parties. They could get away with it. Stephenson had used the same grin for forty years but he could not get away with it any longer. On a dissipated old man it looked grotesque.

'Sublimations . . .' I began and stopped.

'What's that?' he snapped. He looked as confused as Peter Harding had when Nancy used the multi-syllabic word. I think it fitted Stephenson. I could imagine him as the dashing, ambitious young man. Then as the slightly bewildered middle-aged almost-success, who could not quite grasp why he was not achieving what he wanted; who took a long time to realise that his popularity with men and his easy and numerous conquests of women were in fact no substitute; who then had to face up to a life of returning to a forgiving, dominating wife, who did not mind being married to a failure. Perhaps once he had had a flash of self-hatred, and then hatred of her, because she liked him being a little contemptible. It made him manageable. Finally he had settled down to a life of self-knowledge, with a comfortable dose of bitterness.

'Sublime,' I said. 'It must be sublime to have had those compensations.'

He looked at me with the respect the remark deserved, not realising that I had silently joined the ranks of those who patronised him.

'I've been active too,' he went on. 'And very lucky with this constituency. My family's been here a long time. We like local people to represent us.'

'That's rare in England, isn't it? To have a local man become M.P.?'

'Sometimes. There's not much of a problem finding men here. But what we want is to make sure that whoever gets the seat after me has the potential to do something with it.'

'You mean you can choose your successor?'

'I can do a lot to smooth the way.'

'Have you thought of anyone then?'

He looked surprised. 'Yes. Tommy.'

'Thomas?'

'We are talking about the future.'

'But he's not even twenty one yet.'

'Pitt was Prime Minister at twenty four, and if you don't have the right instincts, it wouldn't matter if you were ninety five.'

'Of course, only . . . Thomas isn't at all involved in Cambridge politics. A friend of ours wants him to be chairman of the Conservative Association but he doesn't want it. At least I don't think so.'

'Thomas is well out of that. The private dining rooms at the House are full of clubs made up of ageing Young Conservatives who ran associations at Oxford and Cambridge and are still trying to capitalise on it. I think they'd find the limelight to be a little embarrassing now.'

'Thomas . . . in Parliament . . .'

'I gather you approve.'

I looked at Stephenson. 'I believe in him more than I ever have in anyone else.' That sounded pompous so I added, 'More than his own father does.'

'Most people do,' Stephen said as he got up. 'Wisely.'

I was still sitting there, fingering my glass, and did not notice that the other men were getting up too.

'Come on Neil,' Mr Lyster said. 'We're keeping the ladies waiting.'

The rain finally stopped on my third morning. When he brought in the tray of tea, Thomas said it was time I saw the farm.

'Haven't I already?'

'Not until you've walked across it.'

We started out after an early lunch. I was provided with a pair of Wellingtons and an old coat. Thomas, in his tweed cap and Barbour coat, looked considerably more convincing.

The air was sweet after the rain. We made our way along a field and then along the edge of a wood, where Thomas inspected some traps. The earth was very muddy, but Thomas knew it all so well that he led me over as much hard ground as one could find.

'You know,' I said, as we walked across the fields, 'I can't tell you why, but you seem . . . I don't know, different here.'

He smiled. 'I love Netherbridge. It's the only place I've ever been where I've felt that I know exactly what's right and wrong. A pity it makes me so miserable to come back.'

'Why?'

'Because it doesn't belong to me, and it never will.'

'Aren't you both called Lyster?' I joked.

'It's been called Netherbridge Lyster for five hundred years, but it's still my father's place. I'm only here because I happen to be his younger son. Some day it'll be William's, and then I'll be allowed to visit once or twice a year because I happen to be his brother.'

'But there's so much. Couldn't your father leave you a little of it?'

'As a souvenir? No, thanks. Anyway, every inch must pass intact to William.' He stooped down, picked up a rock, and threw it some distance. 'They don't even deserve to be here,' he sneered.

'Why not?'

Thomas sighed. 'It's a long story. Sometime after the first world war – 1922, I think – it all belonged to my great-grandfather's

110

brother. One day he walked over to the dower house, where his mother, lived and said: "I've sold the place; I'm leaving for South Africa in the morning".'

'You're kidding.'

'I wish I were. But it's absolutely the truth. Great-grandfather wasn't very bright, but he had some decent instincts. We got it all back. But then everything got into an awful muddle. Great-grandfather died just before the war, and even then my grandfather could only scrape together the death duties. The war was the end. Just before my grandfather died – in '48 – he realised that he'd done absolutely nothing about his death duties.'

'So what happened?'

'He decided to flog off what he called superfluous.'

'Like what?'

'Like the great house.'

'The great house?'

'What you'd call the ancestral family home. Netherbridge Hall. It's the house in those paintings.'

'Really? But it looks gorgeous.'

'It must've been, at one time. Inigo Jones and Grinling Gibbons supposedly had hands in it, and it was always said that Capability Brown did the gardens. Christ, you don't think that the Lysters lived in the place we've got now? That's only the dower house.'

'So he sold the great house?'

'No. He destroyed it.'

'What?'

'He destroyed it' Thomas repeated. I wondered how much self-control he was exerting. 'He sold off all the contents – the furniture and the paintings and the silver and even the panelling. That provided plenty of cash for the death duties. And then he simply levelled the place.'

'No!'

'Right to the ground. No house, no house to be taxed. Very simple.'

'How awful for your father.'

Thomas stopped and stared at me. 'Father doesn't care. He says

111

he doesn't even miss it. And William – damn him, he actually was born in the great house – *HE* says that he's glad he doesn't have the bother of it. And they own this place.'

'I wish you could do something about it.'

'I used to dream that I could. My favourite daydream was that William and I would have a duel. Preferably with our fists. And I'd kill him.'

'Thomas!'

'Oh . . . it was only a daydream. William's so gangling and awkward, and I've always been strong. It was too easy, hurting him. Especially since he wasn't allowed to retaliate, because he was older. And by the time we were the right age, I was bored despising him.'

I imagined the revenge my own brother could have wreaked on me, if he had used his fists instead of his tongue. He had beaten me up enough anyway. Then I remembered that Thomas was not simply being sadistic – and that the first compliment he paid me was that he and I were better men than our siblings.

'And then,' he went on, 'there was a whole world to see the difference between us. Father refused to admit it, of course. He used to get apoplectic at my school reports – Radley could see that I was streets ahead of William.'

'You should've been Geoffrey Stephenson's son.'

'Exactly what I've always thought. If I had, Geoffrey wouldn't have been a failure. It really is a waste, having the father I do.'

'Thomas, I really can't believe how members of a family can dislike each other the way you and your father do.'

He shrugged his shoulders. 'I suppose we should love each other or something, whatever that means.'

'Are you serious? About love?'

'Yes.'

'Is that why you're so ambitious? As a substitute?'

'I'm no good at theories. All I know is that if I were Mr Lyster of Netherbridge, I'd be the best man in the world. I'd know exactly who and what I was. If I can't have that . . . then everything's open ended. There's nothing I can point to and say, if only I can achieve that, I'll be satisfied.'

'And so?'

'And so I intend to go on, getting everything I can, until I find out what is enough.'

'I don't know; I've never thought like that.'

'Which is exactly why I love being with you. I can be completely honest. Christ, I can even relax.'

'I'm glad. I ... what about Sally?' I asked in my embarrassment.

Thomas looked annoyed. 'Sally. Sally happens to be the girl I've got the most pleasure out of.'

'Is it just sex?'

'How I wish it were. It would make life much simpler.'

'What do you mean?'

'I mean that being with Sally isn't just physical excitement. She interests me. I know I provoke her all the time, but that's because I find her so interesting. At one point I thought that this was it.'

'Then you are in love with her.'

'Please stop talking about love. It's cloying. I'm talking about something far more fundamental.'

'Such as?'

'It's something that doesn't bother me most of the time. Sex is ... well, sex. But with Sally – and one or two others before her – people I also happen to care about ... you see, afterwards, I feel this terrible ... void. It's not the exhaustion, or the after-sex depression – I know what that is. This is different.'

'Tell me.' This was all eons removed from my own experience, but I wanted to try to understand. I did not think Thomas had ever opened up like this to anyone else; he might never again. It made me feel responsible to him. It was also flattering to be the only person who really knew him.

'I feel nothing.'

'Why?'

'I don't know. I just know that there's this awful void. I've expended everything: emotion, physical energy – even a kind of love. And for all that, I feel dead inside.'

113

'Is that what happened after the lunch party – when you went up to Girton?'

'Yes. How did you know?'

'I didn't, then. But I remember how irrational you were; how irritated.'

'Irritated? I never felt so close to being suicidal.'

'You didn't seem that bad.'

'I couldn't burden you with it, could I?'

'Why not? You are now. I can take it.'

We were ten yards or so from a very large, very old tree. Thomas suddenly sprinted up to it, grabbed hold of one of the lower branches, and chinned himself up, several times.

'What are you doing?' I asked.

'Sometimes I feel as if I'm going to burst. I just have to do something physical.' I remember him leaping up from the piano stool when I said I wanted to marry Susan. 'I'm all right now.'

'But tell me: if you feel that way about Sally, why do you still go out with her?'

'Because I was afraid to give up trying. There she was, lying in my arms, and saying "I love you Thomas; I want to love you more". And I thought, just a little more effort from me, and little more love from her, and I'll be all right. But it was just like coming back to Netherbridge.'

'How's that?'

'I'd like to come back, and feel at peace – not hate William and Father. And I wanted to make love to Sally and not feel the void afterwards. It's like reading a book over and over again – the kind of book where you hate the ending. You keep hoping that this time it'll have the right ending, but it never does.'

'Of course not.'

'If only one could will things to be different.'

'Maybe you just need more time.'

'How much? Sally's probably thinking that she's on the edge of some vast expanse called the soul of Thomas Lyster. But she's not. She's about one inch from colliding with a brick wall. I'm surprised she hasn't hit it already.'

'What'll happen then?'

'I suppose she'll ask me to help her over. I can't. I haven't a clue how to. I can't even say that there's something on the other side.'

'There is.'

'How do you know?'

'If you like, it's my will that there's something there.' Thomas smiled. 'You and Sally will be all right.'

'Christ!'

His anger made me stop. I looked ahead and saw that we were now only a few hundred yards away from the house.

'What's wrong?'

'Do you think she matters half as much as you do?'

I looked at him, bewildered.

'You're the only person I've ever met who makes me want to be better. You've no idea how wonderful it is, being absolutely free to be myself with you. And somehow you understand. How do you do it? Why don't I misbehave the way I've done with every other good person I've known? Every day I can't wait to go back to the room and find you there.'

'I . . . I didn't know.'

'Of course not, I've been far too scared. Scared for the first time – that's paying me back with my own coin. But it's true. The time I got back from Girton I wanted to throw myself at you. That squash game was the next best thing – just being filled with the sense of you.'

'You're not serious.'

'Don't be absurd, Neil. You sat there, just before the Nonagon dinner. You must've realised how I felt about you. I nearly told you then – Christ, why do you think I was drinking so much?'

'I just remember you jumping up when I said I wanted to marry Susan.'

'Yes; I could've killed both of you for that.'

We stood and looked at each other. The flushed, handsome figure of Thomas Lyster seemed to grow until he pushed everything else aside. Then I realised that I was terrified. Twenty two years of my upbringing rose up against six months in England, and won.

Thomas raised his hand and brushed my cheek. His hand had been in his pocket. It was warm and hard against my skin. 'Neil,' he whispered.

I did not speak. I turned my back on him and walked the remaining distance to the house. Alone.

ELEVEN

I walked away from Thomas because that was what One Ought To Do in those circumstances. As I reached the house a sense of panic set in. I was stuck here in Netherbridge, with Thomas Lyster who was either angry at my behaviour or was about to embark on further advances. More than ever before I felt at sea. I would have liked to have had a few minutes to myself, but even that was denied to me. As I strode into the hallway I nearly collided with Mrs Lyster.

'Neil, what good timing. Would you like some tea? Why don't you take off your boots and coat?' I looked down and saw that I had tracked mud into the house. 'Where's Tommy? Have you had one of his really invigorating walks?'

'Yes.'

'Good. Now do put your things away and join us.'

I did as I was told.

'Oh, hello; where's Tom?' Mr Lyster asked without interest as I walked into the sitting room. I hoped that Thomas would arrive before someone seriously expected me to excuse his absence. 'So you've enjoyed your walk,' he went on, while filling his pipe. 'I suppose Tom didn't say much about my efforts here.'

'But you did get an idea of why we love Netherbridge,' Mrs Lyster asserted. She smiled, and I thought that she, too, loved this place, not just as land and house, but as an ideal. 'Of course, I'm a stranger here. I grew up in the north country, although I used to come here to visit my cousins in the summer. I never thought then of being *the* Mrs Lyster.' She said it matter-of-factly. I noticed that she did not exchange any glances with her husband and that she said nothing about mothering *the* Mr Lyster. I wondered if she

117

believed that just deserts had followed primogeniture.

'You're very lucky to live here.' I said.

'What does your father do?' Mrs Lyster asked as she handed me the plate with the tea cake. I put my cup and saucer on the floor next to my chair. My instinct was to throw it against the wall. I had never felt so agitated, and yet here we all were, playing at being conventionally polite English people. I imagined that if I said 'your son has just made a pass at me,' Mrs Lyster would have replied 'Quite; are you ready for more tea now?' Here was England at its strongest and finest and it was driving me insane with irritation.

'My father?' I hesitated, and as I did Thomas sauntered in, looking cheerful, unruffled, and the picture of glowing good health.

'Now there you are, Tommy dearest; we've been wondering about you. Do have some tea.'

'Thanks. I will.' He flopped into a chair and slung one of his legs over an arm, to his father's annoyance.

His attitude was the last straw. I remembered the description of Matthew Jenkins's father as running kettle shops on the North Circular Road. The same could be said for my father, if on a different scale. And the proceeds of that rather large electrical goods business in California – what my grandmother reverently referred to as 'the Empire' – had provided Thomas Lyster with a fine standard of living over the past months.

'My father runs kettle shops,' I said. 'I suppose you'd say that he was in trade.'

No one answered at first. 'I can never understand American business,' Mrs Lyster said. 'That time we were in Venice, we happened to share a gondola with a nice American couple who were staying at our hotel. The husband spent the entire time trying to tell me about his business, but I never could grasp what he did, except that he must've been very sucessful. He made a great show of paying for the entire gondola ride himself. In those days that seemed like a lot of money.'

'My father wouldn't travel to Europe,' I ground on. 'He says that he saw enough of it during the war, and that you don't appreciate what we did for you. In fact, he thinks you're all quite decadent.'

This was an accurate summary of my father's ridiculous prejudices, but never had I dreamed of admitting that he held them, even in a mocking tone. Now I recited them as if they were worthy of consideration. They were not, but I could not think of a more convenient way to insult them all.

'I don't consider that I live in Europe,' Mr Lyster said, 'so I presume that your father couldn't possibly be referring to the state of affairs in this country. I met quite a few Americans during the war and I did find that they had very odd ideas about virility. I couldn't see it. I always thought that man for man we fought considerably better. I still think your technology is likely to work better than your soldiers. Pity we don't have more soldiers. Pity Tom isn't one of them.'

'Oh, Father, do you really think I could make a good job of something?'

'Your name is Lyster. If you don't have a talent for commanding men I don't know what's to be done with you. You might also consider choosing a profession that rewards aggression in the proper circumstances. It might teach you what those circumstances are. Perhaps Mr Fielding will then excuse you from the definition of decadence which apparently includes your mother and myself.'

'But Neil doesn't think me decadent, do you?' He smiled, like a hunter who had closed the trap.

'I've been to England more recently than my father has.'

'You see,' Thomas declared, 'Neil's all right.'

'Of course, darling.'

'In fact, I'm not. I mean, I'm not feeling very well,' I stood up.

'Oh dear, I hope it wasn't something you ate.'

'No. No, it's probably all the changes of water.'

'Has no one put a bottle of water next to your bed?' Mr Lyster asked. 'No one in the family has ever drunk tap water in Netherbridge.'

'I don't know what it is,' I said desperately. I just knew that I

119

had to get out of that room. I wished they would let me go without a diagnosis.

'You're looking flushed,' Mrs Lyster contributed.

I held on to the arm of my chair while they all looked at me with the contempt of the robust for the inexplicably ill.

'I'll be O.K.,' I said. 'But I think I'll just lie down for a while.'

'Of course,' Mrs Lyster comforted me. 'Some people are coming round for dinner, but don't come down if you don't want to. I'll bring something up on a tray.'

'Thanks.' I withdrew, and hurried upstairs.

I felt better just being alone in my room. I took off my jacket and shoes and cravat. I sat on top of the bed, and drew my knees up. I stared at the dreadful pink walls. I tried to sort out my thoughts.

I was bad at doing this. I told Sally the truth when I said that I could look at myself in the mirror in the morning and simply know what was the right thing to do. I was no good at starting from first principles.

I wished I could run away. I supposed I could try to hitch a lift from one of the rare cars which passed the house. There were no buses or taxis or trains for miles around. No, I would not be a coward. I would stay here and stick it out. First I must try to blot Thomas out of my mind. I failed. I kept seeing his expression, as he put his hand on my cheek – hope, fear, desire, all mixed up. It was more powerful than the more obvious image of what Thomas looked like when naked.

If only I had heard from Susan. I could hide behind her letter. I felt deserted, and I was bitter about it.

I was also angry with myself, for having to think in terms of theories. If only I had had some sex in the past. At least I could draw some conclusions from my experience. All I had was my love of Susan, and some fantasies of a very mixed kind.

How had I avoided it so long? It was part of the Berkeley creed that sexual and political liberation were one, and the sooner the wet dream was over, the better. I watched, with equal incomprehension, the drunken fraternity lout, and the young radicals who

120

kissed during lectures and handed in examination papers written in free verse.

Of course there had always been the majority: the nice, clean cut kids who worked hard, worried about being successful and doing the right thing, and respected America's liberal institutions. Most American university novels were written about them, and about their anxious but essentially good-natured process of sexual awakening by the end of their sophomore year.

That majority included my friends, and I was supposed to be one of them. We did not consider sex to be a career. We did not throw tennis shoes at our girlfriends or assume that one body was the same as any other. I guess we didn't even talk about it that much. That was why Rob Berman had assumed that I had had a nice, quiet sex life of my own. He was entitled to assume that; everyone else we knew had one.

I recalled my evenings of turmoil, as I summoned up the courage to make some definite, sexually aggressive act. In the end, I always failed. I left the girl at the door with a kiss and a promise to myself to do better next time. They probably preferred some hulking, self confident Adonis anyway, I thought.

Relief was the word that always came to mind; the same relief that I felt when Caroline's taxi took her away. Caroline. She had told me that men had abandoned their sexual principles for Thomas. I wondered whether I had any principles left.

It was then that I realised what a long, slow rotting away had taken place in the past months. I had come to England too frightened to disagree with the American male ethic. Thomas had laughed that away. He smashed up all the old sexual stereotypes. He got me to read books written by men who did not, like Saul Bellow, feel tortured because they wished to be both virile and an author. He introduced me to people like Peter Harding, who, even in their limited way, coped with the elements of bisexuality. Thomas had set me free to choose.

Even his speech at the end of our walk had given me free choice. He did not claim to love me. He did not ask me to label myself. He simply suggested that two young men, who cared about each other a lot, should have sex together. Well, in his world it was simple.

In a way my brother's own 'conversion' made things easier. The very fact of his letter had started that conversation in which Thomas had trampled on the last of my preconceptions. And I no longer felt a slave to some super masculine ideal.

What seemed most difficult was to do something. I began to see that I had escaped from sex because nothing had ever touched me. No effort or crisis had ever interrupted my scholastic success. I had never been compelled to come to terms with anyone. I had always done the right thing, because then I would be left alone. As a result, there was nothing in particular I felt part of. I began to understand what Thomas was talking about, when he said that he felt dead inside.

I looked at my watch. I was past six. It was time to have my bath, and to change from my tweed jacket and cavalry twills to my blazer and grey flannels. As I went through these motions, I thought of the immediate future. Thomas and I would be sharing a set of rooms for another term. I was to be a guest here for another four days. I ought to apologise for my rudeness at tea.

When I left my room I saw that Thomas's door was open and that the room was dark. I went downstairs. There seemed to be no one about. I went into the sitting room.

Thomas was standing there, with his back towards me, staring at a shelf of china figurines which hung on the wall and which he had already told me he loathed. I closed the door behind me. He took no notice of me.

'Thomas,' I said.

No response. The house was silent. I hesitated for a moment – over what? Where was I to go? I slowly walked to where Thomas stood. I paused at the fireplace.

Finally I went up to him. He did not move. His posture was perfect. I could not see his expression. The tension was awful. Then slowly, and with complete innocence, I put my hand on Thomas's left shoulder.

Immediately he turned round and, slipping his arms around my neck, kissed me. When he finished, he stepped back and smiled.

'Would you like a drink?' he asked happily. 'Mummy and the others will be here in a minute.' He walked over to the side table and began to pour a gin and tonic.

I said nothing. I watched him, as my last opportunity to protest was lost. I was too preoccupied with the realisation that I had become excited the moment Thomas touched me. It only slowly ebbed away.

Just then, four women came in.

TWELVE

The guests that night were a mother and her identical twin daughters. They were described as being from the neighbourhood. As there were no other houses within walking distance, I wondered how 'neighbourhood' was defined.

The girls were just eighteen: fair, pretty, healthy, and completely uninterested in the mental processes. They were also about to start a secretarial course in Cambridge. They were the female equivalent of 'the gentry' amongst Thomas's friends. Like them, Thomas had known the twins all their lives. Their parents had known each other even longer. It was one of those friendships that persist long after anyone remembers how it started. It was kept going by return invitations to dinner, and by meetings at other people's parties and at Newmarket. There was not a spark of spontaneity in it.

Now it was being passed on to the children, on the assumption that they too would get along with people of their own kind. Thomas understood all this. He was willing, within limits, to play the game.

I did not condescend to the girls. We simply had nothing to say to each other. They were likeable, and they had a desire to please. The point of the evening was to extract promises from Thomas and me to look after them. I did not even dislike the social system. I supposed – I hoped – that by making class the basis of friendship, individuals might be allowed to behave as they wished, without fear of being left without human fellowship.

'I understand you and Neil have nothing but parties in your rooms,' the mother said to Thomas during dinner.

'That was last term. We have tripos exams in May. It's nothing

124

but work from now on.'

'Yes, I know what duties undergraduates have' she assured us. No one was impolite enough to ask her to list them. 'But afterwards there's May Week, and you can't work all the time until then. And with those ghastly undergraduates, you're always short of nice girls for parties.'

Sally was an undergraduate and she was not in the least ghastly. I was sorely tempted to say so.

'It's very different in America,' I volunteered. 'It's okay for a woman to be educated there.'

'Really? How interesting. Sometimes I think my girls just live for parties.'

'Oh, Mummy!' they protested.

'But if we do have a party for them,' Thomas said, 'they'll meet our friends, and then Neil and I will never have the chance to see them again. Such a pity.'

Afterwards, in the sitting room, Thomas sat on the floor between the twins. He told them that they would have the time of their lives in Cambridge. He promised to make the necessary introductions. 'Only do tell me, whether you want to meet the men who know how to behave themselves, or the ones who don't.'

We all stood in the hallway as the three ladies left. When they were gone, Mrs Lyster asked me if I had enjoyed the evening.

'Very much. They were so nice.'

'And you're feeling better now?'

'Oh . . . yes, thank you.'

'Good.' That closed the case history.

Thomas raised his arms in a yawn and then patted his stomach. 'I think it's bed for me. Good night.' He kissed his mother, nodded at his father, and smiled at me.

Mr Lyster asked me if I wanted a drink, and we went into the sitting room. Mrs Lyster, who felt that she should not go to bed before any guest, busied herself in the kitchen.

I sat down on the broad, chintz-covered chair, which had silently been allotted to me during tea. Mr Lyster poured each of us a very large tumbler of whisky and handed one to me. He sat in the battered leather chair that was 'his'.

'I suppose the girls were a change from the usual politics,' he said.

'Yes. Of course I liked Major Stephenson too.'

'Geoffrey's probably my closest friend.' Then he added – as if to modify this – 'Of course he thinks the sun rises and sets with Tom.'

'I kind of got that impression too.'

'As far as that goes, you seem to think the world of Tom. If I may say so.'

'He's been a great influence on me.'

'Yes. Yes. I'd prefer you to be the influence on him.'

'What do you think I should do?' I tried to treat it like a joke.

'You could start by seeing Tom as he really is.'

'I think I do.' God, after this afternoon, if I couldn't answer yes to that . . .

'He's probably convinced you that I'm a fiend who hates his own son. In fact, I worry about him. More than he'd admit to.'

'I'm sure you do.'

'Why? Do you think I have cause to?'

I was tempted to tell him exactly why he should be deeply concerned about his son. That might be a way out: to gain a protector in this strange household. Pride stopped me. 'Well . . . where I come from, parents always worry about their children. It's an occupational disease.'

'It isn't where I come from, so when I do worry, I have good cause to. I wish Tom weren't so conceited. It's not as if he's that good.'

'Can't he even be good?' I asked.

'So you do argue his cause.'

'No, I don't, I . . . Damn . . . I'm sorry, Mr Lyster, but there's something about members of your family. You box people into corners and then attack when they try to get out of them.'

Mr Lyster took a sip from his glass. 'I see. You were rude at tea this afternoon.'

I shook my head in despair. 'I'm sorry, I'm sorry . . . I don't

126

know what got into me.'

'Tom has. You're embarrassed, which is something. It shows that you're no good at imitating him.'

'I wasn't trying to, sir. I . . . I was very upset at the time. It was stupid of me to take it out on you.'

'Is anything wrong?'

Now, I said to myself. Tell him. At least say that you have to leave immediately. Again I resisted the temptation. I would settle the matter with Thomas in the morning.

'I'm all right, thanks. But I am very tired. Would it be rude if I went to bed now?'

'Of course not,' He got up as well. 'I've met Americans like you before. You're the best kind, so, you see, I can recognise quality in men when it's there.'

I drained my glass and gave it to him, 'Thank you.'

'I thought I could talk to you.'

'You can, sir.'

'Even after you've spent six months cheek to jowl with Tom?'

'Yes.'

'Well, perhaps we'll talk later in the week.'

'Okay.'

'And don't brood in the meantime.'

'I won't.'

'Good night.'

'Good night, Mr Lyster.' I turned to go.

'Oh, Neil.'

'Yes?'

'You ought to meet my son William sometime. The two of you have nothing in common, but you might find it illuminating.'

I smiled, nodded, and left. As I began to walk upstairs I realised how much whisky I had drunk. Those two quick glasses had come on top of the usual Lyster ration of an evening. This was the fourth night I had drunk two strong gins before dinner, nearly a bottle of wine with it, and three glasses of port afterwards.

Upstairs I saw that there was a light under Thomas's bedroom door. I did not call to him. I went into my own room, got into my

127

pyjamas, and brushed my teeth. I felt weary but incapable of getting to sleep. I was very much awake when I heard a knock at the door.

I threw back the bedclothes and turned on the lamp, but before I could get up or reply, Thomas walked in. He was wearing the large, old silk dressing gown.

'I trust you weren't asleep yet,' he said.

'No, but . . .'

'Good,' He closed the door quietly and, uninvited, sat down on the bed. I lay back upon the pillows. Thomas rested his hand on the far side, so that his body leaned across mine without actually touching it.

'I thought you went to bed ages ago,' I said.

'I thought you would've come upstairs ages ago.'

'I was having a drink with your father.'

'Aha. Anthony Blanche turning Charles against Sebastian?'

'Something like that.'

'Did he succeed?'

'I wish you hadn't come in here,' I said with exasperation.

'Why ever not?'

'Because I'm not in a fit state.'

'You look splendid to me.'

'Don't be ridiculous.'

'I'm not. You look wonderful. What's wrong with you?

'I'm drunk.'

'Good. This is no time for inhibitions.'

'I was sober this afternoon.'

'Yes, and it did you no good at all. Walking off in a huff like that . . . just like a little queen.'

'Get out.'

'Don't give me orders, Neil. Why don't you hit me? Why didn't you hit me this afternoon, if you're going to play the butch American?'

'You're stronger than I am.'

'What makes you think I would've hit you back?'

'All right . . . maybe you would've ducked.'

'Perhaps.'

'I would've felt an idiot.'

'Then why don't you try now. Come on. Hit me.' He grabbed my right hand, which he forced into a fist. Then he unfolded it, and brought it up to his cheek. I touched his taut, dry skin. 'There,' he said, 'that's what my skin feels like. You wanted to know, didn't you?'

I took my hand away, and folded my arms. 'I want to know what's right,' I said.

'Would you like me to tell you?'

'I know your views already.'

'Then what's wrong?'

I turned over on my side, away from him. 'I wish this weren't happening.' I paused. 'Can you understand that?'

'No. Why?'

'For fuck's sake, stop the catechism.'

Thomas sat up, but he did not leave. He pulled a packet of cigarettes from his dressing gown pocket and lit one. He used the ashtray which was gathering dust on my side table. I turned back and looked at him. He seemed almost indifferent. I realised that disappointed me. I preferred him to care. He stubbed out the cigarette.

'I'm afraid,' I said.

'Of course you are.'

We looked at each other for a long time. It was like that moment before the Nonagon dinner, when there seemed to be a physical bond growing between us. This time is was not dispelled. Thomas stood up and took off his dressing gown. His movements were slow, though by now he was fed up waiting for my consent. Then he leaned over me and undid the buttons of my pyjama jacket. He kissed me – lightly at first, but then running his tongue against mine.

'What happens now?' I asked.

'Do you want to find out?'

I nodded. Thomas gently sprawled on top of me, letting me get used to the feel of his body. I rubbed the back of his neck. 'You like

129

it already, don't you?' he asked.

'Shouldn't I?'

'Absolutely. If you don't enjoy this, what will you?'

As he said that it occurred to me that I was rather enjoying it, although not much was happening. Stupid phrases came to mind like 'abandoning myself in desire'. In fact I was as confused and inhibited as any virgin of either sex who has no way of comprehending the extent of the pleasures yet in store.

I was learning immediately that the warm sense of a body next to mine not only made me feel excited; it also made me feel incredibly happy. I was afraid of that happiness for it really only lasted while Thomas was there, and surely this could not go on forever? There was a little playful wrestling which made me feel as if I were a participant as well. Once I cradled Thomas's face in my hands and brought it down on mine. As I did he gave me a smile of pleasure which I knew a lot of people must have seen before. I could not have cared less.

The only thing which worried me was how Thomas would expend his obvious arousal. He must have realised that because he said. 'We're both too nervous for much to happen.'

I thought he was only trying to be kind. He lay by my side and I explored his smooth, broad chest with my fingertips. I felt as much curiosity as pleasure. It was as if I had spent my life as a visitor to a museum, where the rest of the world was a series of exhibits which I could not touch. Suddenly the glass case had been removed, I could feel the texture of the tapestry and the smoothness of the veneering, and know that this was what tapestry and furniture really were. Now I knew what another body was.

All the songs and romantic novels were really quite wrong. I was not transported to some seventh heaven. I could always have fantasised myself there anyway, as the Berkeley dream proved. Thomas had done something much more difficult: he had brought me into the real world. I decided that I liked being there. I also decided that I liked this odd sensation which came in waves. I assumed that this was, at last, lust.

Thomas stayed for nearly an hour. When he left I put on my

pyjamas again and pulled the covers over my chest. With the magician gone I expected to feel a reaction of guilt and self-disgust. Instead I felt extremely pleased with myself and even wondered how this would compare with Susan. I remembered all my fantasies of making love to her passive body, and of her muted responses. They made me feel as if I had been a child far too long.

I was awakened the next morning by Thomas's entrance with the tea tray. As he walked around to my side of the bed I thought to myself, I have been to bed with this man. The thought amused me. It also triggered off a nascent desire to do it again.

'Good morning, Neil.'

'Hello.'

'How did you sleep?'

'I think it's called the sleep of the innocent.'

Thomas smiled and handed me my cup of tea. 'Except that you're not innocent any more.'

'Thank God for that. I'd hoped it wasn't a dream.'

'Would you like me to make it more real for you?'

'Yes, please.'

'Well; Father, as it happens, wants me to do a little chore for him today. One of the tenants died a month or so ago and I've got to go over to the cottage to make sure everything's all right. It's quite uninhabited now. And quite isolated.'

'Oh, Thomas,'

'I hoped you might be glad to hear it.'

We drank our tea. As Thomas got up, he leaned over and kissed me lightly, as if this were the most natural thing for the two of us to do. 'You know, I've never been in love with goodness before. I bet it's dangerous.'

'Why?'

'Because I'm selfish. I've walked out on lots of people. I've never renounced anyone for his own good.'

'Thomas, are you in love?'

He looked at me. 'Who knows? If I am, I think I loved you before I desired you. That's never happened before either.' He picked up the tray and carried it to the door. As he opened it he said,

'You do realise how good-looking you are.'

I hesitated. 'Maybe.'

'He was a strange old man,' Thomas explained as we walked to the cottage. 'He was all alone after his wife died, but when he died, a whole pack of relatives suddenly descended. They've probably taken everything but the bed.'

'Why leave that?'

'Because they couldn't get it out of the house. He built it inside. Carved the bedstead himself.' He put his arm through mine. 'It gives a new dimension to the word, bedroom.'

'They might've dismantled it.'

'I'll shoot them if they have.'

In fact Thomas was right. The old farmer's relations were scavengers, and had picked the cottage clean of all its contents. Nothing remained on the ground floor. Upstairs there were two bedrooms: one empty, and one filled by the huge bed. The relations, who had swept the place before leaving, had also managed to leave a muslin sheet over the mattress.

'What a big bed,' I said. 'How many wives did he have?'

'Two. In succession.'

'Did either of them die here?'

'I don't think so. He certainly didn't.' Thomas opened the window. A gust of sweet, fresh air filled the room. 'He wasn't much of a farmer, so father wasn't sorry to see him go.'

'Neither am I – sorry.'

'In the circumstances, don't apologise.'

Thomas began to undress, and I followed suit. Now that the barrier had been broken, I allowed myself the indulgence of watching all his movements. They were all so quick, strong and easy. He lay down on the bed, and held out his arms to me.

I lay next to him, still rather nervously. 'I want to give you pleasure,' I said.

'You will. You have.'

'I've always been afraid that it would be like Neil looking at

Neil.'

'And was it?'

'Not last night.'

That afternoon it seemed incredible that I had ever looked upon sex as grubby act to obtain temporary relief. I used to hate the feelings of randiness that came to me despite myself. Now, as much as I did not want this ever to end, I looked forward to whatever respite was required before I could start to feel desire all over again. I did want to give Thomas pleasure. I wondered how much he derived from my own fumbling gestures, and whether he found the caressing and the kissing of my body to be as exciting as I did.

I was, of course, almost wholly ignorant still. I saw that Thomas was excited for a very long time. That worried me.

'If you want to come . . .' I started to say.

'I could come in the first thirty seconds, if I really wanted to. If all I wanted to do was to get it over with. But I intend to enjoy this as long as I can.'

At last I lay on my stomach, with Thomas bent over me, gently working against my thighs. His breathing scarcely changed. When he came, I was slightly disappointed that I did not feel more. I rested flat on the sheet, with Thomas lying on top of me, caressing my hands. It was wonderful being smothered by him. He kissed me along my spine, and then sat up. We had placed a towel on the sheet. He went over to his coat and produced another small one.

'Is it very different with women?' I asked him.

'Yes. It's less messy.'

'Is that all?'

He looked at me with mock seriousness. Then he leaned over and kissed me. 'The difference is, my love, that there isn't a brick wall any more. There isn't a void. That's all over.'

'Oh, Thomas . . .'

'I knew you'd do it. I knew it.'

'And that vast expanse which is the soul of Thomas Lyster?'

'All yours, if you want it.'

As we walked back to the house, Thomas suggested,

'I suppose I can forget to give back the key. Then we can say that we're going for a walk, and come here. Or there's always times in the day when the house is deserted. I'll think of something.'

'Promise me this week won't end.'

'I wish I could. But there's all those lovely weeks back in Cambridge. We'll sport the oak and shut out the rest of the world.'

'All of the rest of the world?' I asked.

'Of course. Ten years ago no one would've cared what we were doing. But this is just the sort of thing that people smirk at now. I'm not going to satisfy the prurient instincts of a lot of jealous grammar school boys.'

'I mean, are you going to shut out Sally? And what am I going to do about Susan?'

'Damn Susan,' he said angrily, 'don't you know what you've got to do? Hasn't she failed you?'

'Hasn't Sally failed you?'

He calmed down. 'She tried.'

'So it's over.'

Thomas stopped. 'Neil, what if . . . well, what if I carried on seeing Sally?'

'Why would you want to do that?'

'Of course she won't mean anything more than any other woman. It'd just be playing around.'

'Would it?'

'Well, do you want me to come right out and tell her that you're my lover?'

'No, I . . . I'm just rather new to this. I still have all these bourgeois notions of fidelity.' For a moment I hated him.

Thomas put his hand on my cheek. I should have stepped back. I should have known that the longer he touched me the less will power I would have. 'Neil . . . you know me. And you're old-fashioned. You know the difference between the body and the soul?'

'Yes.'

'Well, you have both. What sort of competition do you think there is between you and someone who just gets the body?'

134

'I just happen to be the first body you had where you didn't have the void afterwards. The more bodies you have, the more likely you are to find a second person.'

Thomas shook his head. 'You are a fool sometimes. If I thought you really believed that, I'd put you on the first train to Cambridge.' Suddenly that was a horrible prospect. Thomas waited for me to speak. When I did not he put his hand through my arm, and started to walk again, as if the matter were now settled. 'Come on,' he said, 'we're incredibly late.'

THIRTEEN

'You're late,' Mr Lyster commented as we walked into the sitting room. 'Did you ever get to the cottage?'

'Yes. Everything's all right.'

Thomas and I took our usual places and Mrs Lyster passed round the tea cups. It was incredible to think that at this same meal only the day before I had been agitated and rude. Now I could kiss my worst enemy.

'Doesn't Neil look tired?' Thomas asked.

'I'm all right.' I said.

'No; too many late nights. I'm running you ragged here. You'll be exhausted by the time you get back to Cambridge.'

Mr and Mrs Lyster, who assumed that Thomas was simply reporting my complaints, looked at me.

'Really, I'm all right,' I insisted. 'You've all been very generous.'

'I haven't done any work since you got here,' Thomas said. 'And when was the last time you opened a history book?'

'Last term,' I said truthfully. 'That's why, when I go back to Cambridge . . .'

'Oh, I think you ought to be in training before that.'

'Perhaps Neil would like a few days of holiday,' Mr Lyster said. 'I presume that's why you invited him.'

'You boys have worked very hard already,' Mrs Lyster added.

By this time even I had caught on. 'I suppose it wouldn't do me any harm if we did a little work here.' I said cautiously.

'Exactly. Mummy, do you have thousands of people coming to dinner the next few nights?'

'Only on Saturday.' It was then Thursday.

'That's all right then. That'll give us today and Friday and Sunday.'

'I thought I should get back on Sunday.'

'The trains are terrible then. Stay until Monday, at least.'

Mr and Mrs Lyster shrugged their shoulders and left us to our swotting. As Thomas had said when I arrived, we were virtually in a separate wing of the house. Neither parent had any interest in our subject and neither thought of disturbing us during our studies. Thomas realised that we could be upstairs much earlier if he did not engage his father in lengthy arguments during dinner. He dropped his aggressiveness immediately and by ten we had retired to work.

It must be said that we did do some work for those three days and nights, but not very much. 'Sex takes such a long time.' I said on Friday night.

'That's because it's an end in itself.'

'You mean there's never an end to it? All my life, I'll just keep wanting it over and over again?'

'My dear fellow, I'm sorry to hear that the proposition alarms you.'

The only difficulty I had was remembering that we were not always alone. I admired Thomas's daring in kissing me at a time when his parents could have walked in the room. I found self control to be more difficult. It was painful that I could not touch him when other people were around.

'I hope you will go into politics,' I told him one afternoon.

'Why?'

'Because I want to see you get everything you want.'

He shook his head, mockingly. 'Just like the others. You want to be able to tell everyone that you've been fucked by the Prime Minister of England.'

Even with all the sex I had been having, it still embarrassed me to have Thomas talk about it. 'Maybe I still will be then.'

'Hmmh. I'll think about it.'

'But seriously, why don't you do something at Cambridge?'

'Like what?'

137

'Peter said you could be chairman of CUCA. In fact there's some odd vacancy coming up, and . . .'

'Don't tell me about it. Leave being chairman to the men who need it.'

'Like Matthew Jenkins?'

'Yes. Exactly. A man who has nothing else. Whose self-esteem rises and falls like an unseasonal frost. Or Peter, who plays at politics.'

'Jenkins worships you, you know.'

'He calls me Tom.' The stranger's unforgivable mistake. 'Anyway, all that man's done is to fall in love with a fairy tale about English youth. He could have done the same thing with Peter or a dozen other blokes.'

'I don't think so. Your opinion really does matter to him. I think all his politicking is just his way of getting your attention. If he thought you liked him, he'd quit tomorrow.'

'That says absolutely nothing for the man. He shouldn't even be in politics if all he wants is my attention. Anyway, I thought you had this theory about him being a dangerous rabble rouser.'

'That's right. Unloved by individuals, he has to seek it in the masses.'

'Oh, stop theorising, Neil.'

'It's quite true.'

'I don't care. And I will not discuss Jenkins any more. The man's a Nemesis. His antics nearly spoiled our lunch party, and now he's spoiling my afternoon.'

'I'm sorry I ever mentioned him.'

'No, you're not. You did it deliberately.'

'Rubbish.'

He threw his arms around me and kissed me. 'Prove it.'

If Thomas's parents suspected anything, they gave no clue of it. On the contrary, his father was clearly delighted with his son's newly respectful attitude, which in fact was my responsibility. I had told Thomas that I was tired of his baiting, and that he could resume when I had left and the flat racing had begun.

'Tom seems to be behaving himself,' Mr Lyster said as we were going into dinner on Saturday. 'You must tell me your secret.' I did not reply.

On the Monday morning, everyone stayed around the house until I was about to leave. While Thomas put my things in the car, I said good bye to his parents. Mr Lyster remained in the doorway; his wife, shivering a bit in only a skirt and jumper, walked a few steps out into the drive. It was a cold morning. I made the farewell short.

'I can't begin to thank you enough,' I said.

'We've so enjoyed you being here,' Mrs Lyster replied. 'Tommy must invite you again.'

Thomas and I spoke inconsequently on the way back to Ipswich. It seemed a waste of valuable time, but neither could think of anything adequate to say. We arrived at the station just before the little local train was ready to depart. Now there was no chance to say anything.

'Only another ten days,' Thomas said. 'That's all that matters.'

'That's all I can think about.'

I returned to Cambridge alone. As I stood in the taxi queue, I looked back at the dull brick facade, and at the boss which bore the coat of arms of my college. There was also the intrusively modern sign, 'British Rail', that failed to set out the name of the city being serviced.

I took a taxi from the station to college, and at the porter's lodge I collected my key. The porter on duty was a square-built man of about fifty who always wore a dark blue suit and a bowler hat. He liked me, adored Thomas, and hated tourists. Each autumn he would buttonhole the new undergraduates, tell us the rules we were not allowed to break, and then how to get away with breaking them. The puritan spirit of the early 1970s annoyed him. Undergraduates who no longer had to worry about gate hours also no longer gave him tips, and in any event they objected to bribing members of their own class. On Thomas's recommendation, I gave him a bottle of whisky at the end of each term.

'Did you have a good holiday, Mr Fielding?' he asked.

'Yes; wonderful; thanks very much.' It was typical of me that I could never remember his name. Thomas would never have such a lapse. 'I suppose I don't have any mail.'

'Good Lord, you have more post here than any other man in college.' No suspicions had crossed my mind when I had made my comment. Nothing had been forwarded to Netherbridge while I was there, and I presumed that that was because no one I knew – including Susan – had bothered to write. Now the porter produced a large envelope stuffed with smaller ones. 'I think you get more letters than any man in the history of the college,' he joked.

I stared at the package. There must have been a dozen letters in it. 'All of these got here in the last day or two?'

'Oh, no; we've been holding them for you since you left at the end of term.'

'But why didn't you forward them?'

The porter smiled blankly. 'We would've, if you'd left us an address.'

'But I did.' I tried not to sound rude.

He shrugged his shoulders and pulled out the exeat ledger. There were several columns on each page, for the name, date of departure, signature, forwarding address, and signature upon return for every man in college.

'We always send on the gentlemen's post if he asks us to. Otherwise it just collects here.'

I looked down the list. I found 'Lyster, G.T.S.' along with his signature in black ink and the address, 'The Small House, Netherbridge Lyster, Nr. Ipswich, Suffolk'. Then I found my own name, and its signature in blue biro. I had left it to Thomas to collect any letters which arrived before he departed himself, and also to arrange for my forwarding. Next to my signature there was not just a blank space but a firm line drawn in black ink.

'I see. I must've forgotten. I'm sorry'.

'The gentlemen are always so eager to get away at the end of term. They forget to do half the things they plan on.'

'Sure.'

'But I was very careful with your post. You'll find it all there.'

140

'Thanks. Thanks a lot.'

I left the lodge and stood in the porch under the great gateway. Ahead of me lay the long stone path which bisected the three redbrick courtyards and which led over the bridge to my own rooms. I stuck the large envelope into the side pocket of my flight bag and slowly made my way down that long path.

I tried not to think about what Thomas had done. I walked through the empty courtyards and over the bridge. The river looked depressingly beautiful. Finally I climbed the tall, spiral staircase. There on the second floor was the sported oak, above which were painted the two, paired names: 'N.P. Fielding' and 'G.T.S. Lyster'. I let myself in.

The sitting room was bare. Mrs Dipper was supposed to do her spring cleaning during the vacation and so we had packed up the books, glass and china. It now looked exactly as it had on that September afternoon before I met Thomas Lyster and before his character had been impressed on the place. I did not bother to go into my bedroom. I put down my luggage, took off my coat, and sat down on the chesterfield.

Hesitantly, as if my fingers would be injured by touching it, I plucked out the first piece of post. It was a card from Rob Berman, who was now in Greece. I did not bother to read it. The second thing was an aerogramme. I opened it just as I realised that it was from my brother.

'April Fool's!' it read. 'You didn't really believe that, did you? Some of the guys put me up to it. We all thought it would make you feel at home with all those Englishmen'.

As a matter of fact I had believed it, and it had made things easier. I felt like someone who had been encouraged to steal by a friend who claimed to be a fence, but who then turned out to be a policeman. I felt angry, although no one in the family could know about Thomas. So my brother did still have the power to annoy me.

That much self-disgust should have sufficed. Instead I plucked out another envelope. It was from Susan. I looked at the postmark. It must have been sent the day she got my cable. I opened it.

'I do love you. More, I think than before. More than when I first wrote that I did. And I do want to marry you, only – how can I say it? – will you forgive me if I say that I want to see you, once more, before I say yes for sure? Maybe I just want to kiss your dear face when I accept; not just stare at a piece of paper. When can I see you? I guess not until our semesters are over in June. I have already made a plane reservation for London on June 8. You see how I can take action once I make up my mind!! Only please write and tell me that it's O.K. to come. Okay? Listen to me reminding other people about writing! But I know myself, and so do you. There is nothing to stop us now.'

For a long time, I just sat there. No one interrupted me. I had nowhere particular to go. It was about lunch time, but I had no appetite. I interpreted my hunger pangs as nausea.

Netherbridge was wiped out. Thomas Lyster was now just a libertine, who had seduced me because there was no one else around and not much going on. I disbelieved everything he told me. He had never thought of starting on me in Cambridge. He wouldn't have: it was too much like hard work. At Netherbridge he held all the cards. It was easy there. And the easiest thing was to stop Susan from spoiling his plans. He was contemptibly lazy.

It was bitterly wounding, to find out that Thomas had refused to give me a free choice. I hated him for it, and as there was no one to plead his cause, my hatred was allowed to cool into a deep, implacable resentment.

At the same time, Susan's former hesitancy now seemed endearing. It was she, not Thomas, who put a value on emotions and sensibilities. Before she knew her own mind, she had given me every opportunity to change mine. Even now I had the chance to withdraw. How different from Thomas, who lured me to a house where I could scarcely resist him, who had slandered Susan, and who had sent me back to Cambridge, sure that I was safely in his power.

Well, he had got it wrong. If Susan had appeared then I would have told her everything, asked to be forgiven, and taken her off to America with me. Instead, I left my room, and made my way to the post office where I had cabled my offer of marriage. I wrote on a fresh cable form,

PLEASE FORGIVE HAVE BEEN ON HOLIDAY JUST GOT YOUR LETTER THE DATE IS PERFECT ONLY NOT SOON ENOUGH I LOVE YOU YOUR FIANCE NEIL.

The postal clerk smiled at me as she read it. I grinned back, sheepishly, feeling happy to be back in that normal world I had always thought was my due. So strong was my sense of doing the right thing, that it never occurred to me to wonder whether I would be able to consummate my marriage.

The next days were idyllic. The weather turned mild, and my room was full of the free air of Cambridge. I unpacked the books and china but rearranged their placing: they were my property, to dispose of as I wished. I worked quite diligently, reading through the required books and taking notes which I intended to be for my own use.

I had lunch and dinner in town, I ran into some of the people who were drifting back. There was a warm reunion with Peter and Nancy.

'Darling, we've just had the most wonderful time at the Hardings',' Nancy told me immediately. 'You know how gorgeous Peter is, but his whole family . . . I mean, his father looks just like a movie star.'

'How lucky for the genes,' I said. Privately I speculated whether my children would have blond hair like their mother or auburn like their father.

'Well, let's hope so,' she said, although Peter was standing there and blushing. 'But Peter keeps saying that he's not really in love with me.'

'I haven't said it recently.'

'You see? And there I was in this lovely house of theirs, lying awake at night and trying to think of what it would be like when Peter decided that he was in love with me.'

'And?'

'I just couldn't imagine. I mean, there's no point getting that excited when you're alone.'

'How was Netherbridge?' Peter asked, to change the subject.

'Fine. They're nice people. And terribly generous.'

'I know. Giles Lyster used to be quite a promising political figure around here.'

'Really?'

'Yes, only he never quite got a Parliamentary seat. Pity. Did you meet Geoffrey Stephenson?'

'Oh, yes.'

'Good man. Under-rated.'

Nancy sighed. 'Honey, I thought you were going to take a vacation from politics this term.'

'Sorry.'

'I have some news,' I said, and told them all about Susan's letter and arrival in June. Nancy hugged me. Peter shook my hand so hard that it nearly came off. We were now as one. I dropped the idea I once had of telling Peter about Thomas. It would only have embarrassed him anyway.

'Just wait till she gets here,' Nancy warned, 'I'll make sure she knows how lucky she is.'

'Maybe she does already.'

'If she doesn't, I'm going to break it off. Just you watch me.'

I was full of love. The phrases of endearment which I had been too shy to bestow upon Thomas were now poured forth on paper to Susan. 'Darling S –' I began my letters, and marvelled at my courage in finally using that opening. While I sat at the davenport, I listened to Wagner and Strauss.

I did not write to Thomas. A letter came from him, but I threw it away unopened. On the day of his return, I went to work in the history library. I left Susan's letter conspicuously on the sideboard.

After the library I dropped in on a friend for sherry. When I finally got back at seven, Thomas was there, alone, reading an early novel by Simon Raven. He sat in one of the easy chairs which faced each other across the hearth rug. I stood behind the chesterfield. In the last few days I had painted a picture of him ic my mind as a twisted and bloated monster. Instead, he was the unrepentant Dorian Gray: handsome, graceful and incapable of guilt.

'Oh, hello. I've been waiting for you.'

'I've been working. In the library.'

'Getting much done.'

'Lots.'

'I saw a letter on the sideboard.'

'Yes.'

'When do you reckon it arrived?'

'About a week after I left for Italy.'

'Did you get my letter?'

'An envelope arrived. I threw it away.'

Thomas nodded. He stood up, put the book away, and put on a tweed jacket which had been lying across the back of the chesterfield. I silently stood my ground. He walked up to within a foot of me and reached out for my arm. I stepped backwards.

Thomas shrugged his shoulders. 'I ran into our pianist friend from Girton on the platform. I offered to take her out to dinner. She said she'd love to see you as well.'

'I'll go and see her tomorrow.'

'Don't you want to join us?'

'No. Thanks.'

He nodded. 'I see that Miller's hasn't brought the piano back.'

'I cancelled it. I can't play and I'd rather not be disturbed before exams.'

'All right.' He walked towards the door.

'Are you sure you can afford to take her out to dinner?' I asked.

He ignored my sarcasm. 'Mummy slipped me a fiver before I left. I spent most of it on a bottle of gin for us. I suppose there's enough left for a grotty meal. I haven't had one of those for ages.'

Then he left.

If Thomas felt anything about my decision he did not say so. Without either of us spelling it out we resumed the position of polite strangers which had been the case in September. Visitors came to the room, but we did not entertain together. Those long, wonderful discussions about our academic work, our ideas and our lives, by which Thomas had been remoulding my character, ceased altogether.

Outwardly, our pattern of behaviour was the same. We breakfasted over the newspapers and then went our separate ways to lectures or the library. If one of us invited people round, he always checked to be sure that the other did not mind. One morning I went quite far and said,

'You know, Thomas, we can still be friends.'

Thomas replied from behind his newspaper.'I'm so glad to hear that. After all, the only thing that matters is your happiness.' His tone of voice cowed me.

I confided in no one, although the tension in the set of rooms was beginning to affect me. Thomas seemed content to resume his old life. Sally left him. In her place there was the succession of 'shop' girls. Thomas was frequently drunk, but never with me. For my comfort, I had Peter and Nancy and their friends. I soon realised how difficult it is to take up a normal social life after an intense affair. Life without Thomas was duller than it had been. If only Susan were in Cambridge already . . .

My communication with Thomas was so limited, that I heard from Peter about his impending speech at the Union, only a day before the weekly posters went up advertising the fact. I was amazed. Union debates are a forum for budding politicians, not for libertines. Thomas might be asked to speak in a funny debate or even on the arts, but in fact he was going to oppose. 'This House would give power to students'. The motion was to be proposed by Matthew Jenkins.

'Is that a coincidence?' I asked Peter.

'Certainly not. I've worked on Thomas for days to get him to speak.'

'Really? Why?'

'Because I know that he'll demolish Jenkins.'

'But does that matter?'

Peter shook his head good-naturedly, and launched into one of his bewildering monologues on the ins and outs of Cambridge politics. It boiled down the the fact that the vice chairman of the Conservative Association was not going to stand for chairman and that no one else particularly wanted to stand either, except for Matthew Jenkins. Ironically, the Association constitution only allowed him to stand because he was a member of the Committee, and of course he owed that primarily to Sally.

'But what if Thomas does crush him?'

'Then of course he'll be chairman instead.'

'He doesn't want it.'

'I think he may be changing his mind. The speech is crucial. No one's satisfied with only one triumph. And people will start to take Thomas seriously.'

Shortly after this I ran into Sally in town. I had seen her since Easter, but only when we passed each other in crowds. Now she was alone and ready to talk.

'I suppose you've seen the posters about the Union debate,' I said.

'Yes. Is Thomas really becoming a political animal?'

'I don't know. We . . . we don't talk to each other very much now.'

She looked at me, and tried to guess how the ground lay before answering. 'Did something happen over Easter?'

'Kind of. It doesn't matter, though, does it?' I had sent her a note about Susan and she had replied with enthusiastic congratulations.

'No. Well, are you going to the Union?'

'I suppose so. What about you?'

'Curiosity's got the better of me already.'

'Who are you going to cheer for?'

'Probably neither.'

'Does Jenkins still make you feel guilty?'

147

'Yes. He's so prickly. And so jealous.'

'Jealous of what?'

'That Thomas is Thomas and Matthew isn't.'

'Gosh, what a masochistic debate. Shall we see how bad this is going to be?' I asked.

'Let's. We haven't seen each other in ages.'

'I'm sorry. It's been a funny term. Come to the set. I'll give you dinner.'

'I'd love to.'

It was the first dinner I had arranged since Easter. It was fun, once more, to order it from the college kitchens. They sent up pate, cold roast beef, trifle, and salads. It was also fun to think that Sally would be in the room again.

She arrived that Monday night looking rather intense. Her hair was pulled severely away from her face. It made her look thinner than she was. I have her a glass of cold white wine and she sat in the chair by the fireplace. Just like old times.

'Are we really going to be alone?' she asked.

'Absolutely. Thomas left about ten minutes ago.'

'Good.' She took a sip from her glass. 'You may not believe this, but it's the first alcohol I've tasted since Easter.'

'You're doing better than Thomas.'

'Is he drunk all the time?'

'No. He's usually sober at least one night a week.'

'Neil . . .'

'Yes?'

'Why have you gone off him?'

'Why have you?'

'Because he was impossible the moment I saw him again. Very good in bed and some nasty remarks in between. I felt used. As if I were a very repetitive one-night stand. He wanted me to walk out on him, but he didn't have the guts to say so.'

'Typical.'

'Oh, Neil, if you'd ever been a woman with him . . .' I got up too abruptly to get the bottle of wine from the side table. 'I'm sorry. I'm probably speaking too frankly. But you are – you were his best

148

friend.'

'Go on.'

'In the end I got tired of it. It was coming to . . . not a dead end, but . . .'

'A brick wall.'

'Yes, that's it. Only there wasn't anything on the other side. But you must know that, if you've stopped adoring him too.'

'Yes.'

'Good.' She smiled at me. Somehow the expression looked familiar. 'I suppose Thomas is just one of those people who go around arousing the most violent love and loyalty because he's so handsome and charming. But he can't return it. I don't even think he has a conscience about it. Just some sense that he has to punish other people for his own inability to love.'

'That's right.'

She stood up. I was leaning with my back to the mantlepiece. She came to within a few feet of me. I felt the same confusion – and some of the same stirrings – that I had sensed when Thomas came into my bedroom in Netherbridge.

'We've both been his victims,' she said. 'The only difference is that I was given the physical gratification. I could hate him for you.'

'Don't. Don't bother. He can't touch us.' I managed to smile at her weakly.

Sally put her hand on my shoulder. This was not to be a re-run of Netherbridge. Here I was the man and more was expected of me. Without requiring further encouragement I put my arms around her and kissed her. I had not touched a woman since January. There was an odd sensation at first at feeling her pliant body rather than Thomas's hard, muscular one, but as I held her the memory of Thomas faded. I could not remember Susan at all.

'Do you remember, Neil? When I said that if I'd been wiser I would've loved you?'

'Wise child,' I said and kissed her again. There was no nonsense here about falling in love with nobility of character. I kissed her cheeks, then her ear and her throat, all very lightly. I returned to

149

her lips. Tentatively my tongue entered her mouth. The response tasted sweet. I held her tighter, slowly realising that my arms felt strong around her body.

'Sally, I . . .'

'Are you going to tell me you're engaged?'

'Well . . .'

'Does it matter?'

'No,' I said, and kissed her again.

We stood there for a moment. She lay her head on my chest and I stroked her hair. I could have remained there forever.

'What's that sound?' I asked.

'Me. Purring.'

'When can I see you?' I asked.

'You are seeing me.'

I smiled at her. I wondered if this was how things were arranged. Matters were going rather quickly. This was no time to postpone them. 'I glanced at Thomas's notes this afternoon,' I said. 'Remind me to tell you sometime what he said in his speech.'

She laughed and looked at me with complicity.

At that moment I heard a scuffle of feet on the stairs. I ignored it at first but the noise came to an end on my landing. Whoever it was stopped at my door and knocked on it. I had left the oak unsported, the invitation to the world to call. There was a second knock, more tentative then the first.

Exasperated, I strode over to the door and pulled it open saying, 'who is it?' brusquely.

It was Matthew Jenkins. He looked extremely uncomfortable in an ill-fitting dinner jacket. 'I'm sorry,' were his first words. I glared at him. Then he saw Sally. 'Hello, Sally,'

'Hello, Matthew,' she said, as exasperated as I was.

I continued to glare. I wished he would go. Thomas had complained that Jenkins had nearly ruined the lunch party and that he was ruining that afternoon in bed in Netherbridge. He certainly had Nemesis qualities.

'I was looking for Tom,' he explained. 'We're speaking on the paper tonight.'

'I know. Thomas left ages ago.'

'Did he? I thought it'd be nice if we arrived together.' He paused. 'Am I late then?'

'He said that he was supposed to be there at six for sherry.'

'Six? I thought it was six thirty.'

'That's what he said.'

He turned to go but as he did he nearly collided with another, burlier figure which came bounding up.

'Jenkins! You look smart.'

'Thanks, Peter.' Jenkins stepped away from Peter Harding as he spoke, although that was the wrong direction. This was one of the first times that they had met since Peter cut his dinner party. I was surprised to see Jenkins look more scared than angry.

'Hello, you two,' Peter said to Sally and me, as he walked uninvited, into the room. 'Gosh, what a spread,' seeing the sideboard. 'It's been ages since I've had a meal here. Looks a bit better than some of that oily Italian muck we had to eat.'

I was speechless. Peter had no idea what was wrong, but at least he looked embarrassed.

'I was only joking, you know, I . . . I just came round to invite Neil to Hall. If you wanted to come.'

'Trinity food is disgusting.' I said truthfully.

He blushed. 'I know, but I owe you so much hospitality. I can't cook and you could go to a far better restaurant without me. But I thought . . .' He stood there, large and grinning and harmless.

There was nothing else to be done. Peter was invited to join us for supper and then the debate. After some charming hesitation, he accepted. I went to close the door. It was then that I realised that Matthew Jenkins had gone. I did not know how long he had stood there while we talked as if he did not exist.

I tried to make the supper a pleasant affair but Peter did not make things easier for me. 'Susan will be here soon, won't she?' he asked almost immediately.

'Susan? Yes; yes, she will. Four – no, five weeks from today.

'Excited?'

'Yes.'

'You don't sound it,' he observed while helping himself to another slab of cold roast beef.

'I am. I can't wait to see her,' I insisted. I avoided Sally's eyes.

It was a short walk to the Union, which was a Victorian Gothic pile with red brick, stone arched windows, and a lot of wasted space. It stood on a tiny green and was reached by walking down a path which divided the Norman Round Church from a toy shop.

The debating chamber was set up to look like the House of Commons: rows of black leather benches rose away from the central aisle at the end of which was the raised dais for the president's chair. The custom of evening dress had degenerated. Now only the speakers and the officers dressed, and they wore dinner jackets.

It was a surprisingly full house for the spring term. Most of them were attracted by the presence of two very well-known M.Ps, who had come up to speak. We three took seats on the benches on the proposing side, in order better to see Thomas when he spoke from the Opposition despatch box.

It was a good-natured audience. They smiled at the President as he came in, leading the Vice President, the Secretary, and the four speakers. Thomas, his face flushed from drink at dinner, paid no attention to the House. He spoke to the Cabinet Minister at his side. He smiled at something Thomas said and then they took their places on the front bench. Thomas carefully pulled at his trousers before crossing his legs. Briefly he looked up at the gallery which ran round the top of three sides of the chamber. There were few people up there. Then he looked towards the President. He did not seek us out with his eyes and he did not look ahead of him, towards Matthew Jenkins, or at the table between them, where the Secretary sat and kept time.

The President was a tall, intense young man with a shock of red hair. As he stood up he turned his head in order to flick back a lock. 'The motion before the House,' he announced, 'is that this House would give power to students. It will be proposed by Mr Matthew Jenkins of Sidney Sussex College. Mr Matthew Jenkins has the ear of the House.'

Jenkins got up and stood by the despatch box. He straightened his shoulders, as if this would do something for the cut of his dinner jacket. I guessed that it was not hired, but that he had bought it cheaply somewhere, because he had been told that one needed a dinner jacket at Cambridge. We were a generation of inverted snobs, but it took someone with a sense of humour to make light of wearing that suit. Jenkins had no sense of humour. He gave the impression of a man who had seriously tried and who had to be blamed for failing.

'Mr President,' he began. Jenkins had an unfortunate voice. It was the sort of whine which would either sound like an apology or a prelude to a rabble-rousing address. I thought it sounded funny: Thomas had imitated it so often that it was amusing to remember that he had been accurate. Like reading *Private Eye* and then hearing how Edward Heath really spoke.

Jenkins performed the usual task of the proposer of welcoming the guests. He then looked very stern and said,

'A lot of people think that it's odd for a Conservative, and a Cambridge Conservative, to propose a motion that power be given to students.' 'Welcome, brother!' shouted a long-haired young man who sat in front of me, and the house laughed. 'Of course, the motion doesn't say which students'. This got more laughter, although I am sure that it was never intended to be a joke. 'But it was a Cambridge man who said that the world had grown old and cold and weary. I think it still is. And I wouldn't trust the men who made it that way to put it right.' There was applause. 'Exclusive power has belonged long enough to men who are satisfied by doing nothing more than moving us from A to B. I ask that some of that power be given to the only people who understand why we're going there – and who have the courage to stop it.'

To my disappointment, the debating chamber was impressed by this. Perhaps I was the only one who had experienced student power and participatory democracy first-hand; who knew that when a lot of single-minded people without practical experience got together, they went nowhere.

No one would have wanted such cynicism tonight. Jenkins

appealed to their self-interested idealism, and they loved it. He did well because he ceased to be himself. In my room he might show that he was hopeless with individuals, but before a crowd he was supreme. Even his voice lost the noisome aspect of its whine. It appealed to the gut. It was the voice of the average Englishman, and the chamber was full of average Englishmen. Intelligent, but dull. Jenkins had learned a great deal since I saw him before the house only a few months before, when the then President had given him a speech as a sop for not having shown up to dinner.

As I looked about the chamber my mind began to wander off in a reverie of train-into-Waterloo, suburban respectability. Then I looked at Thomas Lyster. Impassive, immaculately groomed; elegant in his waistcoat, dinner jacket and wing collar. For months I had identified him with England. Now I felt that it was he who was the outsider, not Jenkins. Not amongst his circle of friends and certainly not in Netherbridge and perhaps someday not in Westminster. But in Cambridge of the early 1970s he did not belong. He had come at the wrong time, when his contemporaries were Jenkin's men. They preferred Jenkins, a man who would tell them that they lived in God's own country and then that he would get on with doing things in the unimaginative way they liked seeing things done. No one waited for the day when they could see Matthew Jenkins humbled.

'As I said at the beginning, it may seem odd for a Conservative to propose this motion. I would remind the house that the youngest Prime Minister was a Conservative, a student at this university . . .'

'Wasn't he also an aristocrat?' the long-haired man in front of me stood up and asked.

'I hope not,' Jenkins replied. There were cries of 'shame' from the Tories present. I wondered if they realised that Jenkins meant the remark.

'Mr President,' he said finally, 'I beg to propose the motion.'

He sat down to a storm of applause. His had been a success it would be very difficult to follow.

'Rabble rouser,' Peter muttered.

Sally smiled at him. 'I think you might say, Peter, that the worm has turned.'

As I heard the President announce, 'Mr Thomas Lyster has the ear of the house', I could not stop myself hoping that he would better Jenkins. It was still aesthetically pleasing to see Thomas walk over to the despatch box, slightly leaning his elbow on it, and taking in the house with a glance before he said a word. He looked too polished though. Young men who appeared that way were not popular amongst their fellows. It was Thomas's misfortune that he had come to Cambridge at a time when he was by definition too smooth. He was being himself, as I well knew; that was enough to arouse suspicion.

'Mr President,' he began, 'it is not for me to criticise the sentiments of Rupert Brooke which were just quoted. No more, I might say, does it fall naturally upon the shoulders of Mr Jenkins, to raise as his own, the banner of a poet whom Henry James called the handsomest young man in England.'

The House enjoyed the malice, but it was not displayed for its benefit. I guessed that Thomas said that for no other reason than to wound Jenkins.

'When we think of Rupert Brooke, we think of war. Of the blood of the Dardanelles. Tonight I also think of the blood of Berkeley and of Paris, and of the fate the proposer has in mind for the Cam.'

'Is the speaker suggesting,' someone stood up and asked, 'that the legitimate demands of students in Berkeley and Paris were a greater crime than the over-reaction of the police?'

Naively, Thomas tried to reply, but he was cut short by the President.

'I am afraid that Mr Lyster cannot accept questions. This is his maiden speech.'

This produced a small uproar. 'Privilege' someone shouted. I later learned that it was customary for aspiring speakers to cut their teeth in the emergency debates which took place before the main debate of the evening. It was a little unusual for someone to be given a paper speech without prior testing. The comparison between Jenkins and Thomas was obvious enough. Some people

155

now thought that Thomas's stardom had been a fix, which of course it had.

'I forgot about that,' Peter said. 'Mistake.'

Everyone calmed down quickly, but it left a bad taste and for a moment it threw Thomas off his stride. It took him a while to regain it, but he did. It was not easy telling a large number of students they were irresponsible.

'Don't tell the university that they're fools, just because they're old; go and show them that you're responsible even though you're young.'

In substance it was no greater than what Jenkins had said, but success in the Union was not based on the cogency of arguments. It depended upon one's style and delivery. Thomas was a young man and he gave the impression that it would be a good idea to give power to him. That was enough to intrigue his listeners.

He might have succeeded no further had he not run out of material a minute before his time limit. He had been afraid that he might run short, and Peter had suggested a short poem to fill the gap. Some speaker had used it a few years before with success, and now Thomas recited the end of Auden's 'September 1, 1939'. It added nothing to his argument, but it sounded good.

Yet, dotted everywhere,
Ironic points of light
Flash out wherever the Just
Exchange their messages:
May I, composed like them
Of Eros and of dust,
Beleaguered by the same
Negation and despair
Show an affirming flame.

It was a tardy but an effective appeal to idealism. Thomas recited poetry much better than he uttered speeches, and his effort produced results. He convinced the House that he was, after all, human. Like then, he was also partly dust — although I wryly thought that Eros took up the lion's share of him. In that single minute he made Matthew Jenkins look strident and presumptive.

It was a superb ending. He paused for effect. That was fatal. In the brief silence, Matthew Jenkins said loudly, 'Very moving'.

It was too much for the House. It burst out laughing. Thomas waited until it finished. Without a flicker of reaction to the blasting of his efforts, he sat down.

I found myself feeling sorry for Thomas even though I knew he would have despised anyone's pity. I could not believe that people had actually laughed at Thomas Lyster. It was incredible. I looked at my companions. Peter's fists were clenched, as if he were ready to beat up every person who had laughed at his hero. Sally looked embarrassed, as if she had seen a public figure stumble drunkenly into the gutter. Thomas was impassive. When the other men gave their speeches he laughed or frowned at the points they made and gave the impression that he was enjoying himself.

Afterwards the speakers were taken to a room for whisky and beer. Several aspiring politicians of both parties came to introduce themselves to the M.P.s. Thomas was alone when we found him.

'Oh, you've come,' he said.

'It was a jolly good speech,' Peter declared.

'Until the end.'

'Damn Jenkins.'

'I wish I could. Sorry, Sally; you must have felt divided loyalties tonight.'

'I wanted both of you to do well.'

'That's what I mean.'

'I know,' Peter suggested, 'let's go smash up his rooms.'

'How charmingly Edwardian of you, but I can tell you that there's nothing at all in his rooms except for some law books and a few sticks of college furniture. The college would cup up very nasty about those Oxfam chairs.'

'Just pretend he doesn't exist,' Sally said. 'You're good at that.'

'I'd be delighted to oblige.'

'After you beat him for chairman,' Peter said.

Thomas looked at him as if he were mad. 'I'm not going to stand

157

against him for anything. Now, if you'll excuse me, I want to have a word with the minister. He used to play cricket with Geoffrey Stephenson, and we became such good friends over dinner.' Thomas turned on his heel and walked away. He and I had not exchanged a word.

The three of us walked together in silence as far as the Round Church.

'Thanks for dinner,' Sally said, while Peter stood just behind me. 'I hope you're still willing to give me lunch tomorrow.'

'Of course,' This was the first I had heard of it.

'It was Fagins' at one o'clock?'

'That's right.'

'Good-bye then.'

I was not thrilled by the prospect of having lunch at the same restaurant where I had entertained Caroline. I believe in omens. Nevertheless, it was fairly free of other undergraduates.

Unfortunately the lunch never really got going. There was no spark as had kindled the whole thing. What had happened in my room was spontaneous.

This was contrived. We were also short of conversation. I had related most of my general news during supper, when Peter had been with us. We could hardly talk about what we were about to do. To discuss plans for May Week and the summer inevitably raised the question of Susan. The obvious topic was the Union debate, but an exchange of views on Thomas was hardly the way to jolly things up.

'What did he say when he came home?' she asked.

'I didn't see him. He got in after I was asleep, and I was up and out before he woke up this morning. He was pretty vicious afterwards, wasn't he?'

She shrugged. 'He was acting true to form.'

'I'd be upset too, if I'd just lost out on a triumph.'

'Back to defending him, then?'

'No . . . I'm just trying to be fair.'

The only thing which lunch succeeded in doing was to get me

drunk. I ate very little, for I had decided that sex was a bad thing on full stomach. It had not occurred to me that being fuddled and smelling of claret was hardly an advantage either.

We took the bus from Castle Hill to Girton. It was the first time I had taken a Cambridge bus. Previously I had made the long journey by taxi or bicycle, preferably the former. It was not an inspiring trip. I was embarrased to try to hold her hand. There is also a depressing effect, on a young man who is drunk in the middle of the day and about to take a girl to bed, to take a slow ride on a bus with a lot of tired-looking people, each travelling alone. By the time I got to Sally's room I would have been happy to leave.

'Would you like some coffee?' she asked.

I feared coffee would make me want to use the toilet at an inconvenient moment, but it seemed rude to say no. 'Sure. Thanks.'

She went out to the gyp room to make two cups, which she brought back. Meanwhile, I took off my jacket and hung it on the back of the desk chair. I sat down as Sally came back. She handed me a cup and sat on the edge of the bed, opposite me. We said nothing.

'Oh Christ,' I said at last. 'I haven't come here to drink coffee. Anyway, I had two cups in the restaurant.'

She put the saucer down, and I did the same. I went and sat next to her on the bed, and put my arm around her shoulder. 'I love you', I said, and, leaning over, kissed her.

I felt somewhat less excitement than I had the night before, but realised that there had not been much of a lead-up this afternoon. I continued to kiss her, and our tongues explored each other's mouths. Without realising it, we leaned back on the bed. I caressed her face and neck and then her breasts, although we were still fully clothed. As my hand moved down her body she twisted.

'Anything wrong?' I asked.

'No. Just an awkward position.'

'Clothes get in the way, don't they?'

'I've always thought so.'

I moved my hand to her back, and fumbled for the hook of her blouse. 'Let me,' she said, and sat up. She took off her blouse and then her bra. At the same time I took off my shirt, vest and tie.

I kissed her breasts. 'Oh brave new world,' I quoted, 'which has such creatures in it.' That line was successful. I began to settle into this part, so I went on to say, 'I'm really going to get too excited this way. And then what will I do?'

Sally got up. I followed her and we both completely undressed. I was encouraged by the fact that I could be amusing in bed with women as well as men. Then I told myself to stop making comparisons.

I looked at Sally a little in awe. It was the first time I had seen, let alone touched, a naked woman in the flesh. Various phrases raced through my mind: 'milky white breasts', 'full and rounded,' 'erect with desire', 'damp with desire' – no, wrong part of the body. Sally did have a lovely body, white and firm and slender. I knew that I was seeing an exceptionally beautiful woman. I admired her flat stomach and shapely legs and the fact that her hips were not too wide.

Unfortunately I was only looking at it. I remembered what the drunken athletes at Berkeley always believed, that just to look at a beautiful woman sets off an irresistible tide of brutal male lust. It did not, but neither was I put off.

We lay down on the bed and let our bodies get used to each other. I began to kiss her. I tried to remember the way Thomas caressed me, then was afraid that if I repeated it I would give away the nature of my sexual experience. This conflict only made matters worse. I could sense that Sally was relaxing more quickly than I was. She was also getting a little excited. The problem was that I was not. We carried on a bit longer and then I broke away. I did not expect to sustain an erection the entire time, but I rather thought one would have happened by now.

'What's wrong?' she asked. I shook my head. 'Don't worry; just let your mind go blank for a moment.' I looked at her fondly. Lightly, she ran her fingers along my thigh and then across my stomach and then up and down the small of my back. As far as she knew I was completely a virgin and she was being very patient.

160

'No,' I said.

'Why don't you just relax for a moment.'

'I feel tired. That must be the problem.' What had all those people said in the movies? Too tired tonight, darling? 'I slept badly last night and I drank too much at lunch,' I over-explained. 'I feel right now as if I could close my eyes and go straight off to sleep.

'Then why don't you? It's all right. Really.'

That was exactly what happened. I had the sort of nap which lasts five minutes and which feels as if one has slept for hours. I also dreamed, deeply. It was the Berkeley dream. I went through all the familiar motions. Once more I drove up the steep hills of San Francisco and then approached the bed. This time I realised that I was naked and also very excited, which had never happened before. I walked over to the bed and looked down on it. There lay Thomas Lyster.

I woke up with a start and looked about, horrified. In this bed I was not excited.

'Neil?'

'Oh – sorry. I just forgot where I was.'

She turned over on her stomach and began to run her hand along my chest. 'How do you feel?'

'A bit groggy. Actually not very well.' I looked at her and nearly cried. I just could not lose this chance. I picked by her hand and kissed it. 'Sally, if . . . if we didn't this afternoon . . .'

'Yes?'

'Oh, the whole thing started off wrong. If only Jenkins hadn't come round. It would've been different.'

'I know.'

'This isn't . . . isn't the end, is it?'

She laughed. 'No, it's not the end. You do take sex seriously. A lot of people do it a lot of the time.'

'I'll remember that.'

'Look, why don't we get dressed and have some tea. You go back to college. And when you feel better . . .'

'Can't I see you in between?'

'Are you expecting it to be so long before you're ready?'

'No. I just wanted to be sure.'

'Come on.' We both got dressed. I stayed for another hour and had tea. It felt like old times.

We left on good terms but my spirits evaporated almost immediately. I walked back, which took an hour, and felt lonelier than I had ever felt before. But I knew one thing: nothing that Sally could ever do would cure it. And if she couldn't, Susan couldn't either.

It was past seven by the time I got back to my room, but it was still light. I found Thomas alone, reading another volume of *Alms for Oblivion*. He had been playing cricket that afternoon. He was tanned and his hair was still damp from his bath. He was wearing a tie and his tweed sports jacket. I presumed that he intended to dine in Hall.

'Oh, hello,' he said.

If this had been any of the evenings since I returned from Suffolk, I would have gone straight into my bedroom or picked up a book myself. Instead I took what had become the podium position in the sitting room: standing up, hands on the back of the chesterfield.

'Thomas, I . . . I think you ought to know that I've just been with Sally.'

'Lucky you. I reckon that I won't be seeing much of her any more.'

'I've tried to have an affair with her,' I blurted out.

He looked at me and smiled. 'Well done. I can hardly fault your judgement. Or . . . were you getting into training for Susan?'

I came round and sat down, a few feet away from him. 'I said that I tried. I failed this afternoon.'

'Failed?'

'All right, I couldn't get it up; what do you want me to do? Draw a picture?' I leaned back. 'It's your bloody fault.'

He shook his head. 'Please, don't ,' he said, and returned to his book.

'I fell asleep while I was there – only for a minute . . .'

'Sounds like a pretty exciting afternoon you had.'

'. . . and I dreamed of you. That's what I meant.'

Thomas closed the book. 'I see.'

I looked at him. 'Why did you make sure that my letters wouldn't be forwarded to Netherbridge?'

'Because I was scared she'd write to you, what do you think?'

'Coward.'

'That's right. It's the first time it's ever happened to me. I've always taken the view that one ought to be quite open about sex: if the other person wanted to go to bed with me, fine; if not, no hard feelings. I wanted you too badly to take the chance that she might write. I went to a lot of trouble, as well, rushing into Cambridge to get your parents' letter, so you wouldn't suspect anything.'

'Stupid.'

'Oh, very, very stupid. I see that now. At the time my judgement was . . . impaired. I read somewhere that people in love also have the power to forgive. I decided that if I failed in Netherbridge it wouldn't matter if you came back here and found a letter. But if I succeeded, then you might see my motives and forgive me. I'm sorry; I'm not very experienced in love. I obviously misunderstood its power. Does that satisfy you?'

I nodded. 'Thomas, I . . . I've been so lonely.'

'What do you think I've felt?' I stared at him. 'Why do you think I went to all that bother about making that damn speech in the Union and getting myself humiliated?'

'I thought you'd changed your mind, and wanted to be chairman after all.'

'How could you believe that? I let Peter think it, because I needed him to fix up the speech. I did it because I wanted to impress you. I was at my wit's end to know what to do.'

'And you thought that would work?'

'I didn't know. I thought you'd been attracted to me because of what I could achieve, and that you'd chucked me because I'd become a coward. Well, what does a coward do except to act bravely? And what could I do in a hurry? Geoffrey's alive. Exam results and any kind of election are weeks away. I can't act or sing, and I can't afford to re-hire the piano. You don't understand cricket. I was really running out of options.'

'I couldn't believe it when they laughed at you.'

He sniggered. 'Neither could I.'

'But I never admired you so much as I did then. You looked so cool and superior. It showed that Jenkins can't crush you. No one can.'

'Except you.'

'Please, Thomas . . . It's funny, I suppose we're both failures now.'

'We didn't have to be.'

'Wasted time.'

'Don't think about that. Think about what's left.'

We both got up. Thomas put his hand on my arm. 'I'm going to let you take me out to dinner and get me roaring drunk. Get us both roaring drunk.'

'Afterwards,' I said very firmly.

FOURTEEN

The affair became part of our everyday life at Cambridge. This required the taking of various precautions, and, in particular, sporting the oak. I remembered what Sally had said, about Thomas making her not care that the rest of the world did not know how wonderful it was to have an affair with him. I found that less easy. I also found that I resented other people being around. Thomas and I couldn't keep our hands off each other. Time spent in company was time spent away from sex.

Lectures had now stopped. It was late spring. Exams were imminent. So was Susan's arrival. I did nothing to put off her trip. I was still willing to tell her everything, but I could not put it on paper. My letters becam evasive.

I felt panic at the news from California. The respective parents were treating it as a real engagement. Mine flew up to San Francisco, met Susan's mother, and wrote ecstatically about mother and daughter. If it was difficult telling Susan about Thomas, it was impossible telling my parents. So I did nothing, and waited for events to sort things out.

The whole Susan situation and the imminence of exams made me tense and worried. Only Thomas's presence made things all right. When I looked too ridiculously morose he insisted on taking me out to play tennis. He was even willing to play doubles with Peter and Nancy, matches which usually ended with long teas in our rooms.

'Don't get me wrong,' Thomas said. 'She's still a frightful woman. But she's also the best female player I've seen. I'm going to put up with her personality until I can beat her.'

The only thing which got resolved was my encounter with Sally.

I wrote to her, explaining that I was still in love with Susan. I blamed guilt and my 'middle class conscience' for my impotence. It sounded reasonable. Sally never questioned it. We ran into each other a few times, and chatted as if nothing had happened.

With all the pressure of things on me, it was a marvel to see Thomas so untouched. He was physically faithful. He worked hard at his books and he resumed the intensive programme of fitness which he had followed at Netherbridge.

He was also impervious to Peter Harding's constant pressure for him to stand for chairman against Matthew Jenkins.

'It's all very well saying no to me,' Peter said in exasperation one afternoon after tennis, 'but a lot of people think that you ought to stand and that you will.'

'Let them. I'm not.'

It was puzzling, after that, to discover that Thomas was keeping up a public pretence that he might stand after all. The politicians came in and out of the room – to my fury.

'Don't worry,' he soothed me, 'I get rid of them as soon as I can.'

'Why don't you tell them you won't stand?'

'Oh . . . they like having something to talk about.'

I never fully understood what Thomas's motives were. I guess he had to react against being good to me; he had to balance that with malice towards someone else. It was easy to imagine what Jenkins was going through: his whole self-esteem teetered in the balance, awaiting the decision of a man who wouldn't acknowledge that he was alive.

I could just see Jenkins in his bare room, sweating over his law books; straining to get a First, not because it would amuse him to do so, but because his ego depended on it. He had to concentrate fully, but he couldn't. Everywhere he was distracted by the spectre of Thomas Lyster. The triumph in the Union meant nothing. It had not made Thomas a bit less handsome, graceful, or attractive to women. And in Cambridge it is difficult to realise that someday you will go to London and never see these people again.

In the meantime he had to bear the fact of Thomas's behaviour. Jenkins had tried so hard. Everything he achieved had been the product of so much effort. Why didn't Thomas Lyster ever try? How, without trying, could he attract all those people who flocked to his rooms and begged to know his intentions?

The whole thing came to a head in the week during which nominations were open. That week ran from Sunday to Sunday. Jenkins was entered as chairman within the first hour on the first Sunday. Thomas stayed silent. By the end of the week, the tension must have become unbearable for Jenkins.

Thomas and I gave our last party on the night of our last exam. It was no Berkeley celebration of passing joints. The room was packed with people getting disgustingly drunk. We began with champagne. We ended with anything alcoholic in sight.

Peter Harding kept saying that Thomas would be the next chairman, until Nancy came up to him and said, 'Come on.' One of the twins, who had come so close to witnessing the birth of my affair with Thomas, confided in me, 'Mummy keeps asking when I'm going to be asked out by you. She absolutely fell in love with you at Netherbridge. I say, isn't this all fun? Thomas is such a great friend.'

The next few days were calmer. May Week had not really begun. Thomas and I spent most of our time together, drinking, reading, and playing tennis. On the Sunday morning after exams – the Sunday that the Conservative Association nominations closed – we slept late. Thomas went downstairs for a bath at about eleven. He returned as I was emerging from my bedroom. We looked at each other and grinned. By this time we knew each other well enough to dispense with preliminaries. If anything, I might have thought how fresh and clean Thomas would be after his bath.

'Neil,' he said.

Thomas took off his bathrobe. He smiled and walked up to me. I was only wearing the bottoms of my pyjamas.

'My place or yours?' I asked.

'In a minute.' He kissed me. When we parted he draped his long arm over my shoulder. 'Come on,' he said, and we turned towards my bedroom.

It was then, while we were both in an excited state, that we

167

noticed by the doorway the unannounced and uninvited Matthew Jenkins.

My first reaction was to break away, but Thomas had guessed that and he held me tightly. We all stared at each other. I was sure that I had not heard any knocking. I could not believe that Jenkins would walk in without being asked to. Unless he was that distraught.

'Oh, Jenkins.' Inevitably it was Thomas who spoke first. 'I suppose you've come to see if I'm standing for chairman. Do you mind waiting a little while? I'm tied up at the moment.'

Jenkins said nothing. The conflict of feelings must have been tremendous, but all he displayed was his first reaction: disgust. Without a word, he walked out.

Thomas waited until he was gone. He put on his dressing gown, opened the door, and sported the oak. 'There,' he said, 'that takes care of that problem. Careless, aren't we?'

'Oh, Thomas.'

'It's all right, Neil. I promise.'

'What do you think will happen?'

'What do I think? I think that deep down in the grey soul of Matthew Jenkins, there's the world's biggest gossip, waiting to come out.'

FIFTEEN

For the first time, I had no wish to go out in Cambridge. I told Thomas this, miserably, and got scant sympathy.

'Look; as long as we act as if nothing's wrong and nothing's happened, no one will dare to say a word to you. If they smirk, cut them.'

'But I'll know what they're thinking.'

'Well, don't give them the satisfaction of imagining that you agree with them.'

Thomas was of course right. No one said a word. For two days we carried on as normal. On Tuesday afternoon he went to see Peter Harding. I know what was said because I was told about it immediately afterwards. By luck he found Peter alone. He was offered tea, and he accepted.

Thomas pretended it was a normal social visit. He discussed the parties he had gone to, and commented on the invitation cards on Peter's mantlepiece. Just as he expected, Peter could not take the matter-of-factness.

'I suppose you know what's going on,' he said.

'No; what's that?' Thomas returned from the mantlepiece to a chair and picked up his cup. 'I've just been to my third May Week party. Not very good. I don't see how they expect anyone to get drunk on that stuff.'

Peter brightened. 'You mean it isn't true?'

'Dear boy, didn't anyone at school ever teach you that antecedents should be identified? What is "it"? and please stop speaking lines from one of those 1940s films Neil always says he watched on television as a child.'

Peter shook his head, and said nothing.

'What is "it"?' Thomas calmly insisted.

'Jenkins . . . Matthew Jenkins is spreading a rumour about you. About you and Neil.'

'Strange chap, Jenkins. I can't imagine spreading a rumour about someone I've scarcely ever met.'

'Thomas, this is serious.'

'All right. Now, stop blushing Peter. You can talk to me, man to man.'

'He's . . . well, it's being said that he saw you and Neil in bed together. On Sunday morning.'

'Peter, I can tell you quite categorically that Neil and I were not in bed together when Jenkins called round. That much isn't true.'

'What do you mean, "that much"?'

'You're the future lawyer. I mean that I've been charged with a great offence and I'm not guilty of it. Is there a lesser charge as well?'

'I don't know what you mean by lesser. What Jenkins is saying isn't quite clear. At least you were . . . Thomas, what happened that morning?'

'You know, Peter, I've never met anyone at Cambridge who gets so embarrassed whenever sex is discussed. A man with your experience.'

'For Christ's sake, Thomas, you didn't come here to have a cup of tea. It's you who want to know how much I've heard.'

'I'm not sure what my motive was. It's always a pleasure to see you. And you make such good tea.'

'Were you naked or weren't you?'

'Not quite naked. Neil still had his pants on. Or maybe it was his pyjamas. I can't remember.'

Peter clenched his fists and brought them down on his knees. 'And I nearly killed Jenkins when he told me.'

'There's every reason to kill people over the truth – it's far more dangerous than the sort of lies you can't substantiate. And it is true. Neil and I went to bed that morning, but not when Matthew Jenkins was there. That would've put us right off.'

'Was it the first time?'

'No. I seduced him at Netherbridge. We had a bit of an argument after that, but we've been going to bed with some regularity for the last month or so.'

'You seduced him in your parents' house?'

'I suppose I'd call it a seduction. He took some coaxing, but not as much as you did.'

'Shut up about that. Tell me, are you going to see Sally?'

'I reckon I'll run into her at some party.'

'She was your girlfriend.'

'And you know perfectly well that she isn't any more.'

'Thomas, go to her. Make it up. Everything will be all right then.'

'Peter, what are you going on about? I don't care what people think. And I have far too much respect for Sally to use her like that.'

'Then you're going to carry on this . . . thing?'

'Yes. I say, would you like to know what we did when Jenkins decamped to spread his dirty little bourgeois tales of horror?'

'I don't want to know.'

'It doesn't matter. You can guess. I haven't changed my technique much.'

'I told you to shut up about that. You know how I feel. Can't you forget that ever happened?'

'No. Why? I mean, it hardly occupies my every waking thoughts, but neither can I forget it. I enjoyed it. So did you. And this puritanism of yours on the subject is revolting. But you're quite safe. Neil's the only other person who knows what a hypocrite you really are.'

Peter stood up. 'It's not hypocrisy. I've become a man. So should you.'

Thomas lounged in the chair while Peter paced up and down in the room. 'You know, Peter, you're still very good looking, but you've got to watch yourself. Men with your metabolism start running to fat the moment they stop taking exercise. You're beginning all ready.'

'It's none of your business.'

'But it is. It's a duty you still owe to me. I want to be able to see you just as you looked then. Do you want to know what that was? Not sick. Not a bit of it. You looked greedy. A greedy little boy: prudish in mind and insatiable in body. I wonder if I dislike Nancy so much because I'm jealous? Do I really still lust after you? I must consider that sometime. What do you think?'

'I think you're disgusting. You have no self-control of any kind.'

'I wouldn't say that. I can be terribly self-disciplined. During the last vac, I ran three miles every day, and lifted weights. Of course it was part of the seduction plan, but it wasn't easy to maintain. The way I've studied for my exams, I think it's quite possible that I could get a First.'

'I mean about sex.'

'Oh that.. I mean, I wouldn't rape anyone, but if they're willing . . .' He shrugged his shoulders. 'But I'd remind you that I've conducted this affair with Neil without any of you guessing a thing. If Jenkins hadn't been so damn worried about that ridiculous election you'd still all be in the dark. You talk as if I were a hopeless libertine.'

'You are.'

'Perhaps, but a libertine with discretion. Ask Neil.'

Peter stopped and stood in front of him. Unconsciously he held his arms out. 'Thomas, I believe in you. Even after that debacle in the Union, I still thought you were the most remarkable man of our generation . . .'

'That's very kind of you, Peter. But I don't see what it has to do with who I go to bed with.'

'To me it does. I thought you'd changed.'

'Don't be absurd. People's natures don't change.'

'Mine did.'

'Hypocrite. If I really applied myself to the task, do you think we wouldn't wind up in bed together again?'

Peter clenched his fists. 'I don't suggest you try.'

'Goodness.'

'I'm glad you're not going to be chairman. No one could've trusted you.'

'But you do trust Jenkins?'

'Yes. He wouldn't have done something like that to Neil.'

'No, and I know why. Now please stop talking as if you had cause to worry about Neil's moral sense.'

'I do. You've ruined it. We've all seen you sponge off his money. You weren't satisfied with that. Now you've destroyed him. He wasn't like that when he first came over.'

'Stop being over-dramatic. Come out and say what you mean.'

'You know what I mean. You know it embarrasses me. You like seeing me embarrassed.' Thomas remained impassive. 'All right, you've made Neil queer.'

'Made him? Do you think I had to rape him? Do you think he wasn't eager? Do you think he isn't a damn sight better in bed than you were? Don't lecture me, Harding. Not when I know how queer you are yourself. And don't clench your fists. I know how strong you are already. I know the feel of your rugger muscles as well as I know the feel of your thighs!'

'Get out, Thomas.'

'Not yet.'

'Get out. Please. While there's still a chance I might speak to you again.'

'No. Not until you take that superior look off your face. At least when I had Neil I knew what a woman – what a lot of women – were like first. I didn't have to wait for that – Nancy to teach me. You must have been bloody surprised the night she had to tell you what went where.'

Peter was now very red. He controlled himself with difficulty. 'At least you didn't ruin me for women. You've ruined Neil.'

'How would you know?'

'Nancy . . . Nancy's been to see Sally. They had quite a long chat. Sally was rather upset and she said a lot of things perhaps she shouldn't have. Apparently Neil tried to go to bed with her last month. He was so anxious to prove himself after you. Only he couldn't prove it. Now she understands why.'

Thomas shrugged. 'I know all about that. It's such a funny story. I never had that trouble with Sally.'

Peter lunged forward. 'If you don't get out . . .'

Very slowly, Thomas got to his feet and walked to the door. 'Tell me, Peter, if I had stood, would you have voted for Jenkins rather than me?'

'Yes!'

'I thought so. You bloody little puritan.'

I might never have known of the conversation if I had not been in our rooms when Thomas got back. He had exercised complete self-control with Peter. He walked back hurriedly and as he did he became angrier. By the time he got back he was angrier than I had ever seen him. Than anyone had ever seen him. I happened to be in the kitchen when he arrived. He immediately poured himself a glass of whisky and then hurled the glass at the fireplace, where it smashed.

'Something seems to be wrong,' I commented.

'Look. I want you to do something.'

'Sure.'

'Never mention Peter Harding to me again.'

'Oh.'

'What do you mean, "oh"?' He was still furious.

'I mean, I expected there to be a bust-up. Now it's happened.'

'Why should you expect it?'

'Thomas . . . we both knew perfectly well what Peter would think when he found out. I've been waiting for the inevitable to happen.'

Thomas smiled hideously. 'It may have been inevitable, but, by God, I made him sweat through it.'

'What happened? Tell me.' He did. 'I'm sorry,' I said at the end.

'That bloody man.'

'But you knew this would happen,' I repeated. 'Why did you make it so vicious?'

'Because I will not have that man judging me.'

'Lots of people are judging us right now. You don't worry about them.'

Thomas waved his arm in the air. 'They're not Harding. He knows what I think of his moral poses.'

'Oh?' Thomas then related what had happened the night of the Nonagon dinner. Of how he had outrun Peter, just to show him that Thomas was still in command. A thought occurred to me. It should have sunk in a long time ago, but it hadn't. I hadn't taken it seriously then.

'Thomas, did you ever like Peter?'

'If I did, it was wasted time.'

'Peter's pretty boring, really, but that never stopped you.'

'He's a bastard.'

'Maybe you never liked him. Maybe you just saw him as the most popular undergraduate of his year. Everyone crowded around him. No one dared stand against him for office. But you were the only person he ever went out of his way for.'

'Spare me your theorising.'

'Maybe I'm wrong, but you liked having him under your thumb. Peter Harding, the man who has everything. And he wouldn't go to the toilet without asking Thomas Lyster, the man who never achieves anything. It's all power, isn't it?'

'Neil, do stop.'

'No. Power. That's the way you see people. Ever since you dreamed of killing your brother.' I paused. 'I'm sorry: you said I made you want to be better. I've failed.'

'And I'm sorry that I seem to have no other attraction for you,' he snapped.

'You're the one who said you have a body as well as a soul.'

'Yes. And you're the only one who's seen both of them.'

'Thomas, tell me: do you think you might get married one day?'

'I suppose so.'

'But she'll expect to think you love her.'

'Cloying; yes.'

'Well, what will you say to her?'

'It looks as if I'll just have to lie, doesn't it?'

'But how could you make love to her?'

He got up, exasperated. 'Oh, sex is sex. You make such a thing out of it. I mean, you'd think I hadn't . . .' He stopped, and then turned towards his bedroom.

175

'Hadn't what?'

'Never mind.'

'Thomas . . .'

He clenched his fists, and then placed his hands on the back of the chesterfield. 'All right. I'm afraid that I haven't been faithful to you the last weeks.'

'What have you done?'

'Looked up a few of the girls I use to pick up. Ones with rooms of their own.'

'Why?'

'Because I liked having sex with them.' Thomas was coterminous with my sexual ego, which he had just destroyed.

'You told me that you didn't feel the void with me.'

'That's right. With those sorts of girls, I never had to worry about that. It was quick sex.'

'Then what the hell did you get out of it?'

Characteristically, he opted for the truth.

'Freedom,' he said.

'What do you mean?'

'Exactly what I said. Neil, I love you . . .'

'Don't say that.'

'I do. That's the point. I love you so much that everything got too intense. I was scared. I had to . . . dilute things.'

'I don't understand.'

'Christ, I wish you would. You've always understood everything else.'

'This isn't everything else. What scared you?'

'What scared me? What gave me the void? But you cured that.' He stepped towards me. 'Now that you know the truth, the fear's gone.'

I stepped away from him. 'Thomas, why were you afraid?'

He looked less pleading. 'That's hardly a question you ask after you've seen how Peter Harding's turned on me.'

'And you think I would have?'

'Why ever not?'

I ceased arguing. The question had left me breathless, like a punch in the chest. I was far too stunned to begin to figure out what it meant for Thomas: to begin to see that it was the key to his whole gloriously arrogant detachment from the rest of the world. If he was going to think that the world was there in order to let him down, he could think it alone. we were silent for some time.

'I want to see Susan,' I said quietly. 'I'm going to the airport, and I'm going to tell her everything, and then we're going home together.'

'Are you really going to marry her?'

'Yes.'

'It won't work,' he said.

'An hour ago, you might have said that. Now now.'

'What if Peter's right? What if I have ruined you?'

'I will not let that happen.'

SIXTEEN

Thomas did not argue with me after that. He left me to feed on my fantasies of Susan. I envisaged us embracing, sitting down together, embracing, and going off in the sunset, hand in hand. I really thought that I could switch from being Thomas's passive lover to Susan's active husband.

I arrived at Heathrow just in time for Susan's flight from San Francisco. I took my place behind the barrier, outside the customs hall. When I saw her emerge, it was a slight shock. For months I had relied on photographs and memories. Both Thomas and Sally had managed to wash my mind clean of her. Now she was actually within reach. She looked wonderful. I could have guessed that she would be the best dressed woman there.

Susan stood with her luggage cart, well on the other side of the barrier. She smiled. She wants a romantic welcome, I thought. Well, at least she's glad to see me. I vaulted over the railing and strode up to her. She offered me her lips. Pursed. As I kissed them, I smelled the perfume and mouthwash which had recently been used.

'Welcome to London,' I said. 'I love you.'

She hugged me, briefly. I took her cart and pushed it towards the taxi rank. She held on to my arm. Several middle aged couples beamed at us.

'Where are you taking me?' she joked.

'London.'

'And then Cambridge?'

'I . . . I thought you'd like to catch your breath first.'

'Okay.'

The drive to London was taken up with Susan recalling landmarks from her previous trips. This seemed natural. We had been apart for a while. Once we exchanged greetings and information, there was a gap, before we could get to the fundamentals.

Everything about Susan was encouraging, but now that the moment had come, I was afraid. I wished we could just sit in the taxi, with Susan nestled in my arms, and have our spirits merge together. Instead, we sat apart and talked. I forgot how much time we had spent talking at Berkeley. So many happy moments with Thomas had been silent. Forget Thomas, I told myself.

The capital was transformed since my last visit in the spring. Those winter trips, with Sally and Thomas, had been exhilarating, despite the dark and the cold. The city seemed at our feet. We were young and happy, and only wanted pleasure. Now, in June, it was hot and glaring. The streets of the West End were packed with tourists. It was their city now.

'London's got so dirty,' Susan said. 'It didn't used to be this way.'

I removed my blazer and rolled up my shirt sleeves, twice. I touched Susan's bare arm.

'It's so hot,' she complained. I removed my hand.

We went to the Ritz. I chose it because I had only ever been there alone. Susan loved the Winter Garden. There was gilt every-where; the waiters were uniformed and deferential; and there were real dowagers, even if they were obscured by the crush of American clientele. It was also cooler. We both felt better.

'Oh, Neil, thank you for taking me here. How did you know?'

'What's that?'

'My mother and I stayed here, years ago. She used to dress me in a pinafore, and then we came down to tea. It's . . . it's the real England to me.'

'I'm glad.' I squeezed her hand. She smiled fondly at me.

The waiter brought us a silver tea pot, milk jug, and sugar bowl with tweezers; then a plate with eight sandwiches – two each of ham, cucumber, egg and smoked salmon, with the crusts cut off the bread.

'You pour the tea, Neil. You're so English now.'

179

It was that old sensation of being in protective command – even of being the man who introduced her to the nice things in life. Maybe I don't have to tell her, I thought. Thomas had said that no one in California was looking over my shoulder in England. Once we got home, how would she even guess what had happened here? I had to get her straight back.

'I'm looking forward to Cambridge so much,' she enthused. 'And this May Ball we're going to . . . tell me again, why is it a May Ball if it's June?'

'It's the end of May Week. You see, the boat races are called the Mays.'

'How interesting. I've brought the most gorgeous dress. Wait until you see it!'

'Susan . . .'

'Yes, Neil?'

'Susan, would you be very upset if we didn't go to the ball?'

'Why? Has it been cancelled?'

'No, but . . . Well, maybe it has.'

'I don't understand. I'd be so disappointed. I wanted to meet all your friends: Peter and Nancy and Thomas . . .'

'I'm not so sure about that.'

'What's the matter?' She looked concerned. 'Have you had a fight with someone?'

'Kind of.'

'Well, we just won't talk to him.'

'It's not that easy.'

'Oh. You still share with Thomas, don't you?'

'Yes.'

'Good. At least I can meet him. We'll go to the ball with his date, and forget everyone else. You know, you haven't written about Thomas lately, but I'm dying to meet him.'

'Thomas? You won't be missing very much.'

'How can you say that? I want to thank him for looking after you for me.'

I leaned back in my chair. I had had the scenario all worked out: I would tell Susan everything, and then we would get on the next flight home. Why wasn't it working out that way?

'Look,' I said, 'I don't want to go back to Cambridge.'

'What do you mean?'

'Everything's gone wrong there. It's been a disaster. I couldn't write to you about it. I just want to go back to California with you. As soon as possible.'

'Neil . . . are you in some kind of trouble?'

'Not exactly trouble.'

'Have you had a fight with Thomas?'

'Well, yes.'

'Then I don't want to see him.'

'Then we'll go back to California? Soon?'

'This is all too much. If I have to . . .'

'Yes. Please.'

'But I've just come six thousand miles . . .'

'Susan, please. I'll make it up to you. I promise.'

'Well, it is all very mysterious. But if you promise to take me somewhere wonderful for our honeymoon . . .'

'Anywhere you like.' I picked up her hand, and kissed it. 'And you will marry me.'

'You know I will.'

'Bless you.'

'But don't you think you better tell me what this is all about?'

'It doesn't matter.'

'But, Neil, it's obviously something terrible. I want to know about it. I don't want to start our married life with a lot of secrets.' I hesitated. 'Come on, I'm here to help. Really. Let me. Please.'

I was won over. I can tell her, I nearly shouted out loud. She is marvellous. I never loved her so much.

'It's about Thomas,' I said.

She nodded. 'You had a fight.'

'Yes.'

'What about?'

I held my breath. 'Our affair.'

'Affair? You mean a party?'

It was so wonderfully absurd of her. 'No,' I tried to explain.

'Thomas and I have been having an affair. We slept together.

'When?'

'Last Easter. You remember I stayed with his parents. And then again, this last term. Until a few days ago. But it's over now. I realise what a pathetic man he really is. I'm yours, completely.'

It was an appalling summary, but at least it got the bare facts out. Susan just looked at me. I wished she would give me some lead. I felt badly that I was throwing all this at her, just after she had got off a long flight.

'I'm sorry to blurt it out,' I apologised. 'It's such a long story, but, believe me, it's all behind me now. Poor Susan, you must be so exhausted. Let's find you an hotel, and you can crash out.'

'No. I want to hear about this.'

'I've told you. You see why we can't go to Cambridge?'

'Do you mean everyone knows?'

'A lot of people do. They're such puritan hypocrites, those people. They'd never say anything to my face. In fact,' I laughed, 'everyone thinks I'm the victim.'

'And are you?'

'You don't think I made the first move, do you?'

'Then did Thomas . . . are you saying that he seduced you or something?'

'I guess he did.'

'And when was that?'

'After Easter. When I was staying with his family. In Suffolk.' Hell, what did the county matter?

'And you say that it happened all over again?' The law student was coming out of her.

'Yes; this last term. He kind of worked on me,' I said. That was partly true.

'But you wanted to do it.'

'It happened, and it's over.'

'But did you like it?'

'At the time . . .'

She shuddered. She was disgusted. No, that can't be right, I thought. Susan was part of liberal, tolerant Berkeley with me.

182

Tolerant? How long had it taken Thomas to overcome my prejudices, quite apart from my inhibitions?

'Darling,' I began, 'you don't know what I've been going through. Everything I ever believed in has been chipped away by Thomas. I'd feel just the way you do, if someone had told me about it last fall. But he worked on me, for months.'

'I thought you had principles.'

'Would I be here with you if I didn't? Susan . . . it only makes sense to me, because I've lived through it. I know it's not fair, springing this on you . . .'

'Neil, it doesn't matter whether you sprang it on me, or whether you broke it to me over a long period. The fact is that you're sitting here, telling me that this man can turn you into putty.'

'Don't say that.'

'I . . . I don't know what to believe any more.'

'Trust me.'

'I did trust you. I trusted you when I said I'd marry you. Now I know what you were doing, before you had the opportunity to cable back.'

'Honestly, I didn't get your letter until I got to Cambridge. Thomas was supposed to have my post forwarded to his parents' house. He double crossed me, and didn't do it. I was furious when I found out.'

'Very well. But you forgave him.'

'I was lonely. And he said . . . he talked about love.'

'So Thomas loves you.' She made it sound disgusting.

'That's what he said.'

'You believed him.'

'Yes.'

'And as long as you believed him, you were willing to sleep with him.'

'I didn't know what kind of person he really is. I guess I didn't know myself very well either.'

'Neil. For the past year, you've been telling me that you knew your own mind. That's why I fell in love with you: because I could trust you; because you were a man of principle.'

'I wasn't lying.'

'You've been lying to someone. It's Thomas or me. Who is it? Who do you love?'

'You. I've always loved you.'

'Even while you were having sex with Thomas?'

'I love you. I love you. How many times do I have to say it?'

It must have been about this time that my will failed me. I had been kept going for months by the mere idea of love. I thought that all I had to do was to repeat it often enough, and the gates of happy marriage would be opened. It had been absurd. I loved Susan as much as I had loved any woman, but it was all theory. I had been lonely and detached, and I wove a dream around Susan to fill the gap in my life. But I had been deluding myself for so long, that I could not yet give up.

Susan put her hands to her forehead. 'I'm trying to think this one out. You say that you love me. You also say that you were telling me the truth when you claimed to know your own mind. However, Thomas seduces you. You find out that he tricked you. I agree to marry you. And then you go back to him.'

'Susan, please stop trying to be logical.'

'Don't you see how this is killing me? I've got to be logical. What else can I do?'

'Think with your heart.'

'Did you?'

'I am.'

'Tell me,' she tried to ask, calmly, 'what would've happened if I'd arrived two weeks ago?'

'How do you mean?'

'What would've happened if I arrived before you became disillusioned with Thomas? Then would you have wanted me?'

That of course was exactly the problem I had been avoiding all term. 'Stop torturing yourself,' I told her.

'I?' She glared at me. 'I?' At this moment, the waiter chose to appear with the tray of pastries. Susan waved him away. 'Don't you see what you're doing to me?'

'Is there no way you can forgive me?'

'Why should I? Can you promise this won't happen again?'

'Yes.'

'Would you have promised me that in April?'

'Of course.'

'But you would've broken that promise.'

'If only I'd been with you then . . .'

'I'm not going to be a policeman for you. The world's full of Thomas Lysters.'

'Let me prove myself.'

'How?'

'You'll know, when I love you.'

'No, thank you.' She brushed me and the offer aside. 'I don't want to see any of the sexual tricks Thomas taught you.'

'And what if it had been a woman?'

'I wish it had been neither. It'll sound funny to you, but I really hoped, Neil, that you'd come to me without any experience. Sex has always seemed so precious and intimate. I wanted to share it with you and no one else.'

It took a while for the full force of the irony to sink in. 'Such a different world,' I mused, 'Thomas sleeps with men and women. So have half his friends.'

'I don't want to hear anything about it. I've nothing against queers, but I don't want to know what they do. It's ugly. Don't you understand?' Her voice was rising now. She was close to tears. 'You've been soiled.'

I was aghast. I was sorry that I had been unfaithful. But so successful had been Thomas's teachings, that it no longer occurred to me that I had done anything wrong. And ugly? How could anyone apply that word to Thomas? Soiled? When I had known nothing but pleasure and contentment with his body?

Susan put her hands up to her face. I looked at her long, lovely fair hair, and at those graceful arms. I thought of the times when I had ached to touch them. I looked at her, and I saw my whole, illusionary youth in her face and movements. It made me feel slightly wistful. Susan had been the perfect person to make believe with. We should part gently, like the dream we had been to each other. But I was anxious now that we should break it off. I was tired of pretending to her and to myself.

'I'm sorry,' she said at last. 'I've probably been very rude.'

'Don't apologise, Susan.'

'This has all been too much.' I did not disagree. 'Neil, would you do me a favour?'

'Of course.'

'Could you see whether I could get a reservation at this hotel? I'd like to stay here for a few days.'

'Certainly.'

'It reminds me of when I was a little girl – with my mother. I was happy here.' She put her hand to her forehead. 'I'm so tired. I can't think anymore.'

'I'll go see about a room.' I walked down the long, wide, elegant corridor, and to the desk. There was a room available, for just three nights. We had left Susan's luggage with the porter. I arranged for it to be taken up to the room. Then I reported to the Winter Garden.

'Thank you,' she said. 'I think I'll go upstairs now.'

'All right.'

'I'll feel better in the morning.'

'Susan . . . nothing will be different in the morning.'

'Are you sure?'

'I am now. As you said, the world is full of Thomas Lysters.'

'Can't you resist them?'

'I . . . I don't think I want to. You can say . . . well, I've decided to stick to what I know.'

She looked at me, trying to smile. She had won the battle. She in fact had won the war. She did not look pleased with her reward. 'What'll we do?' she asked.

'Tell our parents we've made a mistake. We're both very young still.' She nodded, grimly.

We stood next to each other. We both looked at the carpet. 'I hope you'll be very happy,' she said. Then she walked away.

SEVENTEEN

It was an odd feeling, when I realised that emotionally I now belonged to no one. I had cut myself off from all my family expectations. Thomas and Susan, for different reasons, were both lost to me. I sat there in the Winter Gardens, mulling it over. A waiter came and cleared away the tea things. The room began to empty. A few couples were left, sitting on the sofas. I ordered a gin and tonic. It was cold and tasted delicious.

After a long while I noticed, a dozen feet away, a man in his late twenties. He was alone, and staring at me. The stare was neither rude nor conspicuous. I thought he looked like Peter Harding as an aesthete: tall, very slender, pale, with thick black hair, and a rather worn, two piece pin striped suit. I looked away, then back to him. His eyes followed me. At the time it seemed funny, so I smiled. That was enough of an invitation. He got up and came over to me.

'May I join you?' he asked as he sat down in Susan's old chair. 'I'm afraid I've arrived early, and I don't know a soul here.'

There was something wonderfully absurd in assuming that the Ritz was a cocktail party where he might expect the hotel to provide people he knew. Coming at the end of this day, I reacted by laughing very loudly. He was charmed, if slightly taken aback.

'Then it's all right to introduce myself?'

'Sure.'

'I'm Nicholas White.'

'Neil Fielding. Glad to meet you.'

'American, I presume? Just visiting?' He had a smooth voice, which was ostensibly well spoken. For some reason it sounded odd: Thomas's rich accent was the voice of a man who couldn't speak any other way; somehow I felt that Nicholas had had more of a choice in the matter.

'I've been at Cambridge this year.'

'I was at the other place, but it wasn't my fault.'

'Would you like a drink?' I asked.

'Thanks.' He ordered a whisky. 'Are you waiting for someone?'

'I'm completely alone.'

'You must be in the middle of May Week about now.'

'That's right.'

'But you're drinking alone in London.'

'I came down to see a friend.'

'I see. But he isn't coming back?'

'She. Went upstairs.'

He nodded. 'I've just ducked in here for the sake of my soul.'

'Why?'

'I've spent the last three weeks in Birmingham.'

'Is that bad?'

'Have you ever been there?'

'No.'

'Then do yourself a favour.' He grinned. 'Still, it had one or two compensations.'

I ignored the comment. 'So you're glad to be back in London.'

'To say the least. I thought I'd blot Birmingham out completely, so I came in here. I'm glad I did.

'Why did you go to Birmingham?'

'I'm an accountant for my sins. I had an audit. What're you doing at Cambridge?'

'History. But I'll probably wind up as a lawyer.'

'My family wanted me to be a solicitor.'

'Why didn't you?'

'There really wasn't anything I wanted to do. Accountancy's for people like me. It takes up time, but no energy.'

'What do you do in London with your energy then?' I felt bold asking that.

'Go to the opera,' he smiled.

I said that I had been to Covent Garden. We talked about the past season. I had only seen two productions. Nicholas had seen everything. He remembered everything. He compared the performances with those of other singers he had heard, and the productions with what was done in other opera houses.

'Of course,' he concluded, 'if you really like "Die Meistersinger," there really is only the Kempe recording.'

'I'll remember that.'

'I've got it at home. Why don't you come back and hear it?' he offered. 'I'm only in Kensington. The car's there – I'll run you to Liverpool Street for your train.'

'All right.'

There is a difference between not being in doubt as to what is going on, and consciously realising that one is being picked up. I was in no doubt as to what Nicholas wanted. But he was good looking, and his attentions were flattering. Anyway, if this were my fate in life, I'd better start experiencing it.

Nicholas lived in a terrace of houses with stuccoed windows and pillars, and brick walls. They had all been converted into flats. He lived in one on a second floor. He had a big sitting room, with a marble fireplace. There was an upright piano, a huge stereo system, shelves of records and boxed opera sets, and some dinghy furniture.

He poured me another gin and himself another whisky. He indeed put on the Kempe recording. He obviously did not expect me to be interested in the fine points: we started with the Prize Song. A man singing of his idealised love for his golden would be fiancee no longer affected me in the way it did a few months before. It was still magnificent. We listened to the glorious end of the act.

'Who was the friend you were visiting?' Nicholas asked when it was over. He was sitting about a foot away from me on the sofa.

'The girl I was going to marry.'

'Really.'

'We broke it off.'

'Ah.'

I drained my glass. 'We weren't suited to each other,' I said stuffily.

'Do your parents know?' he asked casually.

So this was how it happened. Allusive conversations; a game which we all played together and in which only we knew the rules. I rather liked it.

'No,' I said, and paused. 'I've only just found out myself.'

'Am I the first to know?'

'The first one that matters.'

He smiled at me. He was good looking in a rather inter-war manner, with high cheekbones and thick hair brushed straight back. He was not Thomas Lyster. I did not suppose anyone else ever would be.

'I really did go into the Ritz by chance,' he said, 'and when I saw you, I thought, this is too lucky. Birmingham was so squalid. Rough trade isn't quite me.'

'Thank goodness for that.'

He kissed me. There was a curious mixture of liquors on our tongues. He caressed my cheek. His hand was softer than Thomas's. That didn't matter. Comparing bodies, after all, is like tasting wines: it is only meaningful when you can have one right after the other.

Nicholas had a huge, rather crumpled bed, which was far more comfortable then the absurd conditions I had got used to in Cambridge. I lay there, grinning at him, while he lightly ran his hands over my chest, groin and legs. For such a thin man, he was surprisingly strong. All the surprises about him seemed pleasant ones.

Afterwards we had baths and went out to dinner, to a cheap local bistro. Nicholas asked me to stay the night, but I declined. I had an atavistic urge to go home to my own bed – even if it was a narrow, monastic one. He drove me to Liverpool Street.

On the way to the station, I mapped out in my mind what next year would be like. I would come down to London more often. There would be orgies of opera and sex with Nicholas. And if I didn't have him, I saw no reason not to start making up for the lost years of chastity. But I expected to have him. Every time traffic permitted, he took his hand off the gear shift and placed it on my groin.

'I'll see you in a few days,' I said as I got out. 'As soon as I pack up.' I supposed that I had to spend the summer with my parents, but I was entitled to some holiday first.

'Get your train,' he ordered, 'or I'll fall in love with you right here.'

'Go ahead,' I shouted, as I slammed the door and ran to the platform.

When I got back to college the gates were locked. After a man's day in London, it felt silly to have to rouse the porter – and to hope that he would remember that I always tipped at the end of term. He did, and I was allowed in. I walked across the warm, silent, dark courtyards and up to my room. I went straight to bed.

I slept late. When I emerged, about eleven, I found Thomas dressed and busy packing his books.

'Are you leaving already?' I asked, yawning.

'That seemed more tactful. Mummy's coming over this afternoon with the car. Thinking about everything, I don't mind going down a few days early.'

'You don't have to bother.'

'Are you and Susan really going back on the next 'plane?'

'I'm not going to marry Susan,' I announced. 'She's spending a few days in London; then she's going home alone.'

Thomas stopped what he was doing. 'What happened?' He tried so hard to make his face a blank that I could not tell what he hoped for. I told him about the conversation in the Ritz, and, very quickly, about Nicholas. 'You got yourself picked up five minutes later?' he asked, and started to laugh. He sat down on the chesterfield and literally screamed with laughter. 'Wonderful,' was all he could manage to say. I must have looked as annoyed as I felt, for he told me, 'Oh, don't look so insulted. Don't tell me you've fallen in love with this chap.'

'No.'

'Oh, Neil. I can't wait to see what you're going to get up to next year. I really can't.'

'Go away.'

'I am. I am.'

I turned around and went into my bedroom to shave. When I came out again, Thomas was sitting on his trunk drinking a mug of coffee. I looked at him, and for the first time I thought, this man was my lover. I used to have access to his body as a matter of right. For a moment I was sorry about Nicholas. As long as he was there, Thomas and I would never have another reconciliation. But I don't want one, I quickly added. It's over.

Thomas went home that afternoon. I helped him carry the trunk downstairs to his mother's car.

'Mummy, you remember Neil, don't you?'

'Of course, how nice to see you again. I hope you'll be coming to Netherbridge again. You must get Tommy to invite you.'

I mumbled something, and then went back to the room. There were some gaps where Thomas's few possessions had been, but it was still full of books and china. It all belonged to me. It was one of the few times that year when the room was wholly mine. I felt sad to lose it.

It was now the weekend; the last weekend of May Week. I went to a few final parties. The scandal of Thomas and Matthew Jenkins and I had obviously been forgotten. There were no more suppressed stares. Once, Peter and Nancy approached me. I could think of no way out except to cut them. It was no good trying to pretend that I belonged to their world any more, and I certainly did not want their sympathy.

On the Monday morning there was one letter in the post, from London. I read it over my boiled egg.

My dear Neil,

I'm not going to fool around; you're not that kind of bloke. I'm going to come right out with it. The morning after that marvellous night with you, I saw that I had the signs of . . . well, you know. I went to the clinic and they're pretty sure that I have a good, old fashioned *AND CURABLE* case of V.D. I'm writing because you've got to go to a doctor right away and check. I'm afraid that my 'little compensations' in Birmingham weren't very wise. Please – before you get angry – try to imagine how I feel. I had no idea AT ALL when I met you. I'll understand if you don't want to see me again, but PLEASE PLEASE don't feel that way. I meant everything I said to you. Let me make up for it. Love, Nicholas. There was a P.S. with the address of a clinic in London.

I put the letter down. I looked around the sitting room: that little corner of good taste that Thomas and I had created as a bastion against the squalid, violent, irrational world. I kept expecting someone to walk in; someone in whom I could confide; someone to offer a little comfort. I remained, as always, alone.

I quickly decided that I would go down to London to the clinic Nicholas suggested. It was anonymous. There was no question of going to my doctor in Cambridge. I took a train which got me to London about midday.

I felt lost in the city. There was none of the usual anticipation in my arrival. I became nearly paranoid. Whenever anyone looked at me, I thought, They can tell; They know about me. The 'special clinic' was in Bloomsbury. I took the tube from Liverpool Street. The Circle Line took thirty five minutes to show up. Once it did, the carriages were stuffy with the heat of June.

The clinic was in a basement, by the university hospital. It was extremely dingy. Someone took my name, and I sat down on one of the plastic chairs. I tried to avoid looking at the other men. They were generally young, but all grizzled, grimy and foreign looking. Instinctively, I had put on a tweed jacket and a thick, Viyella shirt. I felt absurdly out of place and swelteringly hot.

Finally I was called into a cubicle. I knew all about that by now. It was far from sound proofed, and I had over heard every conversation that had taken place in it since I arrived. 'When did you last have sex?' 'Do you know who might have caused it?' 'You musn't have sex for three weeks'. I knew the questions by heart.

The doctor was a bored but polite young man. He asked me the usual questions. He examined my genitals, but there were no signs yet. I felt extremely embarrassed, admitting that it had been another man. He, however, could not have cared less.

'Of course, the chances are that you have been infected,' he told me.

'Can I have the treatment then?'

'You don't want to wait – to be sure?'

'No. I want to get it over with now.'

He shrugged. He gave me a piece of paper to take to the hospital around he corner. I had to wait again in the hospital. I did not mind that so much. At least there were genuinely sick people here; not just diseased men.

'Occupation?' the nurse asked.

'Undergraduate,' I replied.

She frowned, and wrote 'student'.

After a very long time, I received my two shots of penicillin, and a prescription for tetracycline. 'Don't drink while you're taking antibiotics,' the doctor warned.

When I finally got out to Gower Street, is was well past lunch. The road was crowded with cars, belching out fumes into the hot, heavy, still air. Now I genuinely felt soiled. I found a chemist, and said I would come back in half an hour to pick up the pills. I went across the street, and telephoned an airline.

'I want to get on a flight to Los Angeles. Tomorrow.'

After checking, the clerk told me. 'I'm afraid that no one has any space on a flight to Los Angeles until Thursday. In fact, we don't have any room on a flight to California all week. Just New York.'

I hesitated for about ten seconds. 'I'll take it.'

'It's tomorrow afternoon. Is that all right?'

'Perfect.'

'Once you're in New York, I'm sure our staff there will make connecting arrangements for you.'

'Thank you, but I don't think I'll need them.'

I would not stay in England. I had no real desire to return to California. I had never been to New York, but last year, while applying to Cambridge, I had also tried to get into law schools. The one at Columbia had accepted me. I would go there, and, somehow, I would get myself in.

EIGHTEEN

The miracle is that I did get into Columbia. I approached the admissions officer with the attitude that there was no question but that I would be let in for that autumn. The man I dealt with was an Anglophile. That helped, to say the least. His favourite city was London. Once upon a time he had had a sad love affair with an Englishwoman. I did not deny that that had been my problem too. His memories of England merged with a welter of male fellow feeling.

Also, that very morning, he had received a letter from the psychiatrist to one of the fall's entrants. Apparently the patient could no longer relate to an institutional situation. With my year old acceptance, I got his place.

'But for God's sake, don't tell any of the minority students,' he urged me.

It was thoroughly unscrupulous of both of us. It was also my introduction to the selfish 1970s. The slush and the guilt of the 1960s were obviously coming to an end.

I then had to square my parents. Their main concern was that I was changing my mind yet again. That they could not cope with. First, I wanted to go to Cambridge. They paid for it. Then I wanted to marry Susan. That was okay. Now I was giving up Cambridge and Susan and going to law school. In New York.

'You'll get killed there,' my mother complained. She, who wouldn't drive through Beverly Hills in broad daylight, unless all the car windows were up, and the doors locked.

'Susan's in California,' I answered.

Now they understood. The real truth was, of course, infinitely more difficult to explain. I was not in the business of creating

195

difficulties just then. They agreed to pay. The concession was a summer at home. I compressed that to a two month stay: I had to scout around New York in June and be back by August to look for an apartment.

It was a lazy, dull summer. I swam a lot and lay in the sun. I saw my old acquaintances. I told them that Cambridge was a stupid, archaic place. They agreed that that sounded bad. I finally got the chance to finish Proust, which I several times tried to hold forth on over dinner.

'So what happened to Susan?' my brother asked whenever I mentioned Proust.

'Hey, when are you going to stop sleeping around and get married?' my father would ask him.

Back in New York, I found a decent, and relatively safe, if expensive apartment, on the upper east side. My trunks began to arrive from England. My living room was half the size of the one in Cambridge. I easily filled it with my books, glass and china. They looked odd, displayed there. They did not provoke any conscious nostalgia, but they did insulate me.

I wanted to feel insulated. I felt that I had experienced life in the raw, and it rather put me off it. My visit to the 'special clinic' had frightened me off sex. That wore off, but by the time it did, my detached way of life was firmly entrenched. Momentum carried it forward, just as it had always done, before I met Susan and then gone to Cambridge.

New York is a surprisingly good place to live like that. Not only is there a crush of anonymous people; it is a city which is beautiful and varied enough to get lost in. I got to know all the elegant streets, and then the older neighbourhoods, whose charm was far more to my liking. I started to build up a serious collection of books. It was the road which Thomas had opened up to me, but I only half-acknowledged it.

The study of law was also pretty time consuming. I was disappointed to learn how uninteresting it was. I understood the subject, and I did well in it, but my imagination was left completely untouched. Law school seemed like a long ordeal, but nothing compared to the prospect of twelve hour days in a fashionable law office.

I discovered that a few of my fellow students had been to Oxford. One confided in me that the only problem with it had been the lack of women, and that when he did find a woman, 'the guy next door complained about the noise'. It was so like Thomas's fears for me, that I used the conversation as an excuse to start writing to him. Thereafter we kept up a restrained correspondence. He gossiped about mutual acquaintances, but told me little of himself. He did say that he got a First in our year. The next year he got another one, went to London, and became a banker. He found it boring, but the bank gave him a cheap mortgage, and they did not mind him 'politicking'.

The only other person I wrote to was Sally. I did not know what her theories really were about Thomas and me. She made no reference to what we had done in Cambridge. She got her law degree, but decided that she hated the subject too. She went to London and found a job with a literary agency.

I spent two busy, emotionally dead years in New York. I rarely read a newpaper. The long, slow road to Watergate was no more cheering than the stories of the three day week in England. There was a General Election there. Thomas wrote that he was 'going mad' with activity. Sally wrote that she wished the Conservatives would stop saying that to give in to the miners would open the floodgates to twenty percent wage settlements. She was becoming more politicised too, but her thoughts were very general. She became aware of the Establishment. She complained that people would not spend the money to buy her clients' novels, which would tell them how rotten they were.

It was Sally who came to New York, in that summer when, in England, the floodgates of twenty percent wage settlements were open. She came with her boyfriend, Chris, a playwright in his early thirties, whom she had met at a literary party. He was rather shaggy, and wore a crumpled white shirt with the sleeves rolled up to his elbows, corduroy trousers, a dirty old cricket pullover, and heavy shoes. I put them up on the sofa bed in my living room.

Sally looked fantastic. She had got thinner, and now wore brightly coloured blouses and tight trousers. It was impossible imagining her in that camouflaging duffle coat, from which Thomas had lifted her room key. She walked around my apartment and shook her head.

'Neil . . . oh, Neil . . . it's still Cambridge in here. I mean, I can remember that jug. You always had white carnations in it. And the bowl, for old invitations cards. And the Nonagon photograph! Surely no one here has any idea that that kind of thing goes on. And don't tell me that they can believe it!' She gave a quick glance to the picture, which included Thomas Lyster, as he had looked when she was in love with him.

'I hear from Thomas from time to time,' I told her.

'Really?'

'Yes. He's a banker, when he's not doing something political.'

'Typical. He couldn't exist unless he was manipulating someone.'

'Who's this, love? Chris asked.

'An old boyfriend. And Neil's mate. Long ago.'

I spent four days showing them New York. Sally was happy to wander round the Museum of Modern Art and the stores. Chris wanted to go the the Village, for reasons of his own.

'I want to hear the voice patterns,' he said. 'It's very difficult, writing dialogue for American characters. But I like the way Americans talk. Of course you, Neil, talk li' e a hybrid.'

'It was Cambridge.'

'I hated the place. I can still smell toffs mile away.'

'Can you?'

'Yah. Don't you notice, the most pretentious people are also the most second rate?'

'Does that mean that the earthy people are the most first rate?'

Chris shushed me. We were in a record shop. In the next aisle a mad old man was talking very loudly to no one at all. Chris was fascinated.

When he was not listening to voice patterns, Chris drank. I had not seen anyone drink like that since Cambridge. When drunk, he complained: about the starvation of subsidised theatre, about the BBC bureaucracy; about his need to tell the world about Life.

I was only alone with Sally a few times. The last was her final afternoon. We had tea in the Winter Garden of the Plaza. A small orchestra played Puccini arias, while the waiters served enormous and expensive sandwiches. It was on far too large a scale to be anything but American, but it was difficult not thinking of Susan and the Ritz.

'Is Chris a good playwright?' I asked.

'He's a genius. He's completely different from everything I've ever seen performed. People write to him, and say that they've re-thought their whole lives after seeing his plays. No one ever did that with Noel Coward, or whoever else we thought was great at Cambridge.'

'He drinks a lot, doesn't he?'

'That's the drawback. Quite honestly, I hate the smell. But he's so intense – he feels so much – he cares so much – sometimes it's the only way he can stop himself from going mad. I'm trying to help him, though.' She smiled. 'I think I'm the only one who really understands.'

'Gee, that's great.' I was not being sarcastic. It really was what Sally had always wanted. And Chris was quite happy to have a beautiful woman to think he was a genius, and to excuse his faults.

'Neil . . . we've changed, haven't we?'

'Sure.'

'I . . . I've just got the impression, the last few days, that you didn't like me so much anymore.'

'Don't be silly. But it was a bit of a shock, after all this time thinking of you as . . .'

'Oh, Christ, just forget the way I was at Cambridge.'

'How can I? What about that afternoon, in your room – do you remember?'

She shook her head. 'Nothing ever happened to me at Cambridge.'

'I wish I could forget about it too.'

'With a sitting room full of ghosts, like yours?'

'Well . . .'

'Neil, you have a wonderful future in a wonderful city. Do yourself a favour, and enjoy it.'

I was about to reply: but I do enjoy it. In a way, I did. But New York's great advantage was that it blocked out the past. I had never really appreciated it for it's own sake. For two years I had tried very hard. It was like loving Susan and asking her to marry me, in the unconscious hope that that alone would make me heterosexual. I could hardly call New York an elaborate sham, but it was a lot of effort, just to stop myself realising that I was in love with Thomas Lyster.

'Sally . . .'

'What's wrong, Neil?'

'What should I do?'

'Go back to England.'

'Really?'

'Yes. Go and get rid of us.'

I arrived in London on a hot July afternoon. Thomas had written that it would be very nice to see me again. He offered me the spare bedroom in his flat. I accepted. Perhaps I was afraid of what that would lead to, and somehow that triggered off the Berkeley dream on the flight. I certainly wanted to show Thomas that I had distanced myself from England. I deliberately left behind the tweed jackets and the Jermyn Street shirts. I brought my Paul Stewart wardrobe: not a million miles away from Cambridge gear, but Thomas would spot the difference.

Thomas's flat was in that unnamed area between Chelsea, Kensington and Fulham, which was full of grand houses converted into flats for bright young professionals. I arrived about half past six.

When I saw him at the front door, I experienced that same shock that I had felt with Sally and Susan. He looked somehow older. The skin on his face was as taut as ever, but he had filled out a lot. The handsome youth had become a superb man. He was wearing one of his New and Lingwood striped shirts, with the sleeves rolled up twice, and jeans – something he had not owned at Cambridge.

'God, you look well,' he said, just as he had when I stepped onto the platform at Ipswich.

'So do you. But I feel dead.'

'Well, come and recuperate upstairs.' He seized my suitcase and led me to the first floor flat. It was exactly the sort of place Thomas was destined to have once he was given enough money. The sitting room had the benefit of a high ceiling and two enormous windows. There were bookcases built on either side of a pine fireplace – the original one had vanished twenty years before. He did not have a lot of books, but they were spaced out in order to look balanced, and the gaps were filled with china bowls. There was a sofa and two chairs, covered in the same green Chiniesoserie pattern as the curtains. Above the mantelpiece was one of the paintings of the great house at Netherbridge.

'Thomas! How did you get that painting out of the house?'

'I took it. Do you know, Father didn't even notice for a month?'

I sat down in one of the arm chairs. It was like coming home, and finding that one's family had moved house. I would get used to it quickly, but not immediately.

'It's lovely, Thomas; really, it is.'

'So you approve?'

'Approve? It's . . . I'm jealous . . .'

'Really? He pulled up one of the short-backed dining chairs, and sat astride it, resting his chin on his folded arms.

'Yes. Because I wasn't here to see you put it together. I'm looking around, and I'm thinking, I bet I know where he found that, because that's where we bought the one that I have.'

'You're probably right.' He grinned at me. If possible, he was better looking than ever. I noted hungrily, the thick veins on his hands and forearms, and how the jeans were stretched against his powerful leg muscles. I had not thought like that in two years. 'I'm glad you're back,' he said. 'There's so much to talk about. I'm such a dreadful letter writer. I've sat down so many times, and just couldn't put anything into writing.'

'How's banking?'

'That's the easiest thing to tell you. It pays the bills, it's boring as hell, and they're marvellous about my politicking.'

'You really are doing a lot of that?'

'Endlessly, it seems. I spent the General Election as personal assistant to an M.P., and there are always meetings to go to.'

'Geoffrey Stephenson must be delighted.'

'Oh. Didn't you know? Christ, didn't I write about it?'

'What?'

Geoffrey . . . he died last month.'

'Oh, Thomas. What happened?'

'Heart attack. At least it was quick.'

'I'm so sorry. You must've been . . .'

'Yes. I was. I loved Geoffrey.'

'And your parents. They . . .'

'Yes, Father looked upset. I think Mother even cried. I've never seen her cry.'

'I really am sorry. And he wanted you to take over after him?'

'Yes. He really was my tutor this last year. He's the one who sent me off to the by-election campaigns, and got me the job during the General Election. He even got me on the candidate's list.'

'What's that?'

'Party Central Office has a list of people they've vetted as suitable. A constituency can technically choose anyone as a candidate, but they almost never do. It was a step – all part of the plan.'

'You mean you were going to run for Parliament already?'

'Only in a hopeless seat. Geoffrey said that I should have that experience, and meanwhile meet everybody. And get established at the bank.'

'That seems fair enough.'

'Yes.'

'And then you'd get his seat?'

'Yes. He said he wasn't going to retire for another ten years or so. The constituency loved him. They wouldn't let him, if he wanted it.'

202

'God, that would've been ideal.'

'Well, it is just about the safest seat in the country.'

I shook my head. It seemed incredibly unfair. After all, their plan was so detailed, and so stuffed with experience for Thomas, that he could legitimately say that he deserved to get the constituency in the end. 'I'm glad you're still active, though,' I said. He shrugged, good naturedly. 'I don't want to wait forever to say that I've been fucked by the Prime Minister.'

He laughed, hugely. So he does remember, I thought. I wondered how much more he recalled. I was suddenly furious with myself for having been away this long. Sitting with Thomas, I could feel how much I had missed his humour and his virility, and even his arrogance. I was jealous of whoever else might have had him to themselves.

'Oh Neil, don't stay away again so long.' He got up. 'Come on, you must want a bath.'

I nodded. There was no point in saying everything now. I had a bath – one of the first after two years of showers – and changed into a Lacoste shirt and beige cotton trousers.

Thomas waited for me in the living room, and laid out on the dining table a cold supper of paté, smoked mackeral, salad and cheese. While we ate, I told him about Sally's visit.

'Sally's having an affair with that man?' He was astounded.

'Have you heard of him?'

'Unfortunately yes. Once or twice I've been stuck in a bath, or somewhere too far away from the radio, and have actually had to listen to some of his plays. He sounds worse, though.'

'She says he's a genius.'

'I think Sally's renounced all the intellectual processes. Her clients certainly have. I'm not surprised, with all the rubbish I used to find on her bookshelf.'

'You two didn't see each other at all after I left?'

'No. I don't know what happened to Sally that summer, but she came back to Cambridge a raving trendy. I was immediately confined to the dustbin of history, where apparently my class belonged anyway.'

'I thought her father was a good, solid burgher.'

'He is, and Sally's bourgeois to the core. I should imagine it killed her to think that she had to eat at the same table as a capitalist lacky. But to think that she used to have sex with me! I mean, at least her father helps capitalism, which is modern; my father supposedly has never heard of the industrial revolution.'

'I'm almost surprised you didn't drag her along to a party anyway, just to mock.'

He suddenly looked grim. 'I didn't give any parties myself that year. I couldn't take her to the ones I went to.'

'Gosh, what did you do?'

He stretched his arms out. He stared at his hands while he spoke. I do not think he realised how close they were to my own. I did, and the proximity, even in my fatigue, drove me mad.

'I drank,' he said.

'You always did.'

'Not this much. I worked during the vacs, I played a bit of rugger – otherwise I drank.'

I put down my cutlery. 'Why?'

'Why does anyone ever go on drinking binges? To forget.'

'What?'

'Whatever it was, it was a blur very soon. I suppose it all started when I turned twenty one. A lot of people get moody then. I suddenly felt as if everything I had ever done came down on top of me. So I drank – and I kept on drinking.'

'And did it get any better?'

'It's the sort of thing that feeds on itself. You know, I began to understand Geoffrey then. Of course I couldn't tell him, but I felt very close to him. I would come back to my room after a night out, and I'd drain whatever was left in whatever bottles I could find. And I knew what it felt like to want to escape. I had no idea what I wanted to escape, but I knew the need to. Christ, I knew it.'

'How long did it go on for?'

'Most of that year. I had to sober up for tripos, and when that was over . . . I just snapped out of it.'

'Thank God for that.'

204

'Yes. I felt released – or unleashed, I don't know. I knew that it would never happen to me again. For the last year, I've felt as if I couldn't waste a moment. There's everything to do, and nothing to stop me.'

'That's the Thomas I knew.'

'I wonder.'

'How do you mean?'

'When you knew me . . . I think I was a little like Peter Harding: you know, he never had to stand against anyone for office.'

'He was untested.'

'Exactly. That's how I was: untested.'

'But you believed in yourself.'

'I still do. Now I'm doing something about it.'

I wondered how much tougher he really was. I was at that point where I felt as if I could stay awake forever. I also knew that I was about to fall asleep. Thomas saw it too.

'Come on,' he said, getting up, 'I'm going to put you to bed.'

'All right.'

We walked towards the spare bedroom. It was really little more than a box room, big enough for a bed and a small chest of drawers. Thomas told me to sleep as late as I liked, and where all he breakfast things were.

'I should be home about half past six. What would you like to do tomorrow night?'

'Let me take you out to dinner. Anywhere you like.'

'Leave everything to me.'

'Thomas . . . you know you can still trust me.'

'Dear Neil . . . if I promise to tell you everything, will you promise to understand this time?' I nodded. He leaned over, and kissed me lightly on the lips. 'Bless you. Sleep well.'

I undressed and got into the narrow bed. I now found that I could not get to sleep. I lay there for half an hour or so. Just before I fell asleep, I heard the front door close. I knew nothing else until nine o'clock the next morning.

Thomas was gone by the time I got up. I made some instant

205

coffee for myself and boiled an egg. Thomas had left *The Times* for me. I looked through it and found that there were a few exhibitions I wanted to see. I did not feel in the mood for museums. There was only one thing I could do that day. I got dressed, found the nearest tube station, went to Liverpool Street, and took the first train to Cambridge.

I had never been there at that time of year. There were no students – not even the few undergraduates who haunted the place during the other holidays, as I had done, in order to work. On the other hand, there were a lot of tourists, every rose bush was in bloom, and the Backs were rich in foliage.

I walked the half hour from the station to my college. The gates, in their Elizabethan redbrick solidity, looked reassuringly the same. I went into the porter's lodge and found that I recognised the man on duty. He was the one who had handed me my pile of letters when I got back from Netherbridge. He still wore a bowler hat.

'It's Mr . . .' he hesitated.

'Neil Fielding.'

'Of course. I suppose you've been back to America, sir.'

'That's right. New York.'

'I thought that was where you came from. You haven't brought your wife, have you?'

'I'm not married.'

'So many of the Americans bring their wives back with them.'

'I'm afraid I'm just a tourist now, on my own.'

'Well, glad to see you back. How have you been keeping?'

'Fine. I'm in law school. And everyone here?'

'Undergraduates aren't the same, but we're all right. Don't let the socialists tell you different.'

I passed through the three courtyards, over the narrow stone bridge, and finally reached my old staircase. I did not go up. I could not bear to see someone else's name painted over my door. I walked out to the Backs, and along the lawn until I could see my old window. That triggered off the memories.

Four strangers had lived in those rooms since then. Once more I felt jealous of the people who had known Thomas in the last two years – perhaps not in that lonely year of drinking, but since he had come down. I was proud of his present ambition, but I hoped it was not an exchange of one compensation for another.

I was glad I had come to Cambridge, and happy to realise that I would never haunt the place, as people did. I would come back again, and have a good wallow. That was all. I had not fallen in love with the place; just with a person who happened to have been there. I thought of what Sally had urged on me. How would I get rid 'of us' now?

I got back to London about five. I bought a bottle of gin and some tonic water and a lemon on the way back to the flat. Once there, I had a bath and changed into my blazer and grey flannel trousers. Thomas arrived just after I put the drink out.

'Gosh, what a welcome,' he said. He was wearing a two-piece, pin striped suit. 'What a sticky day. Would you mind if I jumped straight into a bath?'

'Go ahead. I'll bring you a drink.'

I waited until he had got into the bath. Then I poured a gin and tonic and took it in to him. He was a splendid sight. He had grown particularly thick in the shoulders.

'Thanks. Sit down and keep me company. Tell me about your day.'

I told him about the trip to Cambridge. He said that he had only been back twice; once this last May week, and once for a Nonagon dinner which he – of all people – found too rowdy.

'Was Peter Harding around at May Week?' I asked.

'Peter Harding . . . I wonder what ever happened to him. I haven't seen him in two years.'

'I used to think that London would be as small a society as Cambridge.'

'It can be.' He cradled the drink in his hands, and slid down in the bath so that his shoulders were immersed. It made his knees stick up above the water. 'It depends on what you want. You can live in a world of coincidences . . . or you can keep everyone in different compartments.'

'I think I can guess which one you do.'

'Both, in fact.'

'I imagine you at lots of dinner parties.'

'Some.'

'Come on, Thomas, you're too eligible.'

He looked at me. 'Have I written to you about Miranda?'

'Not by name. Who is she?'

'A girl I met last September. At one of these dinner parties.'

'Last September? And she's still around? That must be a record.'

'I suppose it is.'

'Well?'

'She's very attractive.'

'Thomas, she must be gorgeous, if she's lasted this long.'

'I'm not complaining. She also has a great talent for getting people to do things, without their realising it. Terribly clever.'

'Cleverer than Sally?'

'Perhaps Miranda is . . . shrewd. You know, the more I think about it, the more I think Sally was really uneducated. Miranda hasn't read much either, but somehow she already knows what books have to teach her.'

'She sounds terrifying.'

'That's not quite fair. She's the only child of much older, and very powerful parents. People like that wind up either crushed or pretty formidable.'

'And Miranda's pretty formidable.'

'She will be.'

'Anything else I should know about her?'

Thomas put his drink down on the floor. He started washing himself. I retreated to the doorway. It was becoming increasingly unbearable to see him naked. I could not imagine how I had remained celibate in New York. Talk about psychological blockages . . . even Nicholas was really only an act of defiance to Thomas. It all came down to doing things in relation to Thomas.

'I've made reservations at *Le Gavroche*,' he told me, while drying his hair and body.

'Fine. I don't know anything about it.'

'It's marvellous. Terribly expensive, I'm afraid.'

'That doesn't matter.'

'We can walk from here, if you don't mind a little exercise before dinner.'

'Great.'

Thomas finished drying himself. He combed his thick, damp hair. Then he wrapped the towel around him and went into the bedroom. I followed him. As we got inside he turned around and looked at me.

'It's awful,' he said, 'I haven't asked you anything about yourself. You could be madly in love with someone in New York, and bursting to tell me . . .'

He hesitated tantilisingly. 'There's no one.' He confessed.

'I couldn't touch a man after you.'

We kissed each other. As I caressed his back and neck I felt as if, at last, the glass case had been removed again. We looked at each other and grinned. Both of us had obviously thought that it wouldn't happen.

'Wait.' He stepped back.

'Why?'

'Because you don't know anything more about me than you did when you arrived.'

'Oh, hell,' I laughed. 'what've you done?'

He turned away and started to get dressed. 'Do you know who Miranda's father is?'

'No.'

'He's Lord . . . oh, the name wouldn't mean anything to you. But in the late '50s and early '60s, he was one of the biggest names in the party.'

'Ten years ago?'

'It seems like a long time, but he was one of those men whom the politicians didn't like, but the grass roots absolutely adored. If you'd taken a poll of the people who go out canvassing and who choose candidates, he would've been Prime Minister.'

'What happened?'

'He never came close, but he got a peerage. That was only a few years ago. His constituency was next door to Geoffrey's.'

'Oh?'

'They all think he's a god down there.'

'Still?'

'Yes. He's terribly rich as well. He married an American heiress.'

'Whom you hate.'

'How did you know?'

'The Thomas Lyster theory of the pernicious effect of American women on British political history.'

'I'd forgotten about that,' he grinned. 'As a matter of fact, she did him no good at all. And she does hate me. At least all the money's tied up for Miranda.'

'Lucky Miranda. Lucky you.'

'It's not that simple.'

'You have rivals for her?'

'I did. I'm not worried about them.'

'Of course not. So what is it?'

'You're getting sarcastic, Neil.'

'I had a good teacher. Now what's going on, Thomas?'

'Richard.'

'Who's Richard?'

'Well, you see, last winter . . .'

'God, I think we both need a drink.'

Thomas agreed. He had already put on his shirt and trousers. We went into the sitting room, poured very large gins, and sat in the two arm chairs. Thomas leaned over to a side table and picked up a pack of cigarettes. He lit one.

'I'm supposed to be giving these up,' he said. 'I wanted to get so fit this year. I've become a fanatic about it. Cricket, rugby, weights, running . . .'

'Richard.'

'Yes. Richard. Well, I was playing a lot of rugger last winter. I do love that game. Quite apart from everything else, the sheer maleness of it is so damn exciting.'

'Great.'

'You wanted to know everything. I happen to glory in that kind of thing. And every man who does is homosexual in spirit. Most of them have sex with women, of course, but they don't find them interesting. I wondered for ages which way Richard went. He was on the team I played for, you see. Most of them bored me to death, once we stopped discussing drink and sport. But he was different. Big of course; pale and chunky and . . . your looks and colouring, I suppose. Drank like a fish, and on the pitch . . . Christ, you don't see a killer instinct like that every day. He absolutely loved it for its own sake.'

'Charming.'

He shook his head. 'It was obvious to me at least that there was far more to him. What was that word Nancy used to use?'

'Sublimating?'

'Exactly. Anyway, he doesn't live very far from here. We used to walk home together from the tube after training sessions. We could've driven, but he said he liked the walk. He always insisted on getting off at Sloane Square and walking down the King's Road, which isn't the most convenient way at all.'

'He was trying to tell you something?'

'So it turned out. This went on for weeks, and then one night – January, I think – he stopped at a street corner, pointed up the road, and asked if I fancied a drink.'

'And?'

'It was a gay pub.'

'Were you surprised?'

'Not really. I rather thought that the drink and the brutality were just frustrated sex.'

'Hardly frustrated, if he knows where the gay pubs are.'

'Anyone who lives in the world knows that. It was just his unbelievably inhibited way of making a pass.' He shrugged. 'I brought him straight back here.'

'And had sex happily ever after.'

He nodded grimly. 'I can't help it.'

'Are you actually apologising for having sex?'

'I feel as if I'm losing control. I can't keep away from him.'

'What's his attitude?'

'The same. He's not a million miles away from Peter: he never uses the words gay or queer; all his friends are a hundred percent straight; he makes no demands on my time at all; we just both happen to be insatiable.'

'And you've been carrying on with him and Miranda.'

'Yes. I must say, even I've felt a fair average wreck sometimes. He's incredibly strong.'

'What about the void?'

'I think I've felt it, once or twice.'

'Otherwise, they help you over it.'

He looked at me, astonished. 'No! Don't you understand, Neil? I only ever felt it with someone I tried to love, and couldn't. With everyone else it was just sex–'

'All they got was your body.'

'That's right.'

'Then emotionally, Miranda and Richard don't mean anything more to you than . . . than a Cambridge shopgirl.'

'It's not that simple either.'

'Does he love you?'

'I told you, he won't even admit he's gay.'

'And Miranda?'

'She says she loves me.'

'And you?'

'I lie to her, what do you think?'

I shook my head. 'Do they know about each other?'

He hesitated. 'That's how the trouble started.'

'What happened?'

'I got careless. I broke a date with Miranda because I hadn't seen Richard in a week. He came round just before I was ready to go out and . . . I couldn't send him away. She didn't believe my excuse.'

'What did she do?'

'Came round the flat'

'And found you in bed together?'

'Obviously I didn't answer the door bell. But she told me

212

afterwards, and then she got suspicious as hell.'

'Did she find out?'

'Indirectly.'

'How?'

'She noticed that I changed my sheets too often.'

'Really?'

'Apparently, once or twice, she changed them the morning after. The next night she'd come round, and found that they were changed again. Of course Richard had been here in between. I couldn't risk her finding his hairs.' He shrugged. 'Sometimes you can't win.'

'So what happened.'

'She said I could choose between her and it – it, mind you, not him or her.'

'Thomas, nobody talks to you like that. You would've told her to go to hell.'

'I did. She walked out.'

'And?'

'Life became easier, at first. It was Richard almost every night. I wish he were half as interesting as she is, but I didn't mind. And then . . .'

'Don't tell me. And then Richard began to see that this was a real live, homosexual affair, and if it went on much longer, that's just what he would be.'

'Wise old Neil. I wanted him, and I had to take him on his terms.'

'So back came Miranda.'

'After some suitable coaxing, yes.'

'But you were still being unfaithful.'

'But discreet. No more than twice a week, and only at his place.'

'Where you went last night.'

'Did I wake you up? Sorry.' I shook my head.

'Why did she abandon her principles?'

'She's never admitted that she has. I guess you'd call it a tacit agreement. She knows I'll play the game. There aren't many women like her.'

213

'I bet.'

'Neil . . . I'm engaged to marry her.'

'What?'

'We got engaged, two weeks ago.'

I stared at him. 'It's that fucking constituency.'

'They told me, that a third of the committee wanted me, and a third didn't know, and a third were dead against me. I knew who the opposition was. They're fools, but they all still think that the sun rises and sets with Miranda's father.'

'What a shit you are.'

He got up and came over to my chair, and knelt on the floor. 'Neil . . .'

'You'll have a constituency for life as long as you marry her, and if you marry her, you'll have a rich and beautiful wife. What the hell are you worried about?'

'Because it doesn't satisfy me.'

'Then nothing ever will.'

'If I can't have you, it doesn't matter what I do.'

If I can't have you, I repeated to myself. If I can't be the Mr Lyster of Netherbridge . . . perhaps we were both just excuses, to stop Thomas worrying about his lack of a conscience.

Then he did something unique: he put his head on my lap. In all that time together, he had never made a gesture which would have enabled me to push him aside. He suddenly seemed vulnerable. It was the most devastating thing he could have done. I began to stroke his head.

'You know,' he said, 'Richard looks so much like you. For a long time, I couldn't come with him, unless I thought of you, while I was doing it.'

We sat there like that for a long time. Finally Thomas asked, 'What time is it?'

I looked at my watch. 'Five to eight.'

'Fancy some dinner?'

'Why not?'

He sat up, and draped him arms over my shoulders. 'Then you've really come back?'

214

'Yes. I don't know what the hell I'm going to do here . . .'

He kissed me. 'Let's just think of the celebration.'

We celebrated over the best dinner I ever ate in England. We spent our time talking about the past. We were like two men in the same regiment, who tell each other battle stories once they are safe and sound.

Back at the flat, I followed Thomas to the bedroom as a matter of course. At first I tried to compare our love making with what it had been like at Cambridge. I soon gave up, and revelled in it for it's own sake. Afterwards we lay together: Thomas's chest against my back; his long arms cradling my body. We both fought to stay awake.

At last Thomas yawned. 'Sorry. I do have to go to work in the morning, silly as it sounds.'

'Go to sleep then.'

He turned over on his back. 'Neil I . . .'

'Yes?'

'I couldn't consider myself properly married without you.'

'What!'

'I said . . . I mean, you will come back in the autumn for it, won't you? You will be my best man . . .'

Brilliance Books is a gay and lesbian imprint and we welcome manuscripts on all subjects by gay and lesbian writers.

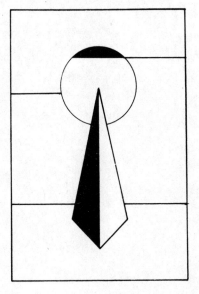